Water

Refuse
Them

LUCIE McKNIGHT HARDY

Water Shall Refuse Them

LUCIE McKNIGHT HARDY

dead ink

dead ink

First published in Great Britain in 2019 by Dead Ink, an
imprint of Cinder House Publishing Limited.

ISBN 978-1-911585-56-5

Cover design by Luke Bird
lukebird.co.uk

Cover photgraphy by Tiffany Combs at Unsplash

Printed and bound in Great Britain by Clays Ltd, Elcograf S.p.A.

www.deadinkbooks.com

For Dom, and for Ted, Ben and Florence.

**All witchcraft comes from carnal lust,
which is in women insatiable.**

Heinrich Kramer, Malleus Maleficarum, 1487

One.

The head in my lap was heavy, and the heft of the forehead and chin sent it tipping forward every time we went round a bend. By the time we got to Bristol my legs were sore and cramped. I licked a finger and swiped at the smear of blood on the thumb of my other hand. The jabbering in my chest had stopped and I was infused with that familiar numbness again.

A mix-up with the trailer meant that we hadn't left home until the afternoon, later than planned. By the time we'd crossed the Severn Bridge it was getting on for six o'clock and the heat was the result of a day's fermentation. The heatwave had been going on for months, each day hotter than the last, and they'd said on the radio that today was the hottest since records began. My dad kept saying how good it would be to get out of the dust and dirt of the city; he seemed to think the drought wasn't affecting Wales.

3

As soon as we came off the motorway and started driving north the roads became smaller and rougher, more like dirt tracks than the roads I was used to. The lanes appeared in my head as arteries, gradually thinning as we got further from the city, the blood being depleted of oxygen as the roads ran out of traffic. Occasionally, we had to pull over to let someone pass, or reverse into a passing place at the side of the road, but we met very few other cars. Then we started the climb.

The slope wasn't too steep at first and the Cortina steamed ahead, but it started to struggle as the track became narrower and harder. The vinyl seats under my thighs were slick with sweat.

My mother was sitting up ramrod straight, her face turned away from us. The whole of the journey she'd peered out of the window as the hedges whipped past. At first I thought she seemed calmer than she had been in months, but then I saw that she was working away at the fabric of her skirt, rubbing it over and over between her fingers and her thumbs.

Lorry slept next to me, his head thrown back and his mouth open, breathing steadily. He was clutching his clown doll and holding it up to his mouth. His stubby legs jutted off the seat, and his bandages were grubby and had started to come loose where he'd been scratching. Blood was seeping through. He'd been worrying away at his legs ever since we'd left home, only stopping when he fell asleep. I knew that under the bandages the sores would be raw and wet.

My dad sat hunkered down in his seat, knuckles white from clutching the steering wheel. He didn't really know where he was going; he was just following the directions his friend had written on a scrap of paper. We had the radio on, the chart show on Radio One. That Elton John and Kiki Dee song was number one for the second week running and I was sick of its relentless optimism. Then the news came on. A story about a toddler who'd been locked in a car by mistake and died of heat exhaustion. My mother's shoulders twitched, but she didn't say anything. My dad turned the radio off and when he spoke I knew it was to fill the silence.

'We're nearly there, Nif. Nearly there.'

When his eyes met mine in the rear-view mirror the shadows under them were darker than usual, his skin dull despite the tan. The hair that hung to his shoulders was longer than it had been in years.

My brother looked at me through half-closed eyes, and dribble ran down his chin. He held out his hand and I took his chubby fingers and squeezed them. He sat up a bit and leant his head against the window.

'Lorry wanna wee.' The voice was small and plaintive and thick with sleep.

'Dad—'

'I heard.'

The road widened to allow an entrance to a field, and the wheels churned up dust as we stopped. I put the head, wrapped in its layers of hessian and plastic, onto the seat next to me. My dad turned around and reached over. He stroked the head gently. Patted it.

I got out and walked round to the other side of the car, opened the door and picked up the bulk that was my brother. He put his arms around my neck and I braced myself to take his weight. He was getting too big to be carried now.

'Nif! Lorry really, really need a wee!'

'OK. Hang on.'

I helped him get his trousers down, and made him lean forward and point himself into the hedge so the stream of piss missed his shoes. When he'd finished, I bundled him back into the car and he went straight back to sleep.

All this time my mother sat in the passenger seat, staring straight ahead, her hand hanging out of the window with a cigarette clamped between two fingers. The fingers of her other hand were turning over the fabric of her skirt, rubbing and stretching.

My dad had lit a cigarette as well, and was walking up and down next to the car. He leant against the driver's door and I stood next to him, enjoying the burning of the hot metal through my t-shirt. He squinted at me, the sun in his eyes. He took a long drag and held it in, blew it out slowly and pointed his face to the sky. The smoke curled up into the still air.

'Why don't you stop cutting your hair, Nif?' He turned his face away from the sun and looked at his feet. He rubbed them around in the dry dirt and his sandals made grooves in the dust. The ragged hems of his jeans traced faint lines after them.

'And those clothes. You've got loads of nice things to wear. Why do you have to go around dressed like a boy?' He took off his glasses and polished them on the hem of his shirt. When he realised he wasn't going to get an answer, he sniffed.

'C'mon, then, Jenny Wren,' he said and put his hand on my shoulder. I shrugged him off. That was his old name for me, the one he used to call me when I was a little kid. I was called Nif now, thanks to Lorry. When he'd first started talking, just after the accident, he couldn't say Jennifer or even Jenny, so he called me Nif and it stuck. We've always called him Lorry, even though his name's Laurence. You'd think he'd be called Larry.

'Not far to go now. Final push and all that,' my dad said. He ground out the cigarette and took a flask of water from the car's side pocket and dribbled some over the fag end, making sure it was properly out. He took a huge gulp of water and his Adam's apple bobbed. He offered the water to me but I shook my head. We climbed into the car and I put the head back on my lap.

My dad started the engine and pulled out into the lane. My mother carried on staring out of the window and nobody said anything for a long while. We turned a bend too fast and I slid across the back seat and into Lorry who woke up and started to wail, grabbing at his bandages. My mother swivelled round and frowned at him, then at me, and I shushed him and patted him and tried to comfort him. After a while he shoved his thumb into his mouth and whimpered a bit before he went back to sleep.

I was glad that I had the treasure bag with me in the back seat, rather than packed away into the trailer with the rest of our stuff. It made me feel safe. I counted off the relics in my head. Even though the incantation wasn't finished, and I still needed another relic to complete the rhythm, the feathers meant it was nearly there. I saw another small smear of blood I'd missed, on the web of skin between my thumb and forefinger, and licked it off. I carried on reciting the incantation, and the repetition of the familiar words made me drowsy, and I must have started to doze off, because a bump in the road made me sit up, instantly awake.

I saw that we were still climbing, the road going up and up. The light by then was waning, and everything was bathed in the insipid flush of the sun just setting. We kept on going uphill, for what seemed like forever, and when I'd counted to

386, and I thought we wouldn't be able to go any higher, we drove over a bump and suddenly we were at the top of the world looking down into the valley. My dad let out a long breath and changed gear and the car started the descent. The heat intensified, as though any breeze there had been at the top of the hill had run out and we were entering a bottle of stale air. It felt as though, on making the descent into this parched and febrile valley, we'd awoken some sort of hostile force.

A sheer drop fell away from my side of the car, the grass all the way down patchy and sparse. A few houses stood on the road, clustered here and there like flies on raw meat, but mostly we passed only tatty sheep that gazed blindly at us as we bumped along. At the bottom of the valley lay a stream, which looked as though it had once been a lot wider and deeper, but had obviously been depleted by the heatwave. Now it was no more than six feet wide and a couple of feet deep, the dry banks on either side steep and bare.

My dad turned the radio on again, but there was no signal, just the buzz of white noise. He switched it off and we followed the road along the edge of the stream. We hadn't passed any other cars for at least half an hour by the time we turned another corner and came to the dirty road sign that announced the name of the village. It was a word I knew I would struggle to pronounce.

As we entered the village, a glowing grey veil hung over everything. There were no street lights here, and everything was held in that suspended place between light and dark. When the road straightened out some houses came into view, their front gardens meagre and poky. In a few, I could see televisions flickering through the windows, and where the curtains hadn't been drawn, the backs of people's heads.

We came to a branch in the road, and immediately in front of us stood a war memorial, carved from the same sullen grey stone as the houses. Everything in the village had a pallor to it, the look of an invalid.

The car swung to the left and, for a moment, a group of teenagers were lit up. They turned towards us, half a dozen of them, their eyes blank in the reflected headlights. They were squatting on the steps at the bottom of the war memorial, each of them clutching a cigarette, the ends glowing like hot coals in the gloom. As we drove past I twisted in my seat. The tallest one—the one with long hair scraped up into a ponytail on the top of her head—caught my eye and held it. Her face was all scrunched up, the features too close together, like someone had taken her face in the palm of their hand and squashed it. She raised her middle finger at me and grinned. I looked away.

The only other living things we saw as we made our progress through the village were cattle, their pale faces luminous in the gloom, surveying us blankly from the other side of a barbed wire fence. We drove past a chapel, a monolithic ugly thing, two high windows standing sentry on either side of a solid wooden door. A pair of iron gates set into the metal fence was secured by a chunky padlock.

'Here we are!' my dad said, and there was a crack in his voice that gave away his relief at finally finding the place.

The Cortina staggered to a halt and crunched over gravel as it pulled into a narrow driveway that was fronted by iron railings. My mother turned around in her seat and looked at Lorry and then at me. The car stopping had roused Lorry, and he stirred but didn't wake up, his bottom lip sticking out like it always did when he was asleep.

'We won't wake him,' my mother said. 'We'll leave him to sleep and then put him into bed when we've got ourselves straight.' She opened her car door, and made sure to close it softly behind her.

I clambered from the car and placed the head, very carefully, onto the seat. My legs felt heavy and sore, and I rubbed them to try and bring some life back into them. My dad got out and stretched. From where we stood, I could only make out the gable end of the house. There was one window up at the top, in what I took to be the attic, a tiny little arched window that was the only thing to break the expanse of stone. Even in the failing light of a late July evening I could see that the curtains on the inside were hanging from the rail, and that the linings were worn and ripped.

The parking space was set up higher than the house and its garden, the cottage cowering away from the rest of the village. Steps led us down from the patch of gravel where we had parked the car to a little path of cracked and weed-ridden flagstones that forked to the left and took us to the front of the house. My dad went first, one hand rubbing at the base of his neck, the keys jangling in the other. A little iron gate squeaked as he pushed it open.

My mother walked in front of me, arms knotted tightly across her chest, bony shoulder blades pointing accusingly at me through her blouse. Her hair had started to come loose from her bun, and greasy brown strands twisted at the nape of her neck.

There was a thick smell in the air, a pungent sweetness emanating from the honeysuckle clinging to the front wall of the house. It smelt like old ladies and decay.

The right-hand side of the house was made of the same sombre grey stone as the other houses in the village, but was even more run-down. A shabby open porch guarded the front door; the slates on its roof had slipped and were threatening to behead anyone standing beneath it. The windows were mottled with dust, their frames flaking and raw, the paint peeling like sunburnt skin.

It was a lop-sided house: a recent, single-storey breeze block extension had been added on the left-hand side and it sat lower than the rest of the cottage and reached back at an acute angle, so from where I was standing, directly in front of it, it looked as though that side of the cottage was disappearing into itself. The more I looked at it, the more I could see that there were very few right angles to this house. The roof over the old part of the cottage was slumped in the middle, and the slates were slipping there. A pair of chimneys rose above the house, massive things that looked too heavy for the fragile roof to bear. Two upstairs windows were offset and asymmetrical. They gazed back at us, as if challenging one of us to be the first to speak.

We stood on a cracked patch of bare concrete at the front of the house, the thick heat still palpable. There was absolute stillness and the air hung heavy and rank and dry about us.

Then Lorry screamed.

He was lying next to the car. He'd managed to open the door and had fallen out onto the dusty gravel that formed the parking area. Wailing, he lay face down in the dirt. My mother took a deep breath and closed her eyes. When she opened them they held the look of disdain she always wore for her youngest child. She looked at him and she looked at me and I ran to Lorry and picked him up, seeing the blood on his knees starting to show through the dust, how his bandaged shins were even dirtier now, the blood on them rusty and brown. My mother just watched, her bony fingers worrying away at the base of her neck, her face a contortion of pain, anger and defiance. Then she gave a little tight-mouthed smile and nodded. I could see how hollow her eye sockets had become; her cheeks looked like someone had taken a spoon and scooped them out.

I turned away from my parents and grabbed a handful of gravel. I didn't want to, but I had to, for the Creed, and I pressed it against Lorry's knee and rubbed it in and he howled again.

My mother didn't react to my brother's wails. Instead, she turned back to the cottage.

'It's fine,' she said, and for a moment I thought she was referring to Lorry.

My dad had been a sculptor for as long as I could remember. In the early days, he'd told me, after he finished art college, he had made a living by painting portraits, commissions from the wealthy and the vain who wanted to be immortalised in oils. He'd made a name for himself and had been quite in demand for a while as his reputation spread, but then he'd decided that he no longer wanted to paint. He told me he found the process of building up layer upon layer of paint restrictive. There was no way of removing what he had created: any mistakes he made would stay there, concealed by more layers of paint, and while they wouldn't be visible, he would always know that they were there. He had instead gone into sculpting, and had used his reputation as a painter to build up a substantial client base. He specialised in busts, first crafting the head and shoulders in clay, before casting them in bronze for those who could afford it, and bronze resin for those who couldn't.

There was one bust he'd been working on for a long time. It had been in his studio at home, and when he couldn't find time to work on it because of his commissions, it would be bundled up in wet hessian and plastic, and sprayed with water regularly to prevent the clay from drying out. It was a sculpture of my mother, a head and shoulders study, and she hated it.

He had started it a couple of years ago and I was surprised that the clay was still pliable enough to work with. He'd explained that it wasn't the same clay as when he'd started, that each time he worked on it he would remove some of the old stuff and apply fresh clay. The inside was hollow, and the skull-shape under the top layer would be set solid and too hard to work with, but the top layers were soft enough for him to mould and shape, his fingers easing and stroking and caressing.

He would work on it intermittently, between his commissions and his teaching at the art college, but my mother refused to sit for him, so he would have to work from memory, shut away in his studio in the evening once she'd gone to bed. He'd collected together some photographs of her, all taken from different angles, and he referred to them occasionally, but she had changed so much since the photos had been taken that they weren't really an accurate depiction of her. Sometimes I'd sit with him, watching as his fingers worked their way firmly but gently around my mother's face, smoothing, soothing. In the last few months, he'd had to take away even more of the clay, and the cheeks had become hollower, the eye sockets deeper. He struggled to keep the sculpture looking like the woman my mother had become since the accident.

It was one of the men he worked with at the art college who'd suggested we go and spend a month over the summer holidays at his cottage in Wales; he'd thought it would do us good to be away from our house for a bit. It wasn't really his cottage, it belonged to his wife, and she had inherited it several years ago from a relative she'd never met. My dad's colleague and his family had never even been to the cottage, and he'd suggested to my dad that, in exchange for a month's free bed and board, he might like to look over the house and see what work needed to be done, and perhaps attempt some of the smaller jobs himself.

My mother, of course, hadn't wanted to go. She'd wanted to stay in our old house in the suburbs, sitting around in her dressing gown, wall-gazing, cigarette in one hand, the other hand up at her neck, scratching away at the place where her crucifix used to hang. When my dad first brought up the subject she'd brushed him off, said it was a stupid idea, and went back to staring into space.

On one of the nights that I'd heard them talking about the cottage, Lorry had woken up crying and saying there were ghosts under his bed. I'd hushed him, stroked his forehead and told him that I loved him and would never let the ghosts get him.

'Mummy don't love Lorry,' he'd said, his voice thick and nasal. Since he'd started talking, just after the accident, this was what he said the most.

'Mummy does love Lorry,' I'd said, stroking his curls back off his forehead. 'Mummy loves Lorry very much but she's just a bit sad at the moment. It'll get better.' The eyes that found mine in the semi-darkness were lit with such a deep and resolute trust that I'd felt the familiar sickness. I held him as he fell asleep, his breathing slowing down and becoming regular, nothing but a faint gurgle coming from his throat.

I was going back to my bedroom when I heard my parents talking, and I stopped at the top of the stairs, just outside the bathroom. The telly flickered away, Morecambe and Wise lying in bed together, but my parents weren't watching it, and the sound was turned down. My mother was sitting on the sofa, her shoulders hunched, one hand holding her dressing gown closed at her throat while the other clutched a cigarette between two fingers. Her nails were stained yellow.

'Linda, it's been nearly four months now. I know that's not long in the grand scheme of things, but we have to allow ourselves to move on. You doing this…' My dad waved his hand in the air in the vague direction of my mother. 'You doing this doesn't help anyone. It's not going to bring her back.'

My mother said nothing. She pulled her shoulders in a little bit more, her elbows resting on her knees in front of her, her mouth puckering as she took a drag on the cigarette.

'So, we go to Wales for a month or so and see if a change of scenery will help. I'm not saying that you have to forget about her. All I'm saying is that going to a different place, without all the memories and the…baggage that come with this house, well, it might make you feel better.'

At first, I'd thought my mother wasn't going to speak, but when her voice came it was cold and quiet.

'I don't want to feel better, Clive.' She stubbed the cigarette out in the ashtray that sat on the arm of the sofa, her fingers grinding the stub down repeatedly.

My dad sighed, rubbed his eyes with the heel of his hand and went down on his haunches in front of my mother. He clasped her alabaster hands in his.

'Can't you see, we have to do something? For Nif's sake, for Lorry's sake. All I'm asking is that we go to Wales for a month. One month. Just until Nif needs to start back at school. We stay somewhere different for a little while, and see if that helps.' My dad had run out of words; the effort had exhausted him. He sank onto his knees in front of my mother.

'Pfft.' My mother's response was merely a harsh exhalation of breath. She tapped out another cigarette from her packet of Silk Cut. She lifted it to her mouth and lit it with her little silver lighter, the one my dad had given her, pulling the smoke harshly into her lungs. She didn't look at my dad. I noticed that the wrinkles around her mouth were getting deeper, etchings radiating away from her lips.

My dad stood up again and he put a tentative hand on her shoulder which she shrugged away. She leant forward and her hair hung down around her face in greasy tendrils. I couldn't remember when I'd last heard her washing in the bathroom.

Then, very slowly, my mother seemed to find a new strength from somewhere. She pulled herself up, her back straight and her shoulders upright. When she spoke, her voice was barely audible in the darkened living room, and I strained from the top of the stairs to make out what she'd said. Behind her, Eric and Ernie's silent sunshine dance came on.

'She should be here, though, shouldn't she? This is where it happened and this is where she should be.' I was surprised at how reasonable my mother sounded. My dad had his head in his hands and he let out a sharp breath of despair.

'She's not coming back, Linda, and that's the truth. She's never coming back and we have to move on and think about Nif and Lorry.'

16

My mother sat for a moment, her eyes unfocused, her breathing shallow and controlled. The hand holding her dressing gown closed started twitching, stroking away at the hollow at the base of her throat, and it was as though all the strength she had been building up suddenly dissipated, and she slumped back down again and gazed blindly at the TV. Even from where I was sitting I could see the desperation in my dad's eyes, but my mother refused to look at him. She sat there on the brown Draylon sofa, deflated, her shoulders sloping as if she'd pulled herself inside out. She looked small, like a child, and defeated.

Sitting at the top of the stairs, conscious of the bathroom behind me, I felt a little stab of satisfaction. This was all my mother's fault.

Over the next few weeks, my dad worked on my mother, gradually wearing her down, until eventually she gave in. Since the accident, she'd lost her resolve, and the feistiness I'd always known her to have had disappeared. It was as though someone had taken a photo of her before the accident but it hadn't been developed properly, like it was underexposed and she was perpetually held in shadow. She resembled her old self, but always there was a fog hanging before her, a veil partially obscuring her that wouldn't lift, no matter how hard my dad tried.

Two.

The smell of the honeysuckle was stronger now, trapped in my nostrils like glue, when my dad shone a torch on the keyhole and fumbled with the keys. A scrape and the door swung open. I was holding Lorry. He'd stopped crying by then, but had his head buried in my shoulder and he was snivelling and whimpering. He was heavy, too heavy for me to carry for very long. I had the treasure bag over my other shoulder and was eager to check the relics, to make sure they hadn't been damaged during the journey. The torchlight played over the walls, seeking a light switch, and flashed onto the faded pattern of the wallpaper, obscured here and there by blooming patches of damp. Finally, a click, and a futile light.

There was a faint smell hanging in the stagnant air, overlaying the honeysuckle, something acrid but not altogether unpleasant. The smell of somewhere that hadn't been lived in for years.

A bare bulb hung from the ceiling and a staircase rose up to darkness on the left. There was a white plastic telephone attached to the wall, the same as the one we had at home. Next to it hung a small mirror. Scuffed floorboards were covered in the tiny tell-tale pin pricks of woodworm. Another door was set off slightly to the right and was closed, although a very faint halo of pale light showed around its periphery. The kitchen. My dad unlatched the door and we stepped through, Lorry's head lolling against my shoulder.

The torch lit up a butler's sink set against the wall in front of us, chipped and ancient. A bright strip light flashed into action and I saw that the inside of the sink was grey, limescale-streaked and unscrubbed. Next to it sat a decrepit fridge, and there was an ancient black range cooker hunkered under an enormous stone mantel on my right. Facing the sink was a window, dust and fingerprints clouding the myriad tiny panes. An old wooden sideboard leant against the wall next to the cooker, but apart from that, a scrubbed pine table in the centre of the room and the four chairs that surrounded it were the only pieces of furniture.

'Here we are then.' I couldn't tell if my dad was trying to encourage us with forced jollity, or if his statement was simply the result of resignation in the face of what he'd landed us with.

My mother stood in what had become her customary pose, one hand wrapped tightly around her waist, the other worrying away at the base of her neck. She was looking at the floor.

'Yes. Here we are then.' Her voice was quiet and gave away only a hint of the reproach that I knew lay within it. My dad put his hand on her shoulder and she looked up at him, and for a moment I thought there was a softening towards him. For a moment, it was like the old days, and I felt like an intruder

19

in their intimacy. My mother even forced out a small, tight-lipped smile, before she shrugged my dad's hand away.

We carried on exploring, going from room to room. From the kitchen, a small corridor led to a tiny living room, the space taken up by a sagging old sofa and two armchairs. I put Lorry down on the sofa and he curled himself up into a foetal position and stuck his thumb in his mouth. I turned on a table lamp, expecting it not to work, but it came on and in the faint light it emitted I could see a bookshelf: a couple of bibles, their black leather covers curling with age, and several hymn books, their pages friable and so thin as to be translucent. All were in Welsh.

'Nif!' My dad's voice cut through the silence.

I retraced my steps to the back hall and saw that there were stone stairs leading down to a small wooden door that stood ajar.

'Nif, I'm down here. Come and see.'

I held on to the iron handrail as I made my way down the steep steps. This room was caught in the same twilight that inhabited the garden, a barely-there glow of gauzy light that found its way in through the corrugated plastic roof. My dad was standing in the middle of the room, the torchlight bouncing around as he took it in. I put my hand up to the side of the doorway and found the light switch. I saw the same bare breeze block walls that I had seen from outside and realised now that this was the single storey extension attached to the side of the cottage. Evidently it had been earmarked by my dad for his studio.

'It's got natural light from the roof, and even running water.' My dad didn't turn around, but I could hear the enthusiasm bubbling in him as he spoke. 'In winter, it'll be horrendous—cold and wet and miserable—but just for a month it'll do.'

'It's great,' I said. 'Exactly what you need.'

'This is where the wheel's going.' He raised one hand towards the centre of the room. 'And the sink's over there, and when we've got your mum settled in I'll fetch the shelves in from the trailer and all my bits and pieces.' When he turned around his face shone with the excited glow of a child, and I saw for the first time that he held the bust of my mother in front of him, clutched to his chest.

I wandered back into the hall and poked my head round the living room door. Lorry was still there, exactly as I'd left him, thumb jammed in his mouth and fast asleep. I crouched down next to him and pushed the hair away from his eyes.

In the last couple of months, he'd changed. His legs were getting longer, and he was filling out. He was talking now and could use the toilet like other four-year-olds. It was as though the accident had forced him to grow up, to shake off his infancy and become a child.

In the kitchen, as I'd expected, my mother was sitting at the table, her fingers rubbing away at her skirt. The window was now completely black, the patch of concrete outside invisible and only my mother's face reflected in the glass, a white oval suspended above an invisible body. She appeared to stare straight ahead, out into the garden, but her eyes were unfocused and blank.

My dad and I roamed the house, inspecting bedrooms and the small dingy bathroom. I was pleased when he said I could have the room in the attic, the one with the little arched window I'd seen from the road.

It was tiny, more like a box room than a bedroom, with a sloping roof and wooden beams, but it was cosy and quiet and away from the rest of my family. I had been right about the curtains: they were ripped and dangling loosely from the rail by a few remaining hooks, so I took them down and bundled them up into a parcel.

The furniture in my room was sparse. A hard, narrow bed faced the window, with no sheets or pillow, and I was glad I'd brought my sleeping bag. Built into the wall on one side of the bed was a cupboard, and a chair stood on the other side, under the slope of the eaves. It looked like a school chair, one of those hard, wooden ones that was built for economy rather than comfort. On the far wall, next to the window, a small stone mantelpiece capped a tiny fireplace.

The window was hard to open, and at first I thought it had been painted shut, and resigned myself to a night of sweaty, restless heat, but then with enough pressure I managed to get the latch up and it swung open. I could see the chapel we'd passed on our way into the village. The night had come in fully now, and the chapel's windows were silvery in the moonlight.

There was a cottage, even tinier than ours, that I hadn't noticed when we'd arrived. It was set back behind a patch of lawn fronted by a rickety picket fence and a gate that was hanging off its hinges. The gable end faced the side of our cottage, and there was a tiny attic window set high up that mirrored my own.

I placed the treasure bag down on the bed and pulled out the shoe box. I took off the lid and then I picked out each of the relics and inspected them in turn.

The robin's egg, tiny and sky-blue, I unwrapped from its cotton wool nest and placed in its own eggcup on the mantelpiece.

Then the magpie's egg, slightly bigger and greenish-blue and mottled: that too had a special eggcup.

The duckling's bill and bone were wrapped in tissue paper. When unwrapped, this had to be folded and made into a pillow for them.

The blue, freckled blackbird's egg had its own eggcup too, even though, like the others, it was barely visible when put inside.

Finally, I unwrapped the feathers of wren, the penultimate relic and obtained only that morning. I lifted them carefully from the folds of their silk scarf and placed them at the end of the row. I left a space at the end, on the far right-hand side. It wouldn't be long. I allowed myself a silent congratulation. The mantelpiece made a perfect altar. It was just what the Creed demanded.

When I went downstairs, my dad had already started unpacking the trailer, and the hallway was full of boxes. We'd only brought the things we really needed for the month we'd be at the cottage: clothes and bedding and my dad's sculpting stuff.

We took a few minutes to explore the contents of the sideboard. A drawer held random items of cutlery. There were bone-handled knives and forks and ornate spoons with elaborately patterned handles and tarnished bowls. Inside the cupboard there were a few assorted glasses and some plates, all with different patterns and all chipped in places, and some with the faint tracery of cracks that comes with age. There were tea cups and mugs, and again most of them were chipped but some were elegantly curved and made of thin, translucent china. The tea cups were stacked, one inside another, and as I reached for them they tipped and the top one fell to the floor and smashed. Shards of china scattered across the flagstones.

'Careful, Nif,' my dad said. 'That's not our stuff, remember?' He shuffled out to the hall with an empty box; that was my chance.

I checked that my mother still had her back to me and, using my left hand, I picked another of the china cups from the top of the stack and tapped its rim against the flagstoned floor. It made a small but satisfying crack, and when I tapped again, chips of porcelain flew off. It wasn't for me, I told myself. It was for the Creed. It needed to balance out the negative energy. Carefully I put both broken cups into a bucket that serviced as a bin.

Lorry staggered into the kitchen, rubbing his eyes and frowning. I picked him up and inspected his filthy legs. The dried blood on his knees from where he'd fallen out of the car was crusted and brown and mixed with tiny pieces of gravel. His bandages were filthy and starting to unravel.

'Shall we get you washed, Lorry?' I asked him. 'Shall we get you nice and clean and into your pyjamas?' He nodded drowsily. My dad came back in, carrying more boxes, but when he saw Lorry he put them down and took my brother from me. He sat down with him at the pine table.

My mother stared out of the window, contemplative, calm.

I thought I could wash Lorry at the kitchen sink, and got his bag of stuff from the hall. I got everything out, the cloths and towel, his ointments and bandages and his pyjamas, and arranged them on the table.

I turned on the tap and a silverfish darted out and scuttled across the sink before slipping down the plug hole. A gurgle and then nothing. My dad got up, hoisting Lorry onto his hip, and peered into the sink. He tried the other tap. Nothing happened.

'It's the drought.' My mother's voice sounded suddenly loud in the quiet of the kitchen. 'I read it in the paper. There hasn't been any running water out here for weeks now. Everyone's having to use the wells and boil up the water from the streams and the rivers. We're not in the city anymore.' It was the most my mother had said in weeks and she sounded satisfied and smug. My dad cleared his throat.

'Well, I suppose we'll just have to make a few adjustments then. We've got a couple more bottles of water in the trailer, they'll do for now. It'll be a bit like camping, an adventure.' His voice was perfectly even, but I knew he was struggling to stay calm. My mother snorted.

'An adventure!' Her eyebrows were raised, in a way I hadn't seen for ages, and she looked at my dad, challenging. She appeared to gain strength from his discomfort, and in the harshness of the strip light the contours of her face were starker, more chiselled, her eyes darker. My dad looked away and kissed the top of Lorry's head.

I fetched one of the bottles of water from the trailer and soaked pieces of cotton wool and wiped them over Lorry's knees, picking out the little pieces of gravel from where he had fallen from the car. He began to whimper, burrowing his face into my dad's neck. I removed his bandages and winced as the crusted blood clung to the fabric, afraid that if I pulled too quickly the scabs would come away whole. I then tended to his other knee, the one that had been undamaged and unharmed, until I'd ground gravel into it. I told myself it wasn't my fault. The Creed demanded equilibrium.

Eventually, we managed to get him cleaned up, and I put ointment on the sores on his legs, where the psoriasis was really bad, and clean bandages over the top. It was better than nothing and I planned to find somewhere to wash him properly in the morning.

Lorry's bedroom was next to my parents' room and my dad had made up a bed for him with sheets and pillows from the car. I carried him up the creaking stairs and put him down gently onto the bed. He looked at me in that drunken way of his, his half-closed eyes slanting up at the sides, and smiled.

'You're a good boy, Lorry,' I said. By now it was gone eleven o'clock and way past his bedtime, but he managed another smile.

'Lorry love Nif,' he said, the thick syllables merging together so that anyone else wouldn't have been able to understand him.

'And Nif loves Lorry,' I said, and I kissed him on his cheek.

We sat, that evening—my dad, my mother and me—around the old pine table. We picked at bits of bread and chunks of cheese. I drank the lemonade we'd brought with us and my dad and my mother drank red wine from the glasses we'd found in the cupboard. My mother had loosened her hair and let it hang about her shoulders, and even in the stark glare of the strip light she looked younger, prettier, somehow softer.

'So, what do you think, Nif?' my dad said. It was the first time anyone had asked for my opinion of the house.

'It's OK,' I said, and then, seeing his eyes darken, 'I think we can make it work.'

'Good girl. That's the spirit. We'll all get a good night's sleep tonight, and in the morning we'll see it in a new light. A new day always sheds a fresh light on things, I find. We can unpack the rest of our stuff from the trailer and you can go out into the village and make friends and it'll be just like home.'

Friends. My dad had just broken the unspoken rule in our house that we didn't talk about friends—or more to the point, my lack of them—but I didn't say anything. He seemed to be made bolder by the absence of a negative response.

'And Linda.' He picked up my mother's hand and held it. 'What do you think?'

My mother looked down at her lap, to where her other hand stroked the fabric of her skirt. When she looked up again, I was surprised to see that her face was glowing and her eyes were alive. She took a breath, a breath that seemed to take forever, and then spoke.

'I think she might be here with us,' she said. 'I can't be sure,' and her fingers fluttered away on her skirt. 'But I can feel something...' She looked down at her lap. I could feel rather than see my dad tense at my side, but before he could say anything my mother spoke again, quietly, as if she was shy, or putting on a child's pretence at shyness.

'I can't quite put my finger on it. There's a sort of a... presence.' She gave a small shrug and a half-smile played across her lips. 'I think she's here with us and she likes it here.'

My dad inhaled deeply, and then let out a long and carefully-controlled breath. He let go of my mother's hand and I knew without looking that his eyes would be closed. When my mother spoke again it wasn't to either of us.

'Yes, she likes it here,' said my mother, her voice hanging for a moment in the stillness of the heavy air. 'It's perfect. I think Petra will be happy here.'

Ah, yes. Petra.

My dead sister Petra.

Three.

The sun poking around in my bedroom woke me early; the light was already insistent and rude. As usual, there on the periphery of my mind was the remnant of a dream, the vague echo of something peculiar and intangible, teasing me.

Lying there, with the sunlight streaming into my bedroom, I wished I hadn't taken down the curtains, but I allowed myself to savour the early-morning sunshine before the temperature rose to an unbearable level. I lay there for a bit until the clamminess of the sleeping bag got too much and I swung myself out of bed.

The relics sat on the mantelpiece in the correct order: *Robin's egg, magpie's egg, duckling bill and bone. Blackbird's egg, feathers of wren…*and then the space where the incantation should have continued. It niggled at me, the vacuum at the end of the rhyme an itch to be scratched. I picked up the robin's egg, the first one I'd found, the first item in my collection. It was tiny, no bigger than my thumbnail, and still the startling blue colour it had been when I'd first found it. I ran a finger over the surface, enjoying its familiar chalky texture.

I had found the nest a couple of weeks after Petra died. It was April Fool's day. My mother had been having a particularly bad day. She was bed-ridden, as she usually was in those early days. Long periods of silence would be punctuated by the sound of her voice seeping out under her bedroom door, a wail that rose in a tremor and then died out. The nuns who tended to her during the first few days after the accident had given up and returned to the convent, offended by her loud and obscene denouncements of their religion. One of them had even gone so far as to imply that my mother had 'let the devil in' and suggested that my dad call the priest. He'd frowned at me to stop me from laughing, and had then resigned himself to caring for her himself.

I had let myself out through the back door, into the garden. Spring had come in with a whimper and we'd become used to the tepid, clammy hand of fog that wafted perpetually over the vegetable patch and the scratchy grass that masqueraded as a lawn. In the distance was the hum of traffic on the ring road.

I was kicking at what remained of the potato mounds, enjoying making the dusty soil fly around, when I saw the flash of blue from the corner of my eye.

The nest was in the most unlikely of places—in one of my dad's old wellies that had been left outside the shed. It was a tangle of grass, moss and dead leaves tucked down inside the boot, and if it hadn't been for the startling colour of the eggs inside I wouldn't have noticed it at all. Gently, barely daring to touch it, I picked up one of the eggs and held it in my palm, marvelling at the weightlessness of it. It was both there and not there.

That was when my dad appeared from the house, dishevelled and broken-looking, and told me to come in and that I wasn't allowed to play outside by myself anymore. I don't know why, but I didn't want to tell him about the nest, and I didn't want him to see that I'd picked up the egg. I'd held it loosely in my hand, behind my back, and he hadn't noticed. He only really noticed my mother in those days, and the empty shell she had become.

That night I went into my dad's studio and took down his book about birds. I'd leafed through the pages until I spotted the picture that looked like my egg. A robin. I'd held the egg up to my bedside lamp, and I'd wondered if there was a baby robin in it. If I cracked it open, would there be a little egg yolk and white, like a chicken's egg but tiny? I couldn't see anything through the blue shell. If there was a life in there I wasn't going to witness it.

For weeks, I kept the egg wrapped up in cotton wool in my sock drawer, and each morning and evening I would check to see if it had hatched, but it never did. I decided not long after I'd found it that it was never going to hatch, but I kept it still—and soon after I started to collect the other relics. I still didn't know then that the Creed was coming to find me.

Standing there in the tiny bedroom in the attic of the cottage, I thought about how much had changed since Petra died. It had only been four months, but in that time, I had become an adult.

I put the robin's egg back in its eggcup and pulled on my clothes—shorts and a t-shirt from the day before, even though they were grubby and smelt a bit. I didn't care what I looked or smelt like; I quite liked the slightly musky animal smell that would rise off me by the end of the day. It was a scent that was all mine and like no-one else's, not even Lorry's, which was warm and sweet like biscuits.

I used the toilet in the dingy bathroom, remembering not to flush but instead closing the lid softly. I crept down the stairs from my little attic room, trying to remember which ones creaked. My parents' door was firmly shut, as it always was at home. I peeked into Lorry's room.

He was lying with the sheets tangled around his legs, his arms thrown back above his head. He'd taken his pyjamas off in the night and they lay in a tangle at the foot of the bed. He looked thin and vulnerable lying there in only his pants, and the bandages added an incongruous bulk to his skinny legs. He'd been scratching in the night and the sheets and the clean bandages I'd put on the night before were already stained with blood. His clown doll sat on the pillow next to him, eyeing me vacantly, mouth downturned.

As soon as I got downstairs I noticed again the telephone that was attached to the wall, the cream plastic and the round dial incongruously modern in this dark old house.

In the kitchen, there were still a few boxes piled around where we'd started unpacking the night before. I thought my dad had wanted to make this place into a home for us, for the month we'd be staying there, and had packed a few familiar things from our house in an attempt to settle us in. But our teapot—the red apples on the side faded and the end of the spout made brown with tannin—looked out of place in this bare room. The wooden chopping board with the carved wheat sheaves; the majolica pot that held the

31

wooden spoons by the cooker; the Formica placemats with their pictures of the Hay Wain: all looked alien against the emptiness of the kitchen.

I put a few things away in a cupboard—canisters of tea, a bag of sugar, some flour—but I couldn't really be bothered. It was a Sunday and there was no telly in the cottage. I pulled on my plimsolls that I'd abandoned the night before in the hall and unlocked the door. I stood on the threshold for a few moments, taking in the empty sky and filling my lungs with the thin air that I knew would be gone in a couple of hours. Already the stillness hinted at the heat to come, and the dreadful sultry swelter that was on its way.

The rusting gate squeaked when I pulled it open, and I winced, waiting for something to happen. Nothing. There was no-one on the lane and the dust lay still. From the verge on the opposite side, a couple of rabbits lolloped out. They were leaner, rangier than the ones I'd seen in the park at home, and they hopped closer, within a couple of feet of me. I remembered my dad telling me that the heatwave had caused a lot of animals to change their behaviour, that they had to adapt to an environment where there was very little water, and that they took greater risks around humans because they were thirsty. I went down on my haunches and held out a hand to them, encouraging them to come to me. They just looked at me glassily, so I kicked out at them and they scampered back into the hedge next to the little cottage on the other side of the lane.

It was set back from the road with nothing but a patch of scorched grass and a dilapidated wooden fence in front of it. The two houses mirrored each other, as though they were whispering together in collusion against the chapel. All the curtains were closed, except for those at the little attic window.

The chapel was painted a dirty white and a coppery discharge was weeping from the walls. The windows reflected the morning sunlight, blank as cataracts. The gates were still padlocked shut and there was a fence running along either side, black-painted railings with curling, fleur-de-lys spikes across the top.

I wanted to see the war memorial in daylight, where I'd seen the girls the night before. The cows in the field stared at me with insolent indifference as I walked along the lane. There were half a dozen or so of the scraggy creatures, and they were suffering from the heat. Emaciated, their ribs bulged rudely through the sandpaper-like skin on their flanks. Their tails twitched at the flies that clustered around them, and which settled on the rims of their eyes and the pale flesh of their noses. Pathetic animals.

I came to a little bridge that I hadn't noticed the night before. There was a low stone wall that ran along the side of the lane where it crossed the stream, that only came up as far as my thighs. I leant over it to inspect the brown water below. There was barely any left, maybe a couple of feet. Further down the stream, where it dragged itself along the valley, a tree trunk swelled out, hanging over the water. There the stream looked deeper, welcoming, somewhere to bring Lorry later, to get him washed. I looked around to see how we would be able to get down there and I spotted a gate which I thought might open into the field that banked the stream. That would do. Sweat was already starting to prickle on my back; I would need a wash later, too.

The war memorial stood erect but sullen in the middle of a patch of faded grass, facing me as soon as I turned a bend in the lane. It was supported by a stone plinth and the steps around the base were littered with empty lager cans and cigarette ends. I looked to see if anything could be salvaged. There were a few fag ends that could be reused so I pocketed them. That was when I noticed the dips all around the base of the war memorial, little concave holes that were about two inches wide and regularly spaced. The stone the monument had been carved from was darker than that used for the houses in the village. It was the same grey, mottled stone, but it looked more worn, and older, as if it had been standing here forever.

Looking up, I saw that instead of forming a pyramid-shaped peak at the top, or a sharp-pointed cross like all the other war memorials I had seen, this one ended in a small, delicate cross, curled at the three ends, like the ace of clubs. The stone was battered and had obviously been eroded over time, and it looked as if it might crumble away at any moment. It looked older than it was possible for a war memorial to be. I placed the tips of my fingers in one of the little dips at the base of the monument and the stone felt smooth against my skin.

In the corner of my eye there was a flash of movement and I heard a clicking sound. I jerked round, expecting to see someone. Nothing, only the relentless stillness and the flat colours of a depleted landscape. Already, I could see the familiar shimmer of heat that rose from the lane, making the grass verge tremble and threaten to disappear.

Time to head back.

We cooked bacon for breakfast on the little camping stove we'd brought with us and ate it sitting round the kitchen table. We drank tea and nobody said very much. My mother came down while we were eating, her dressing gown wrapped tightly around her and held closed against her throat. Her hair was pulled up tightly into her usual bun, and I thought about how she'd looked the night before when we'd sat at this table and she'd drunk red wine and talked about Petra and she'd looked ten years younger. Now she looked ancient. She toyed with the bacon rinds on her plate, pushing them round with her fork. Worms in grease.

After breakfast, I took Lorry outside and we lay on the patch of concrete at the front of the house. It was covered in a web of cracks and frail tufts of dandelions sprouted half-heartedly here and there, the petals wilted and thin. I pulled them up in tufts and threw them onto the scorched grass. I watched as Lorry picked his nose, as he eased out the thick gobbets of dust and snot that accumulated there before depositing them in his mouth. Occasionally, a red ant would scurry past, sometimes carrying a trophy above its head, and I'd use my thumb to grind it into the concrete, causing a pathetic smear of rusty brown to appear against the grey. The heatwave instilled a lethargy in us that was difficult to shake off. We lay torpid in the sun, limbs stretched, lizards soaking up the heat.

Lorry's face was turned up to the sun, his eyes closed. He hadn't said much that morning, but that wasn't unusual. He only really talked to say what he needed, to ask for food and water and the other things that had to be done for him to keep him alive. His hair curled against the grass, the soft blond strands mingling with the starchy yellow hay that encroached onto the edge of the concrete from the lawn around it.

I lay flat on my belly, enjoying the mid-morning warmth on my back, and put my chin on my arm. A grasshopper landed on the concrete in front of me, an inch of green-brown legs and torso. Its feelers twitched and I waited for it to start clicking, anticipating it rubbing its legs together and calling out for a mate, but it stayed silent. I put a hand out to it, but before I could grab it, it hopped away.

It was still early enough for the sun to be quite benign. I turned over onto my back and closed my eyes. An imprint of a bright circle remained in my vision, and little lights danced, bright green against orange. I knew that when I opened my eyes they would still be there for a few moments, temporarily scorched onto my retinas.

To my left the grasshopper started to make its rasping sound, and I turned my head and eased my eyes open, cautious of the sun's glare. The sound stopped abruptly and I couldn't see the insect at all. As my eyes adjusted back to the brightness, my focus shifted and I spotted something glinting on the railings at the front of the parking area, suspended and skewered by the spike at the top of one post, something gleaming white. I lay very still and looked at it. It hadn't been there when I'd got back from my walk earlier that morning.

I pushed myself to my feet, all the time looking at the object, afraid that it might disappear if I let it out of my sight. I never once took my eyes off it as I walked towards it, climbed the steps and squeaked open the little gate. Only when I was within a couple of feet of it could I see what it was.

It was a skull, a bird's skull with a sharp, shiny black beak protruding from the bone. It had been placed on the post so that the spike pierced one of the eye sockets, the skull tilted in an absurd expression of confusion. I lifted it carefully off the fence.

The surface was scattered with hairline cracks, tiny fissures that spread in a web over the cranium. The pearly-white bone held eye sockets that were dark and empty. The skull fitted comfortably into the curve of my palm, but the beak was heavier than the bone, and it tipped forward, the sharp end pressing into the soft flesh of my fingertip. I bent to it and breathed in deeply—at first I thought it had no smell at all, but then I caught the suggestion of something warm and dark and earthy.

In my mind, I recited the incantation. *Robin's egg, magpie's egg, duckling bill and bone. Blackbird's egg, feathers of wren...* I felt sure that the bird's skull was the final relic, the one that would complete the incantation. I left Lorry lying there in the sun and ran up both flights of stairs to my bedroom. I placed the skull on the end of the mantelpiece, next to the other relics. It fitted perfectly.

Four.

I used to enjoy going to church. Of course, I was younger then, but I used to love the ritual of walking up the path to Our Lady of Holy Saviour every Sunday morning with my mother, and the warm smell of incense that would greet us as we pushed open the heavy wooden doors. I'd wonder if the holy water in the little bowl on the side really was magic as I poked a finger in and made the sign of the Father, the Son and the Holy Ghost.

I would dip to one knee before shuffling along the pew, and feel the embroidered prayer stool hard-stuffed under my knees. Then I'd sit on the slippery polished wood and gaze at the enormous crucifix that was suspended above the altar. I used to marvel at how Jesus' face could be formed into such an exquisite expression of tolerant melancholy, while at the same time he wore a crown of thorns and was pinned, hands and feet, to the cross.

Water Shall Refuse Them

The thing I liked most about going to church was the long, drawling incantations, in a language I didn't understand, but which was still somehow familiar. Father Declan's voice was low and monotonous and reassuring, and I would find a tranquillity in the church that I don't think I've ever felt anywhere else. I never really felt very religious; I never prayed at home, or read the bible, so when my mother stopped going to church, after the accident, I stopped going too. For me, the church was about the sights and the sounds and the smells, not about God.

If I had seen a psychiatrist like they wanted me to, he would say that I was trying to impose order on my life by constructing a new religion. He would say that after Petra died, and we no longer went to church, I needed some stability in my life, something to cling to while my parents got on with their grief. To an extent, this hypothetical psychiatrist would be right. I did find that after the accident I needed something that gave me a purpose, even though I already had Lorry to look after, but I didn't need a religion; I had never really had one to start with, not in the full sense. What I needed was something to take control of my life. That's probably why the Creed found me.

Finding the robin's egg had been the start of it, a couple of weeks after the accident, even though I didn't know it then. It was another couple of weeks afterwards that I found the magpie's egg, and then it seemed like a sign.

It was Maundy Thursday. It was also my sixteenth birthday that day, but no-one had remembered; it was only a month after Petra died. I was playing in my bedroom with Lorry, getting him to lie on his back while I rolled a toy car across his belly. I remember the smell telling me that I needed to change his nappy before I made his dinner.

My mother had been getting increasingly agitated all day, and I'd heard my dad on the phone to the doctor that morning. She'd started shouting things, and there were scratches on my dad's cheek when he came out to let the doctor in. When I walked past the door of the bedroom I could see a sliver of her through the crack, lying on the white sheets, mouth open, eyes blank. She wasn't my mother anymore. She was an impostor, a depiction of what she had been, with the inside, the important bit, missing. It was as though someone had taken her away and replaced her with a statue.

I went out into the garden that morning with Lorry, half expecting my dad to come after us and tell us to go back in again, that we weren't allowed out on our own. But he didn't and we made it down to the bottom of the garden. Although the heatwave hadn't really kicked in by then, it was still warm and stuffy for Easter and I only had on a t-shirt and jeans. Lorry was shuffling along, grunting and hanging his tongue out like a dog.

It was Lorry who spotted the axe, lying in a pile of wood behind the shed. The wooden handle was sticking up in the air and had a pale sheen of grey-green mould blooming on it. It was heavier than I'd been expecting, and when I tried to pick it up I struggled against the weight of it and it had stayed jammed in the woodpile. The mould came off onto my palm and I'd wiped it on my jeans. The second time, I lifted the axe with both hands and it came up, scattering little logs from the heap where it had been lying. It was about three feet long and the blade was rusting and dull and huge. I swung it like a pendulum and imagined a woodsman heaving it over his shoulder, maybe Little Red Riding Hood's father, bringing it down under its own momentum onto the neck of the wolf.

It was on the back-swing that the axe caught in the rhododendron bush behind me. A clatter of twigs and small branches fell to the ground, along with a dusty pile of dry mud. Two eggs rolled out from the remains of the nest, larger than the robin's egg I'd found, a greenish-blue with dark olive-green mottling. One of the eggs had cracked and, as I watched, a jelly seeped from it, red and orange and black. I leant down and prodded it with a fingertip, then I used a nail to peel back the shell from around the crack. A tiny beak and two bulbous black orbs were revealed. The creature gave a shiver and then it stopped moving. I picked up the other egg and put it in my pocket.

Lorry started prodding the broken egg with his toe. I grabbed his hand and pulled him away and dragged him up the path to the back door. I already had my hand on the door handle when I heard a flutter, barely there. I turned around and a magpie was standing next to the bundle of twigs. Its head was twisting, first one way, then the other, looking alternately at the egg and at us.

I had a flash of memory of a song my mother used to sing to me, when I was younger, much younger, and was learning to count. We would sit at the dining room window, looking out over the back garden, counting the magpies as they fluttered down and inspected the bonfire.

'One for sorrow, two for joy,' the song started, and then my mother's face would light up and she would hold her crucifix while she sang the next bit. 'Three for a girl and four for a boy.' It was as though she was wishing for another child, or praying—I couldn't tell which—but after that, the song came to take on a special meaning for her and she would look out for magpies wherever we went.

Even then I knew I wasn't good enough for her.

I held Lorry's hand as we watched the magpie inspect its shattered nest. It hopped closer and nudged the smashed egg with its beak. Then it started pecking at the broken remains of its chick.

The bird skull looked at home next to the other relics. That was the thing about the Creed: the newest addition had to go on the right-hand side, never mind how unsymmetrical that made the relics. At first it had really bothered me, like when I found the blackbird's egg which was a bit bigger than the robin's egg and made the display off-kilter. But the Creed said that was how it had to be done and it looked fine to me now.

Of course, I'd been wondering about how the skull had got onto the railings. It looked like it had been cleaned, or bleached somehow, and I was intrigued about who had left it there. The only people I could think of was the group of girls I had seen by the war memorial on our first night in the village, and I wondered if they'd left it as a warning of some sort.

The air in my room was stuffy and dank, even though the window was thrown wide open. I knew that outside would be no better, that even when a rare breeze came, it would be hot, and would carry with it the dust that seemed to settle on every surface, choking all the living things. The heatwave had assumed a permanence in our lives. There seemed to be no end in sight, no relief from the relentless heat and light and the decay it was causing. It seemed strange to think that there had been a time, only a few months ago, when the grass had been green and fresh and abundant, instead of wizened and parched. It was as though Petra's death had lingered somehow, had insinuated its way not only into the crevices of our lives and infected us, but into the wider environment, into the weather and the landscape. By coming to this village, we had not escaped from Petra's death, but had taken it with us.

I remembered Lorry, sitting outside on the patch of concrete, all on his own. I was about to go and check on him when the stillness of the morning was disturbed by the sound of an engine which drew me to my bedroom window. The enormous padlock on the chapel gates winked at me in the sunlight and a second later a car drove up and parked on the verge. It was dark blue and spotlessly clean, as though the owner had very recently removed the dust that clung to everything else in the valley. The driver's door opened and a man got out. Small, hunched, dark-haired, he scuttled from the car. A beetle of a man.

He reached round to the back door and opened it. A little brown and white dog—a terrier of some sort—jumped out and started sniffing around at the grass, its nose snuffling at the verge. The beetle man then opened the passenger door. From my bedroom window, I couldn't see who the occupant was, and the beetle man stood for a moment, waiting for whoever was inside to get out.

A head appeared. A man's head—dark, like the beetle—but as the man pulled himself up to his full height I could see that he was much taller. He held out his arm, the elbow crooked. The beetle man took it and they looked like a peculiar parody of an old-fashioned courting couple. The beetle man led the taller man around the car and they stood in front of the iron gates. A set of keys was produced from the beetle man's pocket and he fumbled with the padlock, and that was when the other man turned around and I saw his face for the first time.

His shuffling gait had led me to expect an old man, but he was in fact not much older than my dad. His dark suit made his face appear pale, almost as white as the shirt he wore. He had black hair, Brylcreemed back over his forehead, and a nose that was long and angular, beak-like and hooked. His mouth turned down at the corners. In his right hand he held a book, small and leather-bound like the ones on the shelf in our living room.

The beetle man hurried in through the gates and turned his attention to the lock on the chapel doors. They swung open and he disappeared inside. Brylcreem was standing just outside the gates, his hands clasped together in front of him, the book held tightly between them. His head was lowered and I thought he might have been praying. The terrier was skittering around in the courtyard in front of the chapel, and then it stopped and cocked its leg against a gatepost.

The sound of an engine announced the arrival of another car before I saw it, but then it appeared and parked on the verge. A man got out from the driver's seat, also dark-suited, and a woman followed from the passenger seat. The beetle man must have heard the car because he came scurrying out from the chapel to meet them.

He greeted the man and the woman, and drew the man towards Brylcreem. The woman hung back, and busied herself with the contents of her handbag, but the man held out his hand to Brylcreem and the beetle man looked like he was introducing him, saying the man's name. The minister greeting his flock, I thought, and it was true, they did look like a flock, but a flock of birds, not sheep. The man, short and puffed-up; the woman, small and neat and dressed in a dark skirt suit, even in the sordid heat, the waist pinched in and the neck with a wide collar. Jackie O but a decade out of date.

More cars drew up and more people arrived, walking along the lane from both directions. Shortly a small crowd had gathered, all dressed in their Sunday best. The women all wore the same sort of suits as the first woman to arrive, greys and navies and variations on black, and some of them also had boxy hats on hairspray-tight hair. The women congregated in a wide circle, their mouths working away, all speaking at once, all pecking out their gossip.

The men stood in threes or fours, silently holding cigarettes between pinched fingers, sucking in the smoke and not making eye contact with each other. One by one they approached the minister who would take their outstretched hand and shake it, his other hand gripping the man's elbow and drawing him closer. He would lean forward and say something into the other man's ear and then release his arm. None of the women approached the minister.

I counted off all the men doing this in the five minutes I stood at the window. A pecking order maybe, an unspoken hierarchy of greetings? It seemed to me that everyone knew the routine, that nothing was left to chance. This ceremony was a well-practised and long-standing ritual.

Then something peculiar happened. The beetle man opened the boot of his car and took out a box, a low wooden tray, the sort you get from the greengrocer to hold oranges. He took out bunches of what looked like herbs—green leaves tied together at one end in clusters, and each about the size of an adult's hand. He passed these around, and when each member of the congregation had one of these bunches, he returned the

45

box to the boot of the car and came back with a bottle and a shallow silver tray. He unscrewed the lid from the bottle and, holding the tray against his chest, poured in a small stream of clear liquid. Then the minister stepped forward and passed his hand slowly over the top of the tray, his eyes closed and his lips moving very slightly, for all the world like he was blessing the water. All the while, the congregation looked on silently.

Then the beetle man held the tray out and, one by one, each of the chapel-goers stepped forward and dipped their bundles of leaves into the water. When they had all done this they turned, en masse, to face the tiny cottage that stood opposite ours. Without a word being spoken, they all raised their bunches and shook them in the direction of the house, causing a fine and barely visible shower of water to hang in the air for a second before it evaporated.

Every one of them had their faces raised to the sky and their eyes closed. Almost imperceptibly, a murmuring began, as though one person had started it and then gradually all the others were joining in. Slowly, it got louder and more insistent. It was impossible to tell where the chant began or ended; it was incomprehensible, words overlapping and obscuring other words. It was a torrent of sounds I didn't understand, like water over a waterfall. Welsh.

Abruptly, as if on an unspoken command, the chanting stopped and the congregation turned back to face the chapel. They followed the minister as he led them in through the iron gates and over the courtyard that stood between the railings and the enormous dark wooden doors. As the doors opened, an immense wail emerged. I thought of my mother and her unholy shrieking in the early days after the accident, but then I remembered: the organ. The animal whine turned into a horrible dirge and the flock of women and the little gatherings of men came together, each couple pairing up as they walked into the chapel, heads bowed, women on the right and men on the left. In turn, they each handed their bundles of herbs to the beetle man, who placed them back in the wooden box. When they had all entered the chapel, the beetle man swung the doors closed behind them and they were swallowed by the darkness.

I didn't stop to think about what I'd just seen. I grabbed the empty treasure bag and pushed a couple of towels into it, and clean shorts and a t-shirt. On my way down the stairs I collected some clothes for Lorry from his bedroom. Outside the kitchen door I could hear the telltale rustle of words: my parents whispering an argument.

Lorry was dozing when I got outside, his face turned up to the sky. I nudged him with the toe of my plimsoll and he lifted a hand to his eyes, shading them against the sun.

'C'mon, Lorry. We're going out,' I said.

He started muttering his resistance to this idea, so I just hauled him up from the patch of concrete. He looked ridiculous in his pants and bandages, so I made him put on the clothes I'd got for him.

As we passed the chapel, the little dog was still snuffling around, but it stopped when it saw us and yapped a few times. It scurried out through the gates towards us and I reached down to touch it, but it shrank away from me, its yellow teeth bared and its hackles raised. It started yapping again, and it only stopped when the howl of the organ started seeping out from the chapel, faint but insistent. The great wooden doors were closed, and the windows were all shut despite the heat, but the higher notes had found a way out through a crack somewhere and they followed us, their insistent whine taunting us as we made our way along the lane.

Even though it was mid-morning, there was still no-one around. It was as though the whole village had gone to chapel. There was no-one sunbathing or chucking their bathwater onto the flower beds, like there would have been on a Sunday morning at home. A few ragged sheep peered at us over the barbed wire that ran along the side of the road, but apart from them the only living things were the magpies, four of them, sitting on the fence. They were preening themselves, dipping their heads under their wings and drawing feathers through their beaks, but they stopped when they saw us and watched silently as we made our way along the lane, their heads sinking into glossy necks.

We came to the stream. Further down the lane, I could make out the war memorial standing stark and black against the hazy blue of the sky. I leant over the low stone wall and the water below moved slowly, thick and viscous. Downstream, where the oak tree hung over the bank, the water swirled darker, deeper, more inviting.

I climbed over the gate into the field, the red paint flaking onto my palms like scabs, and then I helped Lorry to climb over. The grass here was coarse and long and it scratched my legs. I carried Lorry the last little bit, and I made him stand up while I clambered down to a shallow bank that sat under the shade of the tree. I lifted Lorry down after me, and got him to undress, easing the bandages away from his damaged legs, coaxing the dried blood away from the gauze. He cried, but eventually the bandages were off and he stood there, looking at his legs, curious.

Water Shall Refuse Them

At first I couldn't persuade him to go into the water, and he pleaded with me to let him sit on the side and only put his legs in. After a while I lost my temper and I picked him up and waded into the water with him. I dumped him in and he fell over and cried and said he hated me. I dragged him up onto his feet and pushed him in further until he was in up to his belly, snivelling and whimpering. I could have made him go in further, the water at the base of the tree looked very deep, but I pulled him back and made him rub his hands over his legs and his arms, sloughing off the dirt and the bits of gravel that were still embedded in his knees.

When he was clean I gave him a towel and made him sit on the bank. I put my arms around him and kissed the top of his head. The sky was the colour of a sapphire, and it should have been beautiful, sitting there, just me and Lorry under the gaze of the sun. But the heatwave had become intolerable since we'd arrived in this village that had tucked itself away from the world at the bottom of the valley. It was as though the high sides of the valley walls amplified the intensity of the sun. I felt scrutinised by the heat, violated, and this made the dark, gaping water under the oak tree look even more inviting.

I took off my shorts first. I folded them and placed them on the bank next to where Lorry was sitting. I took off my t-shirt quickly and put that with my other clothes. I didn't wear a bra. I slipped my pants off and covered myself with my hands and waded straight into the water. I went in as deep as my hips, drawing in a breath as the cold water lapped at me. I waded in further, as far as my belly, and the swirling stream stroked my hips. The cold rose around me and caressed my back and my arms. Under the water, I circled my hands over my stomach and my thighs, imagining the dirt dissolve and be carried away by the stream. My hands rose up my body and brushed over my nipples, hard beneath my palms.

That was when I saw the boy.

He was behind the tree, about six feet away from me. I could only see the top half of his face; the rest was obscured by the tree trunk. His eyes were deep-set and dark-shadowed and the hair which sprang from the top of his head was mousy and tangled.

My arms flew around my shoulders, an instinctive attempt to hide my nakedness. I glared at him, glad of the water that covered the rest of me. The boy stood up and watched me for a moment; all the while I could feel the heat of the sun on my naked shoulders. Then he grinned and winked, and gave me a thumbs-up. He started walking away backwards, all the time looking at me and smiling, then he turned and ran off, back the way Lorry and I had walked, the long grass whipping at his jeans, his bare back gleaming pale in the sunlight.

Hunkering down, I scuttled to the river bank and grabbed my towel. I threw it round me like a cape.

'Lorry wanna go home.' My brother's voice was a whine through the silence.

I pulled on my clothes, the fabric snagging against my wet skin, and then I dragged Lorry to his feet.

'Come on, then,' I said. 'We're going.'

The cars had all gone from outside the chapel when we got back to the house, but my dad was standing on the other side of the lane, leaning on the fence that ran along the front garden of the little cottage. It looked like he was talking to someone on the other side, leaning forward with one hand jammed into his back pocket. As we approached, I could see that it was a woman.

She had on a bubblegum-pink bikini and her skin was nut-brown, like she'd been sunbathing for weeks. Her hair was blonde and curly and held up in a ponytail on the top of her head. Little tendrils had got loose and sprang around her face. There was blue eyeshadow lighting up her eyes and she was wearing lipstick. She could have been a dancer on *Top of the Pops*.

She stood with one hand on her hip and in the other hand she had a bunch of flowers and leaves that looked as though it was already starting to wilt. They were both laughing, but stopped when they saw me and Lorry, and my dad raised a hand at her and walked towards us.

'Who was that?' I asked.

'Her name's Janet,' my dad said. He was smiling the big oafish grin he used to have back in the old days. 'She's our next-door neighbour.' He lowered his voice to a whisper. 'And she's a non-non-conformist.'

It took a little while for me to work it out, but then I saw the sly smirk on his face and I realised that he'd also seen the chapel-goers arriving that morning.

'She's not one of them,' he said, nodding towards the chapel. 'And she's got a son.' He looked at me sideways. 'He's about the same age as you, I think, and he might be able to show you around.'

I thought of the boy at the stream and must have blushed, because my dad put his hand on my shoulder and rubbed the back of my neck. I shrugged him off.

'Who's the woman?' my mother demanded, as soon as we'd got through the door. She was standing just inside the porch, waiting for us. She was still in her dressing gown and her hair lay on her shoulders in two greasy hanks.

For a moment, my dad's smile looked as though it was going to slide away, but then he found it again and he took my mother's hand in his. It was white and worm-ridden with veins.

'She's our neighbour and she's not from here and she doesn't go to chapel and I think you'll really like her.' His words all came out in a rush and he looked embarrassed, like a small boy.

I looked around the garden for Lorry and saw that he was sitting in a flower bed, rubbing his hands in the dry earth and excavating dead flowers. His clown doll lay on the ground next to him, grubby and forlorn.

'Really, Linda, you'd like her if you'd only let yourself talk to her.' He scratched his head. 'Just try, eh?'

He looked down at my mother's hand, sitting still like marble in his own. She shrugged and pulled her hand away. My dad sighed and pushed gently past her and went into the kitchen. I went to see what Lorry was doing to the flower bed.

The other thing about the Creed is that it makes you do things you might at first think are wrong. For instance, if you drop a cup on the floor and it smashes, you must drop another cup with the other hand to cancel out the negative energy, to make sure that nothing bad will come of it. It's a case of matching the opposites, of finding equilibrium, so that bad luck doesn't breed more bad luck.

So, when Lorry pulled up the dandelion, already withered in the heat and half-dead, and the red ants scattered out, angrily zig-zagging across the dirt, I had a feeling that there was only one way this was going to go. At first, he just scratched at his right hand, incredulity stamped on his face, rubbing away at the palm. He held it out to me, and I saw that a scattering of red dots had already appeared. Then he started moaning, and finally he was sobbing as he scrubbed away at his hand.

'What happened, Lorry?' I asked. Even though I knew the answer, I needed him to say it.

'Ants, Nif. Bite me,' he managed to get out between sobs, angry and annoyed all at once.

'Nasty ants,' I said, and pulled his hand towards me, palm upwards.

'Nif make better.'

'Nif can make it better,' I said, and very gently, I took hold of his arm and pulled him towards me. Slowly, I wrapped my arm around his shoulders and then very quickly I grabbed his left hand and pressed it, palm down, onto the hole left by the dandelion, where the ants were still streaming out. He tried to pull his hand back, but I was a good deal stronger than he was and I forced his hand down, feeling him flinch and squirm as the ants started to bite.

He looked at me in disbelief, the shock at what I had done clouding his pain. I felt the usual bubbling mixture of excitement and nausea when this happened, but I knew that repeating an action, creating balance, was the only way to stave off the bad luck. It was why I'd had to rub the gravel into Lorry's other knee on the night we'd arrived, when he'd fallen out of the car.

Finally, I let him go.

'I'm sorry, but I had to do that. You know that, don't you?'

'You horrid, Nif.' Lorry was snivelling and rubbing his hands together and walking in circles around the small dirty lawn. 'You horrid an' I'm gonna tell Daddy.'

'I'm sorry, Lorry, but Daddy doesn't care,' I said, and as soon as the words came out I realised they were true.

Five.

Sunday lunch was a paltry affair. We'd only brought a few bits and pieces of food with us in the car, and even if there had been any shops nearby, they would have been closed. We had some stale bread which we made into toast, and we ate that with a can of baked beans and some cheese. The fridge was old and worn out and didn't work very well in the heat, so the cheese was sweaty and rubbery. The milk had turned into chunks, so we drank our tea black.

I'd taken Lorry into the kitchen after the incident with the ants, and looked in the cupboards for something to put on the ant bites. I vaguely remembered that people used bicarbonate of soda for things like that, but there wasn't any. Instead I found an ancient bottle of vinegar, the screw top crusted and brown. I used one of Lorry's bandages and soaked it from the bottle, and pressed it onto each of his hands in turn. The smell of vinegar filled the kitchen.

One of the good things about Lorry, one of the things I liked most about him, was his willing acceptance of everything that happened to him as an incontrovertible fact. He didn't ask me why I'd forced his hand onto an anthill to make the ants bite him, or why I'd then done my best to alleviate the pain I'd caused. It wasn't a question of him having forgiven me, he just accepted it, and didn't ask questions, which meant I didn't have to make anything up.

We ate in silence, except for the sound of Lorry chewing and my mother's occasional harsh cough. When we'd finished eating, my mother lit a cigarette and I carried the plates to the sink.

'We need to get some water from the stream for washing up and stuff,' I said, mostly to my dad, but I was hoping my mother was listening as well. 'And the toilet hasn't been flushed in ages and it's starting to smell.'

'No need,' said my dad. 'Janet says there's a well in the field behind the chapel. It's her field, and she says we should just help ourselves. Fresh water, straight from the spring. Means we don't even have to boil it before we drink it.'

At the mention of Janet's name, my mother's mouth puckered around her cigarette, but she remained silent. I could tell that there was a fight brewing between my dad and my mother even though no-one had said anything. There was that static in the air, like before a storm, the sort that only dogs can detect. That was what I was like with my parents.

'Nif, can you take Lorry and go and fill the bottles up? There are a few more of those gallon containers in the studio you could fill at the same time.' My dad pushed his glasses up his nose as he spoke.

'I'm not taking Lorry with me.'

'Fine. Do what you want. Lorry can come and sit in the studio with me.' He looked at my mother, as if expecting her to disagree or complain or perhaps even concur with him, but there was no response. She just sucked on her cigarette and blew the smoke out in one long stream. She looked haggard and had lost the glow she'd found the night before when she'd talked about Petra.

There was a time when my mother was beautiful, and she knew it. She used to have a radiance, a luminescence that drew people to her like moths around a candle. When my parents used to have parties, everyone would surround my mother and she would laugh and throw her head back and shine a light onto all the people around her. The men would be enthralled, and would gather round, tongue-tied like small children.

It was the same when she came to my school. In the mornings, once the twins had eaten their toast and cereal and she'd got Petra dressed and I'd seen to Lorry, we'd all walk the hundred yards or so to Mrs O'Riordan's house. Mrs O'Riordan lived in one of the houses on the new estate, the houses that had been built to cover the waste ground that had lain there since the previous houses were demolished by bombs in the war. Mrs O'Riordan was Northern Irish and had a burr that could sharpen knives, my mother said, but she would look after Lorry while my mother was at home with Petra and I was at school and she didn't charge very much.

Once we'd dropped Lorry at Mrs O'Riordan's house, my mother and Petra and I would walk the short distance to my school, and she'd watch as I went through the dark green iron gates on my own, and then she'd disappear in a cloud of perfume and a swish of hair, Petra clutching her hand and toddling along beside her. Some of the older boys, sitting on the wall by the gates, used to look out for her, and once or twice they wolf whistled. She never looked round, but she would brush her hair behind her ear and draw her shoulders back, and a slight swagger would attach itself to her normally staid gait.

And it wasn't just the boys, either.

At the last parents' evening, just before Petra died, my mother came on her own as my dad had a meeting after work. She sat on the side of the desk in Mr McPherson's office and her long legs dangled down and swung against the shiny wooden table leg. I remember feeling faintly embarrassed for Mr McPherson, who couldn't stop looking at her legs and seemed to be flirting with her, despite the fact that he was married and had five children.

All that had changed since the accident. Now she was dull and plain and bitter.

I went to get the water bottles from my dad's studio. The sun that flooded through the plastic roof had made an oven of the whole room. My dad had been working on the bust of my mother before lunch, and he'd sprayed it with water to keep the clay pliable, but left it uncovered, presumably intending to work on it again that afternoon. He'd been working on the mouth, I could see, and the wrinkles on the upper lip and at the corners were now more prominent, more pronounced. Just like in real life.

When I got back to the kitchen I saw that my parents had taken their argument upstairs, so I stole a cigarette from the packet that my mother had left on the table after lunch. I knew she'd never notice. I grabbed a box of matches from one of the drawers on my way out.

It was a relief to see that the gates outside the chapel were padlocked again when I got there, so that I didn't have to find an excuse to avoid walking through the cemetery, and I looked around for another way of getting into the field. There was a scrappy bit of hedge to the right of the chapel railings, set up on a bank, and I managed to crawl through, scratching my legs and arms a little bit. The raw scrape of thorns against my skin felt good. It was refreshing.

The well was close to the hedge at the bottom of the slope, and the side of the valley reared up in front of me. A couple of spindly trees stood a few feet up the incline, their leaves shrivelled and yellow, their branches still stretching to the heavens, as if praying for rain, or like children, their arms outstretched, begging for their mother to pick them up.

There was the blue plastic bucket like my dad had said. There was the sheet of plywood, weighed down with an old brick, presumably to keep the animals and dirt out. I chucked the brick to one side and prised the plywood up with my fingers.

I expected woodlice to be scurrying around in the dirt underneath, but there was only the spring of grass, slightly greener where the plywood had been and less parched by the sun. The well was just a dark hole in the ground, and I couldn't see how deep it was. The bucket had a long rope tied to the handle, so I chucked it down and heard a splash. I could feel it sinking, and when I thought it was probably full I started to pull it back up, bit by bit. It was heavy and by the time I'd got the bucket to the top my t-shirt was glued to me all over with sweat.

I did this over and over until the four bottles I'd brought with me were full. Then I chucked the sheet of plywood over the well and kicked the brick on top of it. I was flaming hot now and as well as the sheen of sweat on my back there was a flush on my arms and legs, and the saltiness of my sweat made the scratches from the hedge sting. I drank some of the water, the heft of the gallon bottle making it spill over my face and onto my hair and chest. It was different to the water at home, which tasted plasticky and fake in comparison. This water tasted of earth and organic matter and darkness. I lay on the grass and closed my eyes.

In a moment the world turned orange, and little prickles of light danced in front of me. I knew that as soon as I opened my eyes the world would return, brighter than before and colour-saturated. I could still see the shape of the sun even with my eyes closed, a colourless fluorescent disc stark against black.

The black became blacker and my eyes sprang open. A shadow was passing over me. I couldn't make out a face or any features. It was just a head, silhouetted against the bright blue sky. I shot up onto my elbows and shuffled back a bit, trying to create some distance between me and this person. With one hand, I shielded my eyes and there stood the boy from the stream, his face nearly hidden by his long hair as he looked down at me. The sunlight was reflected by his sunglasses and his eyes were obscured. He was smiling.

'What are you doing?' I felt stupid, lying there, all sweaty and wet.

'Nothing. Watching you,' the boy said. In that first word of his I could tell he was an outsider. It sounded more like 'nuffing' and there was no sign of the Welsh lilt I'd been expecting. He took off the sunglasses and stood there, leaning over me.

I struggled to my feet so I could look at him face-on. He was about the same height as me, and his eyes were deep set and looked as though someone had smudged them with their thumbs. He grinned, displaying two rows of tiny, very white, teeth.

'You're trespassing,' he said.

'What?'

'You're trespassing,' he repeated. 'This is my field.'

I snorted. 'Only if your name's Janet,' I said, looking him straight in the eye. His grin had become a smirk.

'OK. So, you've got me there. She's my mum. But it's still our field.'

'She said we could have some water. She told my dad we could help ourselves.'

'Fair enough, I suppose. Glad we got that sorted out,' he said and held out his hand. It was thin and bony and more like that of a woman than a boy.

I took his hand and gave it a faint squeeze, dropping it before the shake had really finished, so he was left with his hand in mid-air. He looked amused, quizzical, and I felt myself sweating even more, watching him as he took me in: my cropped ginger hair, my face on which freckles and spots competed for space, the sodden t-shirt which clung to me, outlining the shape of barely-there breasts.

He was wearing jeans and a denim jacket. No t-shirt. Around his neck hung a camera, one of those new, expensive Polaroids. The sort that prints out a photo straight away, while you're waiting. He eyed the ground for a moment, his eyes tracing over the earth around the well, and up the hill, as if assessing it. Then he jerked his head up at me.

'C'mon. I want to show you something.' He didn't wait for me to answer, but started walking up the bank behind the chapel. He didn't look back.

I followed him up the hill, walking about three feet behind him. Even though it was a steep climb and it was the hottest part of the day, he kept on walking, silent, stopping only once to take his jacket off and tie it around his waist. Even then he didn't look round at me. I was gratified to see beads of sweat starting to appear from under his hair, and soon there was a trickle down his back, running snakelike between the bony contours of his shoulder blades. His skin was pearly-white, almost translucent.

By the time we got to the top of the hill, sweat was running into my eyes and I'd counted to 297. For the last couple of minutes, I'd had to lean forward into the gradient to find the strength to carry myself up the slope, seeing nothing but the scratchy yellow grass and the curling brown of dead bracken, so when we finally reached the top and I turned around, what I saw came as a complete surprise to me.

Laid out below us was the bottom of the valley, a patchwork quilt of fields, stab-stitched here and there with houses and barns, lanes and clusters of trees. From up there I could see the back wall of the chapel, devoid of windows or any form of adornment, set hard up against the bank with only a narrow pathway separating the grey wall from the scraggy grass. I could make out the well, with its piece of plywood and the blue bucket, and I could see the little house next to it, tiny and squat and grey, where I'd seen my dad talking to the woman earlier. There was our house, over the lane from it and further down the slope. The road carried on to the right, dotted with houses, and it curved round and rose slightly where the bridge went over the stream. Then the war memorial.

Like a brown worm the stream ran the full length of the valley, and following it with my eyes I found the place by the oak tree, the place where the boy had seen me naked. I risked a glance at him.

'The village. Lesson one,' he said, still not looking at me.

'What do you mean?'

'Well, you're new here, and you're going to need someone to show you the ropes, right? That's me.' He turned to look at me then and his eyes were half closed, dark behind long lashes. 'I can show you everything.'

'Like what?'

'Like who you should talk to and who you shouldn't. Like where's the best place for getting booze and fags. Like where's the best place to go for a swim.'

I knew I was blushing and he seemed to be enjoying it.

'Like where's the best place for seeing girls with their kit off.' He threw a grin at me and then sat down. He unhooked the strap from around his neck and placed the camera on the grass next to him. Despite myself, I sat down, my knees bent in front of me, and I leant my damp chest against my legs.

I started fiddling with the lace of my plimsoll, but then I remembered the cigarette and the match box in my back pocket and pulled them out. The match flared, the flame almost invisible in the brightness of the sun, and I took a deep pull on the fag to get it to light. It was a bit crumpled, but I took a couple of puffs and held it out to the boy. He didn't say anything at first, just took the cigarette from me between his finger and thumb and put it in his mouth. He took a long drag and let the smoke curl out of his nostrils. Then he spoke.

'So you found it then.' It was less a question than a statement.

'Found what?'

'The gift. I left you a present. I was worried the Christians might get there first.'

I didn't look at him but I could tell he had turned to face me, his elbows resting on his knees in front of him.

'You left it? The bird skull? That was you?'

He didn't say anything but in my peripheral vision I could see him nodding. Then he turned to look at the valley once more. For a few moments, we sat there in silence, both of us surveying the landscape that lay beneath us.

'Why?' I couldn't help asking. 'Why did you leave it for me?'

The cigarette sat between his fingers, the ash long and drooping. He shrugged.

'Because we're the same. You and me. We're on the same team. I knew that as soon as I saw you.'

I took the cigarette from him, and my fingers brushed against his. We looked at each other for a second and then I looked away and took a puff on the fag, conscious of the clamminess of my hands.

'What sort of bird is it?' In my mind's eye, I could picture the creamy smoothness of the mound of the skull, the dark voids of the eye sockets.

'It's a crow. It's not one of my best. My best ones are the ravens. But it's still pretty good.' He was looking out across the valley, his face blank.

'Why? Why do you want me to have it? We don't even know each other.'

He shrugged and turned to face me. The smudges beneath his eyes appeared darker, if anything, in the harsh light of the sun, and his pupils were shrunk to pinpricks, the irises a pale tawny brown.

'You're different. You're like me. We don't belong. We're outsiders. We need to stick together. Form an…allegiance.'

'An allegiance against what?'

He gestured with his hands towards the valley that lay in front of us.

'Them,' and that was all he said.

We sat quietly for a few moments, passing the cigarette back and forth. The nape of my neck was prickling in the heat. I looked across the valley, at the sun-scorched fields on the opposite side, bleached and baked, and at the tiny dots of white, clustering towards the bottom of the valley, which I knew were sheep, their instincts telling them to search for water.

My eyes started to sting from the sweat running down from my forehead and it was a relief to close them and block out the incessant light for a few seconds. Silently, in my head and to myself only, I recited the incantation. *Robin's egg, magpie's egg, duckling bill and bone. Blackbird's egg, feathers of wren, the skull of a crow.* That was it. It was complete.

I wiped my eyes on my t-shirt and when I looked again at the valley below us, I could make out a collection of people clustering around the war memorial. They weren't dressed in the dark sobriety of the chapel-goers from that morning, but wore bright t-shirts and short skirts. I couldn't see very well from up there, but I thought it was the same group of girls I'd seen when we'd driven into the village the night before, and that the tallest of the girls down there was the one with the greasy ponytail and the scrunched-up face.

The boy had seen me looking.

'That's Tracy Powell and her crew,' he said and passed the cigarette back to me.

'Who's she?' I tapped the ash off the end of the fag and took a couple of quick drags.

'She's a bitch, that's who she is. Her mother runs the pub. Local bike, but ugly as fuck.'

He looked sideways at me and I knew I was blushing again. I took another puff on the cigarette.

'See the fat one? Her name's Denise.' One of the girls was noticeably bigger than the others, short and wide and violently clad in fuchsia. 'Guess what they call her?'

'What?' I asked.

'Fat Denise. Clever, eh? She's the size of a house and twice as thick. And her grandad's her mum's cousin. Think about it.'

'I think I saw them before,' I said. 'Last night, when we arrived. They were hanging around the war memorial then.'

'The what?'

'The war memorial. Down there. Where they are now.'

'Ah. That's not a war memorial.'

'What is it then?'

He tilted his head to the side and looked at me through half-closed eyes.

'I'll show you. Tomorrow. I'll come and call for you and I'll take you there and I'll show you what it is.' He ground the cigarette out on the sole of his trainer and chucked the stub away into the bracken. He hauled himself to his feet and grabbed the camera and looped the strap around his neck.

'And that was lesson one on the village. Lesson two tomorrow morning.' He started walking backwards down the hill. 'And bring some fags.'

He turned and started running, the momentum carrying him all the way down. At the bottom, when he was only the shape of a boy next to the blue bucket, he turned and stood facing up the hill, the pale skin of his chest gleaming. His hair stood out in a haze around his head, but I couldn't make out his features at all.

Six.

My mother kept a photo on her bedside table, propped up against the lamp, the edges curling. At the front of the photo was Lorry. He was sitting on my dad's lap and he was looking at the camera. He wasn't smiling and he had his thumb jammed into his mouth. My dad was looking at my mother, who was sitting next to them. It looked as though the photo had been taken a split second too soon, and my dad had just turned to face the person holding the camera but he was still looking at my mother. His mouth was open and he was half-smiling and it looked like he was in the middle of telling a joke.

My mother was looking straight at the camera. She was sitting with her back straight and her shoulders held up. Her hair was loose around her shoulders and even though the photo was in black and white, I knew that she was wearing lipstick, and her mouth was glossy and smooth and full. Her eyes were bright and she looked confident and beautiful, and there was a curve to her cheek, a fullness to her chin. On her lap was Petra. My mother had her arms wrapped around her waist. Even though they were twins, Petra was a lot bigger than Lorry. She was wearing a party dress and she had her hair in bunches. In the middle of my mother and my dad there was me, gawky and freckled. In the background you could make out the Christmas tree, the strands on the tinsel reflecting little points of brightness from the fairy lights, like glitter.

I couldn't remember what Petra's face looked like, whether she looked like my mother or my dad, or like me or like Lorry. The photo didn't help. Where Petra's face should be, there was only a big white smudge, about the size of a thumbprint, where the picture had been worn away. I knew it was the place my mother's lips found when she woke in the night.

Seven.

Toast for breakfast again. I pushed the plate over to Lorry who grabbed a piece and sniffed it suspiciously. The butter had gone off so it was just toast scraped with jam. He took a tentative bite and then jammed the whole piece in his mouth and sat there, chewing noisily.

My mother and my dad were getting ready to go out. They had to get my mother registered with a doctor in town so she could get her prescriptions. The doctor at home had refused to give her a supply of Valium to last her for the time we'd be in Wales, and the unspoken suggestion was that she might stockpile them and top herself. My dad had said they would find a supermarket on the way back and stock up on food.

I'd had the dream again the night before, and I'd woken in the early hours when it was turning from night into day and the light that lit up the little arched window in my bedroom was still pale and fragile. I'd lain there, trying to remember what I'd dreamed, thinking that perhaps, if I could remember it, I'd know for sure how Petra had died.

I knew that there had been an accident in the bath, and I knew that she had drowned, and that it had been my mother's fault for leaving her when she went to answer the phone, but any more than that I couldn't remember. I didn't know who had been on the phone, or why it was so important that my mother left Petra on her own while she went to answer it. The dream, and the memory of the dream, had slipped away, and the more I tried to grasp it, the more it wriggled out of reach.

I'd fetched the relics from the altar and taken them back to bed with me and put them on top of the sleeping bag. I'd laid them out in the correct order and said the incantation four times. I'd tried rubbing the crow's skull with my thumb while I said the incantation but still nothing. That was the thing about the Creed: it didn't make everything obvious straight away. It made me work things out for myself. Only by trying different things, experimenting, would I discover its secrets. In the end, I decided this approach wasn't going to work, and I gave up and put the relics back on the altar. At some point, I must have fallen asleep again, because my mother and my dad were already dressed when I went downstairs. It was a couple of days since I'd seen my mother in anything other than her dressing gown, and she looked different in her clothes.

She hadn't said anything else about Petra since our first night at the cottage. She still spent most of her time in her bedroom on her own, or if she came down for meals she would sit and fiddle with the hollow at the base of her throat, where her crucifix used to hang. But this morning she was different.

There was a new lightness to her, something indefinable which suggested that the darkness was starting to lift.

She was wearing jeans that should have been tight around her hips but which were held up with one of my dad's belts. The blouse she was wearing I recognised as the one she'd had on in the photo, the Christmas photo with Petra. The last photo we'd taken as a family before the accident. The blouse was made from a thin, silky material and it used to cling to her breasts and the curves of her stomach. Now it hung like a shroud.

My dad said a few things about not leaving Lorry on his own and being careful not to annoy the neighbours, and then they went, leaving it up to me to make Lorry his breakfast.

'Don't eat with your mouth open,' I told my brother. He looked up at me, and chewed-up toast spilt from the corners of his mouth.

Sunlight pushed its way through the grime on the window. My dad had cleaned it yesterday, but hadn't done a proper job of it and the glass was smeared and streaked and made everything outside appear blurred. He'd looked around the house to see what jobs or repairs he could do to repay his colleague for letting us stay there. He'd started a list, with things like *fix roof*, and *repair pointing*, but later he'd crossed these out and replaced them with little jobs: *repaint kitchen window, clean gutters, dig up concrete*. Already he'd made a start on removing the old paint, and had scraped a neat pile of white shavings onto the path outside.

I started clearing the breakfast things and put the plates and tea cups in the sink. I hefted one of the gallon bottles up onto the side of the sink and poured water on top of the crockery. I could smell myself as I worked, each movement causing another wave of my scent to rise to my nostrils. I lifted the collar of my t-shirt over my nose and took a deep breath and relished the animal sourness.

A sharp tap on the window made me jump—I spun round and there was the boy from yesterday, the boy from the stream and the well, his face blurred by the smears on the window. I found myself blushing, feeling like I'd been caught out, and I wiped my hands on my shorts and went into the hall. The little mirror there told me I was still ugly, still freckly and spotty and spiky and ginger.

When I opened the door, the boy stepped straight in without saying anything. The Polaroid camera hung from his neck and it bounced against his chest as he walked. I stood back, on impulse, and he went straight past me and through the doorway to the kitchen. Lorry was still chewing his toast, and he looked up, worried. The boy went over to my brother and crouched down on his haunches so he was at eye level with him.

'Hey, little feller. What's your name?' he asked.

Lorry looked suspicious, and put both hands over his face.

'It's OK. I'm good with kids.' I didn't know if the boy was talking to me or to Lorry, but then he stood up and took a ten-pence piece out of the pocket of his jeans.

'Hey, look,' he said, and Lorry took a hand away from his face, leaving one eye uncovered.

The boy put the coin between two of the fingers on his left hand, and with a rippling motion, passed it over his fingers, up and over each of his knuckles, until it had come to settle next to his little finger. He turned his hand over and repeated the trick, sending the coin scurrying across the undersides of his fingers, his palm upwards and open.

By then Lorry had taken the other hand away from his face and was looking at the boy in wonder.

'Magic, Nif,' he said, and he beamed at the boy.

'It's not magic, Lorry,' I said. 'It's a trick, that's all.'

'Don't believe her, Lorry. It's magic alright, and I'm a magician. Mally the Marvellous at your service,' and he clicked his heels together and gave a little bow.

Lorry was clapping his hands in excitement and saying, 'More magic, more magic.'

The boy put his hand behind Lorry's ear and produced another ten-pence piece, which he gave to my brother. Lorry turned it over in his hand and looked at the boy very seriously.

'Magic man,' he said.

'Lorry,' I said, 'It's not really magic. Real magic is...I don't know...turning people into animals and making things disappear and stuff, not just chucking a coin around.'

'I don't think your sister likes me very much,' the boy said to Lorry in a theatrical whisper, and he ruffled my brother's hair.

I turned to the sink and clattered the breakfast stuff around. I scraped crumbs off the plates and wiped jam off the knives. I pushed a musty grey cloth around the insides of the cups and put everything on the draining board, and then I turned around and faced the boy. He had his hands in his pockets and his hips thrust forward and there was that grin again. He'd been waiting for me.

'So, lesson two today then, eh, Nif?'

I found myself nodding, unable to take my eyes off him, this peculiar boy with shaggy hair and eyes like bruises and the tiny pointed teeth of a rodent.

*

We walked along the lane from the cottage in silence. Mally let Lorry hold his hand and my brother was enraptured, alternating his gaze between Mally's face, the Polaroid camera, and the lane in front of him. He was mesmerised. It was still early, but a couple of people were out in their gardens, watering flower beds and cleaning windows. I thought one man had caught my eye and I gave him a nod and a little half-smile, but he quickly looked away and went back to tinkering furtively with the hosepipe that lay on the grass in front of him. Somewhere a lawnmower buzzed and a grasshopper creaked out its song, but everything else was silent.

The war memorial stood black against the limpid sky. Small and inconsequential curls tipped the points of the cross, as though put there as an afterthought, and the pillar tapered, wider at the bottom, until it reached a large plinth that was encircled by the stone steps. The whole thing was worn and chipped; it looked ancient.

The three of us stood at the bottom of the monument, the plinth now cleared of the cigarette ends and empty lager cans. Lorry had let go of Mally's hand and was clambering up the steps. I put my fingers in one of the little concave dips at the base of the monument and marvelled at how smooth the stone there was.

'You're right,' I said. 'It's not a war memorial, is it?'

'Co-rrect,' said Mally, feigning the voice of a quiz show host. 'And for your next point, can you tell me why you think that?'

'Well, it's far too old for one thing. The stone's really worn and it's all crumbled away in some places.' I went on before he could interrupt. 'And there are no names or dates, and that's the whole point of a war memorial, isn't it? To remember the dead.'

He was looking mock-serious now, frowning and nodding his head.

'So, young lady, for another point, and to win the game... can you tell me what it is?'

I stood back from the steps and looked up at the cross at the top. I felt as though the answer was there somewhere, would be obvious when I knew it, but I couldn't think what it could be and shook my head.

'Shall I tell you?' Mally was looking excited, like a kid with a secret he was bursting to share.

'Go on, then.' I sat on the stone steps and stretched my legs out, enjoying the light touch of the early sun.

'It's a plague cross.'

A faint breeze blew on the back of my neck, lifting the hairs there. Lorry climbed down from the steps and wandered over to the other side of the lane. He started gathering up clusters of sheep's wool that had snagged on the barbed wire fence.

'You know about the plague, right?' Mally said. 'Sixteen-hundreds and all that. Bubonic plague all over Europe? Hundreds of thousands of people died. A quarter of the population of London was wiped out.'

I nodded. 'Wasn't there a massive fire that stopped it, though?'

'That's right. It did, but by then it had already spread to other parts of the country. This village had it really bad—I mean, really bad—and most of the people living here caught the plague and died.'

He looked at me from under his eyelashes and then he looked down. I followed his gaze and saw that his fingers were rubbing the inside of one of the little indentations in the plinth.

'When most of the village was either dead or dying, there was no-one to grow the crops or look after the animals. People from the nearby villages wouldn't come near, for fear of being infected, and so the people from this village needed to be able to buy food without passing on the disease.' His voice had lost the showman's swagger, and had taken on the patiently explanatory tone of a teacher.

'They built this cross thinking it would protect them and they'd put their coins in the little dips all around the bottom, in order to pay for the food. The traders would take the coins and leave the food and everyone was happy.'

He sat down next to me and I was conscious of my dirty t-shirt and the acid smell that lifted to my nostrils.

'They put vinegar in the holes where the coins went. They thought that vinegar would kill the plague germs.' He snorted, as if affronted by the sheer naivety of these people, hundreds of years ago.

'But we're miles from London.' I thought of the journey we'd taken only a couple of days before, the car eating up the miles as we'd driven through the heat. 'How did the plague get all the way over here?'

'It found a way in.' He looked me right in the eye. 'It came in from the outside. You see, however hard they tried, the villagers couldn't keep all the *evil* out.' He said the word 'evil' with relish, drawing it out and making it sound dramatic. He was grinning. 'And that's why they hate us. You and me. We're outsiders.' He shrugged. 'We're evil.'

'I haven't even met anyone here yet—apart from you,' I said. 'Why would they hate us?'

'Trust me. They will. If you're not from around these parts, you'll get no welcome here. You and I need to stick together.'

Without warning he sprang up and pointed the camera at me. Before I could move away or put my hand up over my face, there was a click.

'What's that for?' I asked, conscious of my spiky hair and spots.

'Call it a souvenir,' he said.

'A souvenir?'

'Yeah. A memento of when we first met.' He had turned the camera around and was looking intently at the slot at the bottom, waiting for the photo. He looked up at me and he was grinning again, tongue just visible between his teeth.

'Come with me. I want to show you something.'

He grabbed my hand and pulled me to my feet. His fingers were surprisingly cool. We started to walk back the way we had come. I dragged Lorry away from the fence and saw that he'd accumulated a little pile of greasy, dirty wool that he clutched in one grubby hand. As we walked over the little bridge Mally kept on fiddling with the camera, impatient for the photo to appear. We walked in silence for a while, the dust lifting from the lane beneath our feet, the grass on the verges defeated and parched. A pair of rabbits stumbled into the lane and stared at us vacantly. Lorry ran after them, his hands outstretched, and they dragged themselves lazily away from him and disappeared into the cows' field.

Mally hadn't even seen them. He was still playing with the camera.

'We're friends now, Nif,' he said. 'And friends have to stick together. What you have to remember is that there are three sorts of people in the village.' Now he looked over at me. 'There are the outsiders: you, me, our parents. There have been others, but they've never stayed for long.' He went back to tinkering with the camera.

'Then there are the normal villagers. Well, I say normal, but most of them are weird. My mum says they're inbred and that affects their…mental faculties.' He looked at me again, cross-eyed, and rapped his knuckles against the side of his head. Despite myself, I smiled.

'They're mostly harmless, that lot. People like Tracy Powell and Fat Denise and the rest. Not a lot going on upstairs but not too much of a problem.'

The camera started to make a churning sound. Slowly, the photograph appeared from the slot, just a grey square in a white rectangle. He pulled it out gently and wafted it in the air, waiting for the picture to appear.

'And the third sort?' I couldn't help asking.

We were standing outside the chapel by then, nothing inside visible through the blank, unseeing windows. The gates were resolutely padlocked. My parents' car was back, parked on the little gravelled area at the top of the stone steps.

'They're the ones you have to worry about. The chapel-goers.' Mally tossed his head at the chapel as he said this, and I thought about the day before, when I'd seen the congregation arriving, and the strange ritual they'd performed. 'They're the troublemakers. You see, they hate everything about me and my mum because we're outsiders. It has nothing to do with religion or with not going to chapel. There are plenty of people round here who don't go to chapel and they all manage to get along. It's because we're different, that's all.'

'So why do you stay here, then? If no-one likes you, why do you and your mum insist on staying?'

'Sheer bloody-mindedness on my mother's part,' he said. 'She knows that they don't like us here, don't want us here, but she's always been one for antagonising people.'

'What about your dad? Where does he fit in?'

'He doesn't. I never knew him. Didn't stick around. Disappeared before I was born.'

'Did you ask your mum about him?'

He smiled a tired, resigned smile. 'Of course. Each time she'd give me a different answer. Travelling salesman, just passing through town. Lorry driver, likewise. Airline pilot. Every time I asked her, she'd come up with something different, so I gave up asking.'

We were outside his house and he turned to the gate in the picket fence and pushed it open, the bottom of it scraping along the yellow grass. I noticed a pattern that had been scratched into the wooden gatepost, an arrangement of sets of concentric circles, overlapping and intertwining, that made me think of the simpler patterns I used to make with my Spirograph.

'Welcome to Chez Mally,' he said, with an ironic twist of his eyebrows, and he bowed down and swept his arm in a magnanimous invitation to enter. I felt no surprise that this peculiar boy lived in the house opposite ours. It was inevitable.

Eight.

Mally led me straight round to the back of his house. I'd taken Lorry over to our cottage and watched as he walked down the stone steps and in through the front door, and now it was only the two of us. I was surprised to see a small, very tidy garden, enclosed by a low fence. There were brightly-coloured flowers growing around the edges, thriving in what should have been bare soil. Pinks and oranges, purples and yellows screamed in the sunlight, and in neat rows grew various herbs, their leaves dark, moist and vibrant. I realised with a jolt that I hadn't seen anything as lush and vital for weeks. The colours were wanton and extrovert.

The top half of the stable door was open and I could see in to a poky kitchen. Most of the room was taken up by a Formica-topped table, but around the edges were sideboards and cupboards, a sink and an electric oven. Bunches of herbs and flowers hung from the beams, forming a canopy of dried and withered vegetation, and they brushed the top of my head as Mally led me over to a narrow flight of stairs in the corner of the room. He led me up, but he paused outside a closed door on the first landing and put his finger to his lips. Then he made a drinking motion with his hand and stuck his tongue out and I guessed that meant that his mother was in bed with a hangover. We carried on up to the second floor.

Mally's bedroom was cool and dim. There was a pungent smell, not unpleasant, but dark and woody and earthy, like the smell of the crow's skull he'd left me. I walked straight over to the window and I wasn't surprised that I could see right into my bedroom, which was lit up by the sun.

His bed was pushed into the far corner, away from the window, and he took the camera from around his neck and put it on the bedside table before sitting down on the bed. His face was blank as he passed me the photo he'd taken of me, which was now fully developed, and a cursory glance told me I hadn't got any less ugly since I'd last looked. I tossed it back at him and he slid it onto the bedside table, on top of a pile of magazines. He lay down and put his arms behind his head, watching me. I stood with my back to the window, leaning on the window sill.

'So? What did you want to show me?'

'Look around you. What do you see?'

For the first time, I looked properly at the room. Apart from the bed and the bedside table there was a desk and a chair in the far corner, a narrow wardrobe and an old pine cupboard about the same height as me. There were haphazard piles of books leaning against the wall, and above them were tacked a few posters: Bowie as Ziggy Stardust, Deep Purple, Pink Floyd.

There was a record player on a stand and a stack of 33s. An electric guitar was propped against the end of the bed.

On the wall next to the bed was a collection of Polaroid photographs, mostly three-quarters shots of people. They were arranged in a grid, each meticulously and evenly spaced from its neighbour. Stepping closer, I saw that they were people I vaguely recognised, people I'd seen outside the chapel. The photographs all had the same orangey-brown glow, and in all of them the subjects were either looking away from the camera, oblivious to the photo being taken, or were covering their faces with their hands. In a couple of the pictures the people looked like they were shouting at the person taking the photos, their faces contorted in anger. It was obvious that none of the subjects had wanted to have their photo taken. In the white strip along the bottom of each picture a date was scrawled in a looping hand.

'Why do you have all these?' I asked, leaning closer and examining each of the photographs again in turn.

'Because it annoys them,' he said, and he gave a small chuckle.

'What do you mean?'

'The chapel-goers. I told you. They hate us. They can't stand us because we're outsiders.'

'Are they really that...' I searched for the right word, 'narrow-minded?' He snorted.

'Narrow-minded doesn't even start to cover it. They think we're eccentric. They take that as a threat. Because we're not like them, they think we're bad.'

'Why do they think you're eccentric?' I asked. 'You seem pretty normal to me.'

'Aha! That's it!' His finger jabbed at the air in front of him.

'You think we're normal because you're an outsider as well. You're just like us, and sooner or later they'll turn against you as well.'

'What do you mean "turn against you"? What have they done to you?'

He leant forward, his hands on his knees.

'They have these…rituals, I suppose you'd call them. Little things they do when we're around. It's like they're trying to intimidate us or something. Fucking nutters.'

I thought about the day before, when I'd watched the minister and the beetle man and all the men and women congregate outside the chapel, and the peculiar performance with the bunches of leaves and the water and the chanting. That had all been directed at Mally's house.

'So, you take photos of them, just to annoy them?'

'Yeah. Why not?'

'And how else do you pass the time? I mean, there's nothing to do here, is there? What else do you do?'

He was quiet for a moment, and looked at me, the dark smudges around his eyes sinking into shadows. Then he sprang up from the bed and darted towards the cupboard that stood against the far wall. He rummaged in a jar on top until he found a key, which he used to unlock the doors. They swung open.

Lined up along the top shelf, and right at my eye level, was a row of bird skulls. Larger than the crow's skull Mally had given me, five of them, all similar but not identical, each one having small variations in size and colour. Their beaks were all jet black, polished and glossy, and the eye sockets were huge shadows hanging in the stark white of the bone. He picked up the one that was in the exact centre of the row. It was a bit smaller than the rest, creamy beige and slightly dirty-looking.

'What is it?' It seemed only right that I was whispering.

He didn't answer my question, but reached for my hand and opened out my fingers. 'Do you like it?'

I was surprised by the weight of the skull, which filled my palm, the shiny black beak jutting preposterously forward. I held it up to my face and looked into the empty eye sockets.

'Watch this,' Mally said. There was a narrow shaft of sunlight piercing the window and settling on the bed in the far corner. He took the skull from me and held it up, angling it so that the sunlight was channelled through the eye sockets. The light that landed on the bed seemed stronger, more concentrated.

'Good, isn't it? It's a raven, by the way. A raven is the only one that's shaped like that, that'll let the sun go right through it.' He gestured at the row of skulls along the top shelf.

My eyes travelled along the raven skulls and then down the shelves in the cupboard, each one containing between half a dozen and twenty or so skulls, all categorised according to size. Mally explained that there were jackdaws and magpies, blackbirds and starlings. The tiny ones on the very bottom shelf were mostly blue tits and chaffinches. I thought about the relics on the altar and a new feeling bubbled up inside me. It was something I hadn't felt in ages, a feeling of quiet anticipation, of there being something to look forward to, but not quite knowing what that was. It was like Christmas was approaching but I didn't know what I was going to get.

'Why have you got all these?' I asked. 'I mean, what do you do with them?'

'Nothing, really. I just like having them.' He shrugged. 'They look nice. Don't you think they look nice?'

'Yes,' I said. 'Yes, they do look nice. Very nice.'

I took my time examining the skulls, picking up each one in turn, marvelling at their smoothness, their elegance, the sheer perfection of them.

'Where do you get them all from?' I asked.

'Round and about,' he said, and there was a sly grin forming on his lips.

He went over to his bedside table and opened the drawer. He pulled out something shiny; it was a wire, long and thin, and it was coiled up into a tight circle. He explained how he'd made a noose out of the wire and lain in wait, sometimes for hours, using worms as bait.

'The birds come and look at the worms. They're tempted, you can tell, but they hold themselves back. I think they're suspicious. Sometimes they sense that something's wrong and they fly off, but usually they go for it. They're greedy, you see?' He was standing next to me, looking at me through those long eyelashes, and I looked right back at him.

'So what happens?' I asked. My stomach felt hollow with the familiar sensation of thrilling nausea.

'What do you mean?'

'What happens when you trap the birds?'

Mally looked at me for a long time, like he was trying to decide whether to tell me something. Gently, he took the raven's skull from my hand and placed it back in the cupboard. He was standing very close to me. The shaft of light coming through the window had shifted slightly, and shone into his eyes. He didn't blink, and his pupils were pinpricks, tiny dots against the pale brown irises.

'The bird puts its head out to pick up the worm. What it doesn't know is that I've pinned the worm to the ground. Just a little pin, right through its middle.' The backs of his fingers brushed against the fabric of my t-shirt where it covered my stomach. I didn't flinch.

'Carry on.'

'The worm wriggles. It wriggles and wriggles and wriggles but it can't get free.' His hand moved deftly under the hem of my t-shirt and I felt cool fingers on the skin of my belly.

'The bird can't help itself. It wants to eat the worm so it pulls at it, it keeps on tugging at it. Eventually the worm might break in two, or the pin might slide out, but by this time I've got the noose lifted up around the bird's neck.' His hand was moving upwards under my t-shirt, stroking my flesh.

'And then I pull the end of the wire, slowly at first, gently, so the bird doesn't realise what's happening. Slowly, gently, and all the time the noose is getting tighter and tighter.' His breath was hot on my cheek.

'And then, very quickly, before the bird knows what's happening, I pull the wire and it tightens around the bird's neck and it's trapped. Trapped in the wire. And then I pull it tighter, and more often than not, the wire will either throttle it or go straight through. Straight through the bird's neck and cut its head off.'

He took his hand away from my stomach and stood back. My breath was quicker now and I turned away from him so he wouldn't see. That's when I saw the photo, peeking out from one of the magazines on the bedside table.

Only half of it was visible, and it had the same orange tinge as the other photos, the ones on the wall. But it was different, because this time it was a photo of me, taken when I'd been at the plague cross early on our second day in the village. I picked it up. In the white space at the bottom was written the date: 1

August 1976. Just the day before. In the photo, I had my back to the camera, and only part of one side of my face was visible, just my ear and the curve of my cheekbone and the end of my nose. In the background was the bottom part of the plague cross, the plinth and the steps.

Mally saw me looking, but he didn't say anything. He took the photograph off me and placed it gently on the bedside table, next to the photo of me he'd taken that afternoon. Then he sat down on the end of the bed and picked up the guitar. Without plugging it in, he started plucking at the strings with those long, slender fingers, playing the same tinny chords over and over again. I looked over at the open cupboard, at the skulls arranged in a perfectly symmetrical display. Something fluttered in the pit of my stomach.

Lorry was spreadeagled, asleep on the patch of concrete at the front of the house when I got back. He looked small and vulnerable lying there, his arms up above his head. His clown doll was discarded at his side, so I picked it up and placed it on his chest and went straight into the kitchen. I was starving and thought I could make a sandwich for me and Lorry to share. My mother was sitting at the pine table, smoking, and she looked up when I walked in and smiled. The shadows under her eyes seemed to have lifted, and the lines on her forehead looked softer, less pronounced.

'Hi Nif. How are you?' It was the first time she had asked me anything in ages. I must have looked surprised, because her smile got wider and she ground out her cigarette in the ashtray.

'Come here.' She held her arms out to me and made a beckoning motion with her fingers. Her arms when they settled around me were hard and bony, yet surprisingly strong. She held me tightly and breathed in, her face pressed into the side of my neck. When I pulled away I saw that her eyes were wet.

'Can you feel her, Nif?' I felt suddenly cold. 'Can you feel her? She's here, isn't she? Petra's here. She's come back.' She was smiling properly now, a placid smile that covered her whole face and made her eyes shine.

It was like when we used to go to church and she would listen to the priest and his mutterings in Latin, and she would look peaceful and contented. She would step up to Father Declan to take communion and as she opened her mouth, her pink tongue ready to take the wafer, she would have such a look of pure elation on her face that I thought back then I wanted to be confirmed, to have the same experience of joyful contentment as my mother did. When she would walk back to take her place in the pew, her step would be light and she would look like she was gliding.

She had the same look on her face now, and her eyes were gleaming behind the tears.

'Petra's come back, and she says that she's forgiven me.'

I sat with my dad that afternoon as he worked on my mother's sculpture. He had angled a spotlight onto the wheel where the head sat, even though there was enough light seeping in through the coagulated moss on the corrugated plastic roof.

He'd already removed much of the clay that he'd built up. He said the heat had made it harder than usual and difficult to work with. I watched as his fingers applied the new clay. The dark orange substance built up in layers, substrates, the head starting to take on its new form. He placed strips of clay under the eye sockets, and above them, using his tools to carve them once they were in place. He used his fingers to press onto the forehead, pulling back to ease the clay flat. His thumbs worked away under the chin, pulling the substance upwards and outwards, making the neck swanlike and graceful.

It was the eyes that fascinated me the most, though, and I knew that when he had formed the brows and the cheekbones and smoothed the skin, and was satisfied that the line of the nose was perfect, he would take a metal-headed tool, a piece of thick wire shaped into a loop and secured at the rough ends to a wooden handle. Meticulously, he would insert the metal end into the eyeballs, his fingers working slowly and firmly to ease out a lump of clay. This would create both the iris and the pupil. Both would merge into an unseeing void. But this afternoon he was still not satisfied and my mother's eyes remained intact, uncarved.

Nine.

A couple of months after Petra died, my dad decided to take me and Lorry to the park. We'd hardly left our house up until then, and I think he could tell we were both bored with playing in our bedrooms. The back garden was still out of bounds.

Small feet greeted us on the pavement outside our house. It was half-term and the street was packed with kids, their brightly coloured t-shirts a relief to my eyes after the gloom of our house. The air was full of the clatter made by roller skates and skateboards. Our neighbour, Mrs Akhar, was standing on the patch of grass outside her house—when she saw us, a flicker of a frown crossed her face and she'd looked as though she was going to say something to my dad, but then she'd turned away and busied herself with watering the lilies that grew in the little border at the front of her house. Her mangy cat was rubbing itself up against her legs and eyeing me suspiciously. We'd never had pets of our own.

All along the street, gaggles of children had gathered, and as we approached them they parted to let us through. It was as though we had some invisible force field around us that made them move aside—they all stopped talking and stared at us, and a few whispered things behind their hands. I copied my dad, who walked with his head down, not looking at anyone. Lorry skipped along in front of us, oblivious.

Leaning against one of the gateposts at the park were two girls I recognised from school. Older girls, sixth-formers. As we got nearer one of them called out, 'Hi, Jenny,' and the other one put her hand over her mouth to stifle a giggle.

A week or so after the accident my dad had said that perhaps it would be a good idea for me to go back to school. He'd thought the return to a routine would help me get back to normal and that schoolwork would take my mind off things. I'd gone along with it, but I'd only stayed a couple of days. The other kids had all suddenly wanted to be my friend.

I think, in a way, there is something attractive about death, a glamour that attaches itself to those who have experienced it and which makes it appealing to those who haven't. Girls would come up to me in the playground and ask if I needed help with my homework. I'd be in the canteen and they'd come and sit down at my table. These were the ones who had sneered at me or bullied me, right up until the time that I became interesting because I had a dead sister.

I'd ignored the girls at the gatepost, and my dad, Lorry and I had walked along the wide tarmacked path that ran around the lake. There were sprinklers going in the flower beds, and as we walked the fine haze of cold water landed on my face like mist from the sea. I stopped and turned my face to the sprinkler, which had already moved away on its back-

and-forth trajectory. My dad said something about how the park authorities were probably getting the most out of their sprinklers before the hosepipe ban kicked in, how our area was one of the last to introduce the ban which already covered most of the South East. He was saying anything to break the silence that hung between us.

The ice-cream van was in its usual place and there was a line of kids snaking back from it. Without us even asking my dad had gone to stand at the back of the queue. From where we stood, I could see the jetty from where rowing boats were launched into the lake. The open space around it was always crowded with birds: ducks and geese and even swans sometimes. They congregated there as people came with their bags of bread, and the birds would flap and squawk and occasionally peck each other in their enthusiasm to get to the food.

We'd got our ice-creams and had walked in silence to the jetty. There must have been about a dozen people there that day with their bags of bread and the birds had gathered in a mad frenzy of feathers and quacking. Some of the ducks were followed around by broods of ducklings, little brown balls of fluff, the yellow stripes on their wings miniature lightning bolts. We'd stood in the middle of the hubbub and Lorry had started chasing geese, his ice-cream held in one hand, the other flailing wildly in front of him. For the first time since the accident my dad was smiling, but his eyes were wet as well.

It wasn't long before Lorry tripped over and his ice-cream went head-down onto the tarmac. He'd tried to pick it up, but my dad ran over and grabbed it, said it was dirty and put it in the bin. Lorry had started wailing—people looked at him and smiled and frowned, and my dad had to go down on his haunches and tell him he'd buy him another one.

It was the sound from behind me, a great whooshing noise, that made me turn around. A swan was flapping wildly a few feet from me, its wings sending ripples through the air as it tried to slow down for landing. It came down heavily, its enormous orange feet thumping onto the ground, the momentum from its own massive weight carrying it forward into the flock. One of its wings sat lower than the other, and trailed along the ground at an awkward angle. It was injured. It staggered onwards, and where its giant feet had hit the ground there lay the broken body of one of the ducklings, crushed into a brown and yellow smear on the tarmac.

Its mother was oblivious, and had wandered off, her depleted brood trailing after her. My dad was still fussing over Lorry and I scooped up the duckling in my hand. The tiny bill was still warm when I stroked it, but the head was set at an impossible angle to the body, and the soft down was flattened and congealed.

It wasn't easy getting the duckling back to our house. I had to hold it loosely in one hand, trying not to crush it, but at the same time needing to keep it hidden. Luckily, Lorry had grazed his knee when he'd tripped over, so we didn't stay any longer at the park. When we got back home and my dad was dealing with my brother, I went straight out to the back garden and dug a hole with a trowel. I dug it under the bush where I'd found the magpie's nest a few weeks before: it seemed appropriate somehow. I even made a little cross out of two twigs tied together with dry grass, and put that on the top.

When I went back three weeks later and dug it up, the duckling was nothing more than a collection of tiny fragile bones, connected by a thin covering of sodden down. The beak came away in my hand when I picked up the tiny corpse. It was shrivelled and grey. The feet were curled in on themselves, the tiny webs now absent, but the miniature claws were still in place. I reburied most of the body, a pathetic clump of bones and down, but I kept the beak and one of the feet and put them in the shoe box under my bed.

That was the night I cut off my hair.

Ten.

We'd driven past the pub on our way into the village, but I hadn't noticed it then. Although it had only been a few days, it seemed like forever since we'd left our cosy terrace in the suburbs and come to Wales. Now I could hardly remember what my bedroom looked like, or the skinny strip of garden that ran away from the back of our house, or the orange glow of street lights that stopped the darkness penetrating every corner.

We'd eaten our dinner and piled the dishes in the sink. That evening we'd feasted on the spoils of my parents' shopping trip: beef stew heated up on the camping stove, with tinned peas and Smash and hunks of soft bread. There was chocolate mousse in pots and cream from a can and there was ice cream that my dad had bought as a treat but which had melted in the broken freezer compartment, so we drank it straight from the tub. My mother came out of her room, and we all sat together at the pine table. My dad drank wine and told a joke about a parrot and my mother smiled. She hadn't mentioned Petra again.

I think that's what made my dad suggest that we should all go to the pub. At first my mother wasn't convinced, said she was tired and wanted to go to bed, but my dad persisted and finally she went upstairs to get herself ready. It was still light outside, and the heat was dirty and still, and the smell coming off me had got thick and stale. I changed my t-shirt and then, on a whim, put on a skirt I hadn't worn in months, that my dad must have packed for me. He raised his eyebrows when he saw me, but he didn't say anything. When my mother came downstairs she'd brushed her hair, and I thought there was a trace of lipstick on her mouth, as though she'd put it on and then thought better of it and wiped it off again.

The pub wasn't far from our house, only a couple of hundred yards back along the lane, and as we walked I noticed again how it got dark earlier in the village than it did at home. At first it bothered me, as if this little corner of the world was different somehow, unworldly and set apart. Then I thought that it was because of the deep sides of the valley that surrounded it and rose up around us, meaning the sun dipped below the horizon earlier. When we left the cottage, the sun was inching down towards the top of the hill, watching us as we walked along the lane and starting to infuse the sky around it with a pearlescent rosy glow.

When we got to the pub it was easy to see how I'd missed it. It looked like an ordinary house from the outside. It was set back slightly from the road and made of the same stone as all the other houses in the village. There was a painted wooden board over the front door with an amateur, childish painting of what might have been a dragon.

A gang of teenaged boys had congregated outside the pub. Five or six of them, they were spotty and pallid and all had long, greasy hair. They lounged against the wall and as we walked towards the door their eyes roved up and down, assessing and appraising, first me and then my mother. My dad made eye contact with the tallest one, the one nearest the door, and held it as he pushed the heavy wooden door open with his shoulder.

At first I thought we'd walked into someone's front room. There was a massive stone fireplace, an inglenook, with a huge empty grate. Upturned horseshoes were nailed into the enormous wooden beam that ran across the top of it, and the middle of the beam looked scorched, as though an ancient fire had once taken hold there. There were circles scratched into it, large ones and small ones overlapping each other, identical to the ones I'd seen scratched onto the gatepost outside Mally's house.

The long wooden table in front of the fireplace was flanked by two benches, each of which was occupied by two men, who turned as we came in. Their faces weren't hostile, merely blank, as they looked us over and turned away again. They could have been any of the men I'd seen since we'd been in the village: small, dark and compact, dressed in dirty tweed jackets and flat caps. Each man held the butt of a cigarette pinched between the finger and thumb of one hand. In their other hands, they held a splayed collection of playing cards. No-one spoke.

The room was lit by two strip lights, like the ones in the kitchen of the cottage, and it was too bright to be cosy. There was a dartboard on the wall to our left, and a door past it with a sign for the gents. An empty wooden settle spanned the wall at the back, and on our right, on the far side of the fireplace, stood a doorway. There was no bar. The walls were empty, unadorned except for grubby marks that ran around the room at waist height. The floor was of massive grey flagstones, chipped and stained, the grooves between them holding who knew how many centuries' worth of dirt.

I think if my dad had been sober we might have turned around and left then, but the wine he'd drunk with dinner had made him bold. Still carrying Lorry, he headed for the doorway in the corner. We followed.

The room we walked into was darker than the first, and if anything stuffier and even warmer. There was another empty fireplace to our right, backing onto the one in the other room, and arranged around it was a motley collection of armchairs and small sofas, ancient and slumped, covered in discoloured velour and Draylon. The occupants of these chairs, half a dozen men in dark suits clutching black-covered books, looked startled to see us, as if we should have somehow had our presence announced. These ones looked like the men I'd seen outside the chapel: hunched and sombre. I thought they must have been reading when we walked in, but now they shut their books and put them away, sliding them into the crevices left by the cushions on the armchairs, or slipping them into jacket pockets. There were no drinks on the small table in front of them.

'Good evening,' said my dad. His earlier jollity seemed to have left him, and now his voice faltered.

The man who stood up and stepped forward seemed to assume the role of leader and as he moved into the light I could see that he was the man I'd seen outside the chapel, the little beetle of a man. The one who had helped the minister. He was short, barely taller than me, and his chin receded so much it disappeared into his neck. He leaned past my dad and spoke softly into another room, a room that was behind where we stood and that I hadn't noticed when we'd walked in. I couldn't work out what he was saying, but thought I heard him say 'Tracy' and I craned my neck to see. The girl from the plague cross came out, wiping her hands on an apron.

She looked at us; there was something confrontational in her expression. I saw again how her features were all too close together, like someone had taken her face and pushed it together, and when she looked me up and down, I noticed that she was very slightly cross-eyed. Her greasy yellow hair was tied up in a ponytail at the top of her head and a line of pimples dotted her hairline.

When the beetle man spoke to my dad his voice was quiet, but the room was so still there was no need for him to raise it.

'Tracy here will help you. If you don't mind, we're in the middle of a meeting and would welcome some privacy. Perhaps you would care to sit in the other room.' It was less a question than a statement, and his words, while being fluent, were slightly too formal, too strained.

Tracy stepped forward. 'Wha' d'you wan'?' She had her arms crossed over breasts that were straining to escape from a grubby white vest. Her apron did little to cover her thighs which poked, mottled and meaty, from the bottom of a denim mini skirt. 'My mam's not 'ere so I can only do you beer or pop.'

'I'll have beer please.' My dad looked at my mother and for a moment I thought she might smile, but she simply shrugged and said, 'Pop.'

'A beer and three pops, then,' my dad said to Tracy. 'How much is that?'

'Settle up at the end. That's 'ow we do it 'ere.' She turned around and, manoeuvring her hefty thighs around a battered table that seemed to do service as a bar, slid into the little room.

The beetle man was still standing, still looking at my dad with a little pinched smile attached to his face. His lower lip was bulbous and wet, and as I watched, his tongue popped out, pointed and surprisingly pink, and darted around the edges of his mouth. The minute gesture his hand made towards the doorway we'd come in through seemed to dismiss us. In the shadows behind him, one of the men shifted in his chair and in the meagre light I recognised him as the man I'd seen outside the chapel. The minister.

He was sitting hunched into his chair, as if his tall frame made him too large for the room. Again, I noticed that the skin of his face was pale and pulled taut over his features as though it had been stretched, like a canvas on a frame. His black hair was still Brylcreemed back over his high forehead. He turned towards me, and that was when I saw his eyes.

They were milky white. He was blind.

The beetle man moved his hand again in the direction of the door and my dad must have taken the hint this time, because he ushered us back into the strip-lit glare of the front room. We took our place on the long settle, all four of us in a row.

When Tracy came back in she had a pint of stagnant-looking brown liquid and three bottles of violently-pink fizz. All three bottles had straws jammed in the tops. She glared at each of us as she handed them out, and when it was my turn there was a flicker of puzzlement there as well, as though she recognised me but couldn't quite place me. I thought of her giving me the finger as we drove into the village and felt a quiet surge of satisfaction at knowing she didn't remember me.

The card players carried on with their game, and the silence lay heavy.

I was reminded of what Mally had told me about there being three different sorts of people in the village. There were us, the outsiders, ranked along the settle. There were the villagers, keeping themselves to themselves as they played their card game, not attempting to socialise, but not antagonistic either. And then there were the chapel-goers, who had hidden themselves away in the back room, engrossed in their meeting and concocting whatever rituals they performed that Mally had told me about and some of which I'd witnessed with my own eyes.

Lorry started babbling, making noises that sounded like they could be words but weren't, and my dad shushed him and frowned. My mother lit a cigarette and took deep drags, alternating between the fag and the straw that stuck up out of her bottle of pop. Even in the glare of the strip lights, the lines around her mouth seemed shallower, somehow, smoother. Her eyes were brighter and I could tell that she'd washed her hair because it was glossy rather than greasy, and sat in waves on her shoulders. It was as though her belief that Petra had come back—had forgiven her—had somehow reversed the ageing process and started making her young again.

We sat like that in silence for a few long minutes. It wasn't easy to make conversation, even if we'd wanted to, sitting as we were in one long line. Lorry finished his drink and blew through the straw, sending little drops of spittle sailing into the air. My mother looked around for somewhere to put out her cigarette, and my dad took it from her, cradling his hand under the tower of ash. He carried it over to the fireplace and squeezed himself past the bench to lean in and throw in the fag butt.

When the front door opened, there was a bit of a creak but the air didn't even move. The woman who stood in the doorway was wearing a red dress, nipped in at the waist and cut low at the front, the colour a shriek in the harshness of the strip lights. She had on stilettoes and stockings. It was the woman I'd seen my dad talking to, the woman who lived in the cottage opposite ours. Mally's mum.

As she stepped over the threshold, she must have caught one of her heels, because she lurched to the side. My dad lunged forward and caught her by the elbow.

'Janet!' His voice rang out in the silent room, and I think even he was surprised at how loud it was.

The woman looked up at him, her head moving slowly backwards and forwards, her eyes trying to focus. Finally, they must have managed it, because she put her arms around his neck and pulled him into an awkward embrace.

'Hello Clive,' she said when she'd let him go. 'Out for a couple of drinks?' She looked amused, but the smile kept sliding around on her face, as though she wasn't in control of it. Her eyes too slipped in and out of focus, and when she walked towards us she staggered slightly, before correcting herself.

'Is this the family, then?' She leant down and peered at Lorry, then at me and then at my mother, who looked back with raised eyebrows and a downturned mouth. The woman clutched at my dad's arm and drew herself up to a standing position. She waved a hand at my mother.

'I'm sorry for your loss, my dear.' The woman slurred the words and they came out in one convoluted string, but their meaning was clear. My mother's face drained of blood.

My dad was starting to say something when the door to the other room opened and Tracy darted in, surprisingly agile for someone of her build. She smirked at the woman, and looked her up and down, like she had done to me.

'I'm not servin' you, Janet White,' Tracy said, the smugness in her voice palpable. She had her hands on her hips, one foot crossed over the other. Her tiny eyes looked like raisins pushed into dough.

'Ah, go on Tracy. Just a half bottle of Scotch to take out. Won't kill you, will it?'

The card players had abandoned their game and were watching this exchange with interest.

Tracy crossed her arms over her chest, her cleavage reaching up to her double chin in the process. She shook her head.

'Absolutely not. You still owe my mam for that bottle last week. She said not to let you 'ave nothing more on tick till you've paid for that.'

The woman started rummaging in her handbag, a silver glittery thing that was wildly incongruous in the front room of the pub. She pulled out a couple of grubby pound notes and thrust them at Tracy.

'Go on then, take it. Take my last couple of quid and give me a half bottle of Scotch. That's all I've got until Thursday when the family allowance gets paid, but you have it.'

Tracy took the notes and held them up to the light, as if checking that they were real. Then she looked slyly at the woman, her little pig eyes glinting with menace.

'That pays your debt, all right, but it won't get you anything else tonight. Reckon you'd be best going home and sleeping that lot off.' Tracy looked pleased with herself.

The door to the back room opened and the beetle man walked in and stopped in front of Janet.

'Miss White,' he said, and his lip was drawn back over his teeth as he formed the sibilant whisper that revealed Janet's unmarried status. 'Don't you think behaviour like this should be carried out in the privacy of one's own home?' He sounded superior and pleased with himself, and I felt a bit sorry for Janet as she looked at him, her head swaying as she tried to focus on those sharp eyes.

'I suggest you do as Tracy says and go home and sleep it off. Perhaps this gentleman would care to escort you?' He looked at my dad, who raised his eyebrows but didn't say anything. I could tell that we had cemented our position in the village as outsiders, as far as the beetle man was concerned. 'I'll settle up for you with Tracy,' he said, and there was a finality in his voice that made my dad nod.

It was dark when we left the pub, but it was a clear night and there was a bright moon. The lane shone grey. Janet had one arm around my dad's neck and she stumbled all the way, occasionally tripping and causing him to pull her up again by the elbow. I was carrying Lorry and we walked behind in silence. My mother hadn't said anything at all, and she walked a few feet behind us, her hands crossed over her chest and clutching her shoulders, glaring at the ground. Her mouth was pulled into a pout, like a cat's bumhole. She looked old again.

When we got to Janet's house, my dad managed to push the gate open with his hip and we all trooped up the path. My dad leant Janet up against the wall at the side of the front door and took her bag off her and rummaged around for a key. Before he could find it, a light came on and then the door opened. I tried to hide in the shadows.

'Mally. Y're a good boy.' Janet's voice was still slurred but now it was fogged with sleepiness as well.

'Hi, Mum.' Mally's voice sounded fresh and clear in the still heaviness of the night. 'Hi, Mr Allen. Find her in the pub, did you?'

I was shocked that Mally knew my dad. When had they met? I shrank further back into the shadows, glad that Lorry had fallen asleep.

'That's right, Mally. She's in a bit of a state I'm afraid. Can you get her up to bed, or do you need a hand?' I heard my mother let out a sharp breath behind me.

'That's fine, thank you, Mr Allen. It's not like I haven't done this before.' In one move he hoisted the semi-conscious woman over his shoulder and patted her backside.

'C'mon Mum. Let's get you up to bed.'

My dad raised a hand to Mally and turned to go.

'Thanks Mr Allen. For getting her home, I mean.'

I blew out a silent breath of relief that he hadn't seen me.

'Bye, Nif. See you soon.'

We walked across the lane to our own cottage. Even though it was fully dark now, there was no respite from the sun. It was as though the long afternoon had just been a preparation for night-time, accumulating and reinforcing the fingers of heat that penetrated the darkness and settled on my shoulders.

I left my mother and my dad arguing in the kitchen. I put Lorry to bed and went to my room in the attic. From the window, I could see the moon reflected in the windows of the chapel, white orbs held in black. The smell of the honeysuckle was invasive and found its way into my bedroom where it stayed, cloying and somnolent. The smell was more aggressive at night, as though the darkness concentrated the scent—it became sweeter and more pungent, and muskier, like the incense in church.

On Saturday mornings, when Father Declan was holding confession, the smell of the incense would be at its height, as if it could somehow help to seek out sin. All morning at home my mother would be twitchy and alert, and I knew she had been rehearsing her confession, plucking from her conscience the sins she had committed during the week since her last performance. I would sit on the back pew to wait for her, right at the end, next to the statue that was tucked into an alcove in the wall. It depicted the Virgin Mary, blue robes flowing and an expression of unremitting piety on her face as she clutched the Sacred Heart, a single tear falling onto her cheek. The church would be mostly empty at that time, and it was usually just the flower arrangers who would be there, preparing the church for Mass the next morning, and the odd sinner, awaiting their penance from Father Declan.

Mr McPherson was the only one of the teachers who went to Our Lady of Holy Saviour; all the others went to St Francis on the other side of town. He'd quite often be there on Saturday mornings to take confession, and would nod to me as he went past and then take a seat and wait for the confessional box to be free. He wasn't bad looking, Mr McPherson. He had lots of dark brown hair that curled around his forehead, and a moustache that Burt Reynolds would envy. Usually my mother would hasten out of the box, her face a study in humility, and she would sit next to me and take out her rosary and start muttering, counting off on her fingers the required numbers of Hail Marys the priest had demanded of her. After a few minutes, Father Declan would appear, and beckon Mr McPherson into the confessional box, but not before he'd cast a worried look in my mother's direction.

All this time, I'd sit watching the Virgin Mary, willing her to move, like she did in those villages in Ireland and France. My mother's fingers would be tapping and fidgeting, twisting the beads. Long minutes later, Mr McPherson would come out of the confessional box and walk down the aisle towards the door—he was always in a hurry, scurrying, trying to get away from the dank interior of the church and back out into the sunlight. He'd invariably cast a glance at my mother, and I'd feel her tense as he walked past, but she'd never look at him, never open her eyes. She would just carry on muttering her prayers, her fingers twisting and writhing in her lap, and all the time the lusty smell of incense would pervade the church.

On the other side of the lane, Mally's house sat in darkness, except for a light on the second floor. I picked up the crow's skull from the altar and ran my fingers over the shiny-domed mound. I didn't feel anything different, anything peculiar from it. I placed my fingers into the hollows of the eye sockets, and I thought of Mally. As I knew it would, a shape appeared at his bedroom window, a dark head silhouetted against the pale light.

Eleven.

'Tell me a secret, Nif.'

We were lying on the bank by the stream. Lorry was sitting with his legs in the water, giggling as the shallows lapped at his thighs. He'd been in a foul mood all morning, scratching away at his legs then crying when the blood started showing through his bandages, but he'd perked up when Mally appeared at the window after lunch. Now he was content, and the water was soothing the sores on his legs.

It had taken quite a bit to persuade me to go to the stream, but Lorry had begged, had clutched at Mally's hand, and he'd seemed so happy that I gave in.

'Tell me a secret, Nif.' Mally was lying flat on his back, his arms behind his head, eyes closed. I sat with my legs crossed under me, facing the stream, feeling gangly and awkward.

With the sun in my eyes I was squinting, but I could still see Mally. He looked fuzzy through my eyelashes.

He'd taken his shirt off as soon as we got to the river bank, and the skin on his chest was smooth and hairless. He was pale and wiry and his chest was slightly concave. Pigeon chested, my dad would have said. Three small moles were strung in a line across his stomach, like Orion's Belt. His jeans were tattered and ripped at the knees, and the frayed hems were cloaked in dust.

I bit my lip and tried to think of a secret to tell him. I thought of the girls at school and how they'd all wanted to befriend me after Petra died, how they wanted an association with death that would perhaps bring it closer to them while also keeping it at bay. Not yet. It was too soon to tell him about Petra.

He sat up, propping himself up on his arms. Light danced from the ripples that Lorry was making in the water.

'You do have secrets, don't you, Nif? I mean, everyone has secrets.'

'I suppose so. What about you? What's your secret?' I focused on my hand, the fingers pinching at the dried grass, pulling it up in tiny bundles.

He laughed softly. 'I already told you my secret.'

The skulls appeared in my mind, lined up on the shelves of Mally's cupboard, gleaming in the sunlight. I carried on pulling at the grass, clearing a little patch of dusty earth. Lorry was still standing in the stream, splashing and giggling to himself. I could sense that Mally was lying down and I risked a glance. He had his forearm resting over his eyes, shielding them from the sun, and that half-smile had formed on his lips.

'What kind of a name is Nif, anyway?' he asked.

'That's rich, coming from someone called Mally.'

He snorted out a laugh. 'It's short for Malcolm,' he said. 'I know. It's a shit name, isn't it?'

'My real name's Jennifer,' I said, and suddenly I realised that I hadn't called myself that for months. 'Only the teachers call me that, though.'

'Are you going back to school in September?' he asked, rolling over onto his side and looking at me.

'Dunno. Probably not. I don't want to go but my teacher, Mr McPherson, thinks I should sit my O-Levels.' I thought I'd said too much, that I might have to tell Mally about not going to school because of Petra, but he didn't ask and rolled over onto his back again. 'What about you,' I said. 'Where do you go to school?'

'I don't,' he said. 'I haven't been to school in years. My mum's taught me everything she knows. All the rest I get from books and telly and stuff. There's no need for school. Pointless.'

We sat in silence for a few moments, enduring the sun's heat. It was the hottest part of the day. People said that midday was the hottest, when the sun was directly overhead and the rays were more direct and the light wasn't diluted by the atmosphere as much. But I knew that it was now, in those couple of hours in the early afternoon, after the sun had spent the morning baking the ground and boiling the air, that was when it would get so hot that there was nothing else to do but stay as still as possible and wait for the sun to go down.

Lorry knew this too, and he got out of the stream and came and lay on the grass with us, placing himself at a right angle to Mally, his head resting in the curve of Mally's back, his clown doll lying on his stomach. I was dozing, when Mally's voice dragged me back to consciousness.

'I think I might get pissed tonight. You up for that?'

'Maybe.'

I'd been drunk before, of course. After Petra's funeral, we'd had a wake at our house. My mother hadn't been able to go to the funeral and had stayed at home, sedated, with one of the nuns to keep an eye on her. I remembered standing with my dad outside the church, him with one hand on my shoulder, the other on Lorry's, none of us saying anything. I remembered Lorry, his bandages coming undone and trailing absurdly from the hems of his too-short trousers, the only trousers he had that were a vaguely dark colour. I remembered Father Declan muttering in Latin as the coffin was carried down the aisle, the sweet heady smell of incense furring up my nostrils. And I remembered the tiny coffin, white and impossibly small, being lowered into the ground.

Mrs Akhar made fish paste sandwiches for the wake. It was mostly people from the church, and a couple of my teachers who'd turned up out of obligation and then sat around on the periphery, fidgeting and trying to think of something to say. Mr McPherson came and looked awkward, not knowing what to say to me or my dad. He hadn't stayed long. My dad just wandered around, shaking hands and accepting condolences, all the time his mouth set in a blank line.

There was a make-shift bar on the dining table, but no-one was really drinking much. I nicked a bottle of whisky and smuggled it up to my bedroom. I remembered sitting on the bed and twisting the lid, the tiny cracking sound as the metal tabs broke. At first the smell alone had made my stomach churn, and when I took a gulp I'd gagged on the taste, sweet yet bitter at the same time. But then I'd got used to it, and carried on swigging, throwing my head back and chucking the stuff down my neck. The last thing I remembered was Ziggy Stardust gazing down at me from my bedroom wall, and his lightning streak zooming in and out of focus.

When I woke up the next morning I was lying on top of my bed. The sheets were rancid with vomit. That was the first time I had woken with a sense of déjà vu, that nagging feeling of having experienced something important while I slept, but not being able to pin it down.

Much later, when I went downstairs, I knew I was red-eyed and stank of alcohol, but my dad didn't notice anything different about me. He had my mother to look after.

I half opened my eyes and looked at Mally through my eyelashes. 'Go on then. Why not? Let's get pissed.'

He looked pleased, and shuffled forward conspiratorially.

'So where are we going to get the booze from?' he said, in a theatrical whisper.

'Dunno,' I said. 'My dad drank the house dry last night, and I reckon your mum's probably done the same thing at yours.'

'Leave it to me. Mally the Marvellous will make some booze appear as if by magic.' He clapped his hands and bizarrely, for a split second, I expected something to appear, a bottle or some cans or something.

He sprang to his feet and grabbed his shirt.

'See you tonight. Nine o'clock. At the plague cross. I'll see if there's anything in the house my mum hasn't drunk.'

He tied his shirt around his waist and ran off across the field without looking back.

I recognised the car as soon as we got back to the cottage and saw it parked outside the chapel. A dark blue Austin Allegro, spotlessly clean and devoid of the dust that seemed to be everywhere, the chrome bumpers glinting blatantly in the sunlight. It had been the first car to arrive on Sunday when the villagers had congregated at the chapel. The little brown and white terrier was sitting on the back seat, and when it saw me and Lorry it jumped up, teeth bared, and made high-pitched yipping noises which escaped from the crack where the window had been left open. I went closer and tapped on the glass and the dog went berserk, throwing itself against the window, quivering with rage and frustration. Lorry started looking agitated, twisting his clown doll between his fingers, so I gave the dog a middle finger salute and we walked over to the cottage and down the stone steps.

The sun was still high in the sky and sweat was trickling down my chest and pooling under my breasts. I was clammy and my throat was dry and parched. What was left of the lawn at the front of the house had been desiccated even more by the sun, and there were now little bare patches where it refused to grow at all. I made Lorry sit down on the patch of concrete and went to get him a drink of water.

The front door was already open and there were voices coming from the kitchen. I stood in the hall and through the crack in the kitchen door I could just about make out the side of a man's face. Clean-shaven, pale, a chin that disappeared into a wattled neck. The beetle man.

'It's not appropriate.'

'With all due respect, I don't think it has anything to do with you.' My dad's voice was quiet and calm but there was a waver in it, and I knew he was struggling to keep his temper under control.

'But they're impressionable. Especially your daughter. Who knows what ideas that boy's filling her head with?'

'She's a sensible girl.' Again, my dad was trying hard to keep his voice low and steady. 'She won't do anything silly.'

'It's not only her I worry about, Mr Allen.' The beetle man's voice, which had been pleasant and light, now took on an insistent tone. 'There are others here who are in danger of...' When he paused, his little pointed tongue darted out and licked his bulbous lower lip. 'In danger of succumbing to certain...charms.'

I heard my dad make a huffing sound, and then there was silence. A chair scraped and I could see my dad through the crack in the door. I guessed he was standing with his hand on the latch.

Another chair scraped, slower this time, as if the occupant was taking their time standing up.

'It's just a friendly warning, Mr Allen, that's all. Nothing more than that. I would hate for your time here to be spoilt by any...unfortunate circumstances.'

'Thank you for your concern, Mr Vaughan, but I'm sure we'll all be fine.' My dad's voice was clipped, but the tremor was still there.

'We'll pray for you then. We'll have our usual service on Sunday and our minister, Mr Beynon, will ask the congregation to hold you in their thoughts. To hold you in their hearts, to keep you safe. We'll ask God to cherish you.'

A third chair screeched and I realised with a start that there was another person in the kitchen. My mother. When she spoke, her voice was raw and brittle.

'You'll not ask your god for anything on our behalf, Mr Vaughan,' she spat. 'We don't need your god. What use was he when my Petra died? Did he "cherish" us then? No, he did not. He took my daughter from me and gave me no comfort, nothing, so don't you come here telling me about your god.' My mother took a deep intake of breath, as though talking for so long had exhausted her of air. Through the crack in the door, I could see my dad raise his hand to his eyes and rub them. Then my mother spoke again, and her voice was cold and clear.

'Get out of this house. And take your god with you. Neither of you are welcome here.'

I only just managed to dart up the stairwell before Lyndon Vaughan marched out of the kitchen and into the hall. My dad went after him and caught him by the arm as he was stepping over the threshold. The beetle man swung round to face him. He was even paler than usual.

'It's the medication,' my dad said. 'It makes her say things, things she doesn't mean. I'm sorry.'

The beetle man stared at him for a few moments, then his little pink tongue darted out again and slid across his lower lip.

'Mr Allen.' I was surprised at how calm his voice was. 'You're new here and I can understand that there is a certain… naivety to your actions. However, we have a way of doing things that I think you should bear in mind. I'm sorry that I asked you to escort her home. That was foolish of me. I would strongly advise that you and your family have nothing to do with Janet White and her son.'

My dad stood watching as Lyndon Vaughan left, the only sound in the stagnant air the squeal of the gate.

A silence descended on the cottage. My mother put herself to bed, claiming that the confrontation had exhausted her. My dad escaped to his studio and didn't appear until much later, his face grey and lined, his hands clagged with clay.

I lay with Lorry on the patch of concrete and together we drifted off to sleep.

Twelve.

Petra had been dead for ten weeks before I decided what I was going to do. I had already spotted the blackbird. At first, I'd only heard it from my bedroom window which overlooked the long expanse of back garden, the bird's fluting song drawing me to look for the source of the melody. After a few minutes I'd spotted it, a black, glossy flutter of feathers that hopped around on the dusty path, bright eyes ringed in the same sunshine yellow as its beak. It would inspect the ground, its head twisting on its neck, each eye focusing in turn on the dry soil. Sometimes, it would scratch at the ground, a cloud of dust would fly up, and if it had hit the jackpot it would scoop up a worm in its beak and disappear behind the shed. I watched it closely from then on.

My mother was on the Valium all the time by then, and I rarely saw her. Mrs O'Riordan had said she couldn't cope with

Lorry anymore, on account of her arthritis, so my dad had him at home with us. In truth, my dad had his work cut out with trying to persuade my mother to eat and wash and occasionally get out of bed, so I was left in charge of Lorry. I didn't mind.

It was the spring bank holiday Monday when I decided to do it. It had seemed auspicious: it had been a bank holiday Monday when I'd found the duckling, relic number three, and already the incantation was forming in my mind, even though I didn't know then what it was. It had a nice tempo to it, a rhythm that begged to be continued. Seeing the blackbird seemed like a good omen, one that I couldn't afford to let slip by.

I'd given Lorry his lunch and cleaned him up. He'd suddenly started using the toilet a couple of weeks before, and he wasn't in nappies at all by then, so that was one less thing I had to do. I put him to bed for his nap and closed the door, aware that if my mother woke up and started screeching she'd wake him and that would be the end of it. She was Valiumed up to the eyeballs, though, so little chance of that.

I let myself out into the garden and looked around for the blackbird. For a little while I felt sorry for it, but then something came over me, a burst of energy that drove me onwards. I know now that it was the Creed, telling me to go through with it.

I'd hidden myself behind the shed, hunkering down on my haunches, and I waited for the bird to appear. The sun was high in the sky by then, and sharp needles of heat were piercing my scalp. The grass under my feet was brittle and stiff where it curled over my sandals. My legs were getting tired and I'd been considering giving up when the blackbird appeared, about twenty feet further down the garden, and oblivious to me. I stayed completely still, barely daring to breathe, and watched as it started strutting over the barren earth of the empty vegetable bed. The weight of my parents' grief had meant that they had no desire to encourage new life and nothing had been planted that spring.

After a few minutes of hopping and scratching, the blackbird must have spotted a worm, because it bent down and started tugging at something in the soil. Eventually it managed to free it from the earth and gave what I thought was a little celebratory dance, hopping on its brittle legs a couple of times, before fluttering off. I stayed still and silent, and watched as it flew towards the holly bush that sat next to the washing line. It settled on one of the branches and eased itself through the jagged leaves, and the worm caught on a spiked edge before the blackbird tugged it free and disappeared.

The nest had been easy to spot, once I knew where to look for it. I parted the holly branches, spiking my fingers a couple of times but not really caring. The nest was tucked back towards the trunk of the bush and it sat balanced on the y-shape made where two branches joined. It was cup-shaped and the outside was a jumble of small twigs and grass. The blackbird was sitting on the edge, the worm still dangling from its beak. When it saw me, it flitted away, its wings bashing cruelly against the glossy green holly leaves. Another bird, brown and puffed up, regarded me warily from the inside of the nest, peering over the edge with furtive eyes.

I reached forward and tipped the nest, and rolled it to one side so I could better see the inside. The mother bird took exception to this and jumped up, flapped, and squeezed through a gap in the holly leaves, abandoning whatever it was that was housed in the nest.

Pink-slimed, a few small nubs of feather. Three chicks lay in the nest, their preposterously large heads swaying blindly on spindly necks, massive black orbs of eyes covered by a pink membrane. I drew my hand away, sickened at the sight of these monstrous creatures, and as I did so the nest tipped fully over, and sent the chicks sprawling into the maze of jagged leaves, falling through the narrow gaps that lay between the branches. They hit the floor, one by one, and each caused a tiny puff of dust to rise.

I ran back to the house, my heart thumping in my chest and aghast at what I'd done. I locked myself in my bedroom and it was only later that I spotted the scratches on my arms where the holly leaves had made contact, deep red lines adorned with tiny crimson berries of blood.

Over the course of the next couple of weeks, the idea of the Creed started to form in my head. It wasn't something I consciously decided upon, rather it chose me. Gradually, it seemed, little pieces of information, ideas and suggestions, fluttered into my mind and melded together to create a whole that was greater than the sum of its parts.

One morning I'd been sitting at the kitchen table, eating my Ready Brek, and *flash*—into my mind had popped the word 'relic', to describe the eggs and the duckling. A few days later I was lounging on the sofa with Lorry watching a news story about the IRA blowing up the Irish Ambassador, when the word 'incantation' had appeared, hovering in the air in front of me. It was inevitable; it had been decided that I was to discover the Creed and there was nothing I could do about it.

The Creed chose me.

It was the Creed that made me summon up the courage to go back to the blackbirds' nest exactly two weeks after I'd found it. I had failed to obtain the fourth relic, the one that was needed to continue the rhythm of the incantation.

I had read my dad's book about British birds, and found out that blackbirds could have as many as three or four broods of young every year and I thought that there was a fair chance they would have another lot of chicks by then.

This time the birds weren't there when I approached the nest. I'd made a bit of noise as I walked down the path, whistling, stamping, that sort of thing. I didn't want to see the mother and father blackbird again, didn't want those bright eyes glaring at me when I did what I knew I had to do.

There were no chicks in the nest, but there were four eggs, blue and freckled, barely bigger than the tip of my finger. It would be easier this way.

I'd lifted the eggs out carefully, one by one, conscious that the warmth of them meant that the mother was not far away. I thought of my own mother, catatonic in her bedroom, oblivious to all that was going on around her, shielded by her drugs from reality. And I thought of how she'd let Petra drown.

I ran towards the shed, the eggs cupped in both hands and stopped about ten feet away from it. I picked up one of the eggs in my right hand. I drew my arm back and threw it with all my might at the side of the shed, thrilled at the minute explosion of reddened-yolk and slime as the tiny missile hit the wooden planks. I did the same with the second and the third.

And then the fourth egg I very carefully carried to my bedroom and put in the shoe box with the other relics.

Thirteen.

'I had a sister,' I said.

Mally said nothing; he just picked up the bottle of gin he'd brought with him and made a little 'hmm' sound that might have meant 'go on'.

We were at the plague cross. It was late and the sun had long since sunk behind the high-sided valley walls, but a pale blue haze remained on the horizon as a clue to where it had disappeared and its heat still palpated in the air around us. Mally had sat down next to me on the steps, his thigh touching mine, the denim rubbing slightly against my bare leg whenever he moved.

'She was called Petra and she was Lorry's twin.' I knew that my dad had told Janet about Petra—her approach to my mother in the pub had made that clear—but I didn't know how many of the details he'd told her. Mally swallowed and

I could see his Adam's apple stick out for a moment before it receded again. We'd been drinking for half an hour or so and I felt light-headed but quite calm.

'She was only four when she died.' I hated myself for talking about my sister like this, as though she was some part of a game, and if only I knew how to use her properly, how to say the right things about her, I'd win. 'She drowned. It was an accident.'

Mally sniffed. 'I know,' he said.

'Why didn't you say?'

'I needed to see how much you would tell me. To see if you trusted me with your secrets. Do you trust me, Nif?'

I took the gin bottle from him and put it down on the plinth. I was starting to feel the effects of the drink. I picked up his hand and turned it palm up, and with the tip of my finger I traced the lines, deep and cracked with dirt. The life line, curving around the bulge at the base of his thumb; the head line, long and deep and arcing across the expanse of his hand; the heart line, shorter and fainter. And the fate line, a barely-there indentation at the base of his palm.

'Perhaps,' I said. 'Perhaps I trust you.'

He laughed softly and rubbed his hand on his jeans and picked up the bottle again.

'Go on,' he said. 'Tell me about Petra.'

I tried my hardest to remember what Petra had looked like, to remember any detail about her that I could tell Mally. Instead of memories, there was a just a vacuum, as though my mind had wiped all the information it had held about her. I felt numb.

'I can't. I can't remember. I know there's something there, something I should be feeling, something I should be able to remember, but there's nothing there.'

Mally looked at me sideways, quizzical. I went on.

'You know when you go to the dentist to have a tooth out, right? And he gives you an injection? And for a while you can't feel it, but you keep on chewing away at your lip, because it's weird and you can't feel anything. It's a bit like that. I can't feel anything at the moment, can't remember anything. But I think that if I keep trying to remember, keep picking away at my memories, it'll be like the anaesthetic has worn off and I'll get the feeling back again.'

Mally looked thoughtful. He lifted the bottle to his mouth and took an enormous slug.

'Enjoyin' that are you?'

The voice was harsh in the twilight and carried easily over the twenty feet or so from where Tracy Powell stood, her feet planted squarely apart, hands on hips. She had her gang with her: Fat Denise and the other girls I'd seen her with on that first night. It seemed like weeks ago, rather than just a few days.

She was walking towards us, a swagger in her step that she hadn't had that night at the pub. Her hair was up in its greasy ponytail and as she got closer I could see the ring of pimples that sprouted around her hairline. She blew out a huge pink bubble, and the gum popped and splatted against her nose. She sucked it back into her mouth and her friends giggled.

'Well, if it isn't Beelzebub's nephew.' Again, the girls laughed. Mally was looking straight down at the ground, his head hanging down, hair hiding both sides of his face. I didn't know what Tracy was talking about, but I felt Mally tense next to me. Tracy turned round to the girls and said something in Welsh. It was just a collection of sounds to me, none of them intelligible. It wasn't like when Father Declan used to say the Mass in Latin. Even though I couldn't understand it, that would be a warm, reassuring mumble. This was harsh, the consonants clacking out of Tracy's mouth causing her cronies to hoot with laughter.

She turned back to Mally. 'It's the Prince of Darkness 'imself. Our own little Lucifer.' Tracy was enjoying herself now, and it wasn't until she got closer to us and noticed me that she did a double take. 'I know you,' she said, her mouth pursing round the vowels. 'You were in the pub the other night. New folks. Tried to listen in on old Lyndon Vaughan's meetin'.' She blew out another bubble and let it splat against her face.

Mally looked up and brushed his hair away from his face. 'What meeting?'

'Never you mind.' She smirked and her features sank even further into her doughy face. 'Just your new friend here and her family, sniffin' around where they're not wanted. A bit like you and your mother.'

'Fuck off Tracy.' His voice was small, quiet, indistinct in the stale air.

'But it's true. Nobody likes you around here. I know the chapel lot think you're bad, that your ancestors brought some bad shit to the village, but I just think you're a twat. Nobody asked you to move here. Why don't you just fuck off back to whatever shithole it was you came from and leave us alone.'

'Tracy, just leave it, right, it's not worth it.' Mally was still speaking quietly, but he had his hands clenched in his lap, the knuckles white.

'Oh, it's fuckin' worth it, alright. I'd like to see the back of you. We'd all like to see the back of you and that whore of a mother of yours.'

As Tracy turned to acknowledge the wave of laughter from her cronies, she didn't see Mally spring up and land a solid punch straight to her face.

It connected with the side of her chin, knocking her head round with a loud click. He went for her again, this time a blow to her nose, which made a delicious crunching sound. She fell onto the ground, blood seeping from her face, both hands held up in defence. Her gang gathered around her, twittering and shushing, aghast and outraged.

'Don't push it, Tracy, alright?' Mally stood back and wiped his hand on his jeans. Then he grabbed my hand and pulled me to my feet.

We left them there and we walked back along the lane. As if we both knew what was going to happen, we stopped on the bridge and Mally put his hands on my shoulders. Gently, he turned me to face the stream, the hills now dark, the sun long gone. I could make out the looming shape of the oak tree, the spot where he'd seen me naked. I felt the bulk of him behind me, his breath warm on my neck, but his hand was cool as it snaked down the front of my shorts, and I tensed, waiting for the inevitable. His fingers found me quickly and eased their way down, rubbing softly at first then harder, rougher.

When it was over we walked back along the lane and the night was finally starting to cool. All the time neither of us had said a word.

Fourteen.

I was washing the dishes after lunch when there was a knock at the door. My first thought was that it was Mally, and I left the brown-clouded water and the smeared plates and, drying my hands on a tea-towel, went into the hall. Standing next to the open door, blonde hair glowing in the sunlight, stood Mally's mother. She pulled a smile onto her face.

'Hi. It's Nif isn't it? I'm Janet. I'm told we met the other night at the pub.' She looked slightly shame-faced, but her smile stayed in place. 'I have to admit I don't remember much about that night.'

'I'll call my dad,' I said, and I turned around to fetch him from his studio. Janet spoke quickly.

'No, no, it's fine. It's your mum I wanted to see.'

'My mother?' I pictured her, lying in bed, gazing at the wall.

'I wanted to…apologise for my behaviour. I'd had a couple of drinks, you see, and I didn't know what I was doing.'

'I'll see if she's awake,' I said and turned to start up the stairs. Then I stopped. 'You'd better come in,' I said, and stood back to let her into the hall. I stepped round her and she followed me into the kitchen. I could see her looking around, taking in the stained sink and the vast old range cooker. That was when I noticed that she was holding a bunch of flowers, pinks and purples that could have come from a meadow if it hadn't been for the heatwave, so I guessed it was more likely that they had come from her own garden. It occurred to me that she was a bit like one of her flowers, lighting up the gloom of the kitchen with her blonde curls and eyeshadow and her bright red vest. She saw me looking and shrugged.

'Just a little something for your mum. I'm trying to make amends.'

'I'll go and get her.'

My mother wasn't lying in bed as I'd expected, but was sitting at the dressing table. She had her back to the door, but even though I could see my own reflection in the dressing table mirror when I walked in, she didn't appear to notice me. She was brushing her hair in long, smooth strokes, and smiling that placid, contented smile she seemed to have found in the last few days. She didn't start as I walked up to her, but her eyes met mine in the mirror.

'Janet's downstairs,' I said. 'You know, the woman from the pub the other night?' I wanted to say 'Mally's mother' but I didn't think my mother would remember Mally and I didn't want to say his name to her. 'She's come to say sorry, and she's brought you some flowers.'

My mother put the hairbrush down, gently and deliberately, onto the dressing table. It was only when she stood up that I noticed she was wearing proper clothes again and not her dressing gown: a flowery dress that I hadn't seen her wearing for months. It was too big for her, and its strange familiarity was both reassuring and unnerving.

Janet was sitting at the kitchen table when we went down. The flowers were lying on the table in front of her, and when she saw my mother she picked them up. I held my breath, unsure of what my mother's reaction would be. I wondered who was going to speak first.

'I came to say sorry.' It was Janet. 'About the other night in the pub. I think I must have made a fool of myself. I wanted to come sooner, but I felt a bit embarrassed.' She held the flowers out to my mother. 'Anyway, these are for you. A kind of peace offering, I suppose.'

She was still holding the flowers out in front of her, the bright colours vivid in the gloomy kitchen. I held my breath, silently daring my mother to do something dramatic. Instead, she reached out her hand and took them. She didn't look at them, but passed them to me, all the while looking at Janet. Most people would have looked away then, or would have said something to clear the silence, but Janet gazed back at my mother, and there was something powerful about the silence, some sort of energy that pulsed between the two women.

I rummaged in the cupboard and found an old green jug, a bit chipped around the rim. I tipped in water from a bottle and placed the flowers in, the stems already starting to wilt in the heat, the heads drooping slightly.

I don't know what happened to my mother to make her thaw. Perhaps she thought she needed a friend, a companion for the time we were going to be staying in the village, or maybe she just felt better about everything, now that she thought Petra had forgiven her, but she suddenly looked softer, less angular.

'Would you like a cup of tea?' she said, and Janet took a couple of seconds before she nodded her head. Then my mother did something even more unexpected. She picked up the kettle and filled it from the water bottle. She placed it on the camping stove and lit a match. She held it to the gas ring and the blue flare hissed into life in the silence of the kitchen. It was the first time I had seen her do anything for herself for ages, and she seemed a bit self-conscious of her actions. When she reached for the teapot, her fingers gripped the handle deliberately, as if unsure whether she could take the weight of it. She picked up the cork-topped pot we kept the teabags in, and very briefly she faltered as the lid failed to shift. Then her hand twisted again and the cork came loose. She reached her fingers inside and pinched out two teabags.

All this time, Janet and I had been watching her intently, but we both turned around as the door to the back hall opened and my dad came in, wiping his hands on his trousers. At first, he looked surprised to see Janet, then he looked worried, and then he adjusted his face and smiled.

'Making tea, Linda?' He sounded overly-casual, like he was forcing himself to say something mundane.

'I just came round to say sorry for the other night.' Janet was quick to speak, as if to explain her presence to my dad before he asked.

'That's good of you,' he said, 'but really, there's no need.'

'I was apologising to Linda.' Janet's voice was louder than it should have been, and sounded petulant in the silence of the kitchen. My dad looked at the floor and sniffed.

129

'Of course. Well, that's good of you.'

All this time, my mother had been standing with her hands clasped together, looking at the kettle, waiting for it to boil. As the steam started rising from the spout, and the tell-tale bubbling sound became louder, she looked at my dad and Janet in turn, then she spoke.

'Thank you for the flowers, Janet. They're lovely. Now let's all have a cup of tea, shall we?'

That afternoon, my mother and Janet stayed talking for hours. My dad soon realised that he wasn't welcome to join in their conversation, and took himself back to his studio. I hung around in the kitchen for a bit, forcing myself to drink the weak tea my mother had made, and looking at Janet out of the corner of my eye, as she and my mother chatted about recipes and gardening.

It was hard to believe that she was Mally's mother. She was all blonde curls and pink lipstick and tanned flesh that bulged around the straps of her vest. She was wearing flip flops, and even her toenails were painted a frosty pink. As she sat there at the kitchen table talking to my mother, their conversation at first stilted and strange, and then lapsing into a more comfortable exchange, I saw how different they were: Janet was fair and tanned and plump, my mother dark, pale-skinned and painfully thin, and yet there seemed to be an instant bond forged between them.

Over the next few days, my mother and Janet grew closer. They spent hours together, huddled over our kitchen table or theirs, their heads close together, blonde and brunette almost mingling. They would smoke and drink tea and gooseberry wine, and they would whisper and laugh and cry and hug each other. They would walk along the lane, arm in arm, in companionable silence, and all the time my dad would shut himself in his studio, working on the bust. Sometimes he would emerge and do a few half-hearted things to the house: scraping the paint from the windows or weeding in between the flagstones of the path, but mostly he would just sculpt.

Fifteen.

When I was younger, I used to see if I could make myself cry by imagining myself dead. I would picture my dad and my mother at my graveside. He would have his arm around her shoulders and she would be engulfed in grief, shaking, hands over her face, as they lowered my coffin into the ground. It would be a drizzly autumn day, and the trees that ringed the cemetery would be empty except for the rooks that roosted there. Father Declan would be there in his cassock, the hem damp and muddied, an open bible in his hands as he read the words of committal in his lugubrious tone. My mother would scatter a handful of dirt onto my coffin, and then a handful of rose petals, and then she'd collapse into my dad's arms, the grief too much for her.

I tried to do this now, lying on my back with my arms behind my head, watching the swallows that darted and swooped against the cloudless sky. I used to be able to summon up a few tears just by thinking about it, by thinking about how sorry they'd be if I died. This time it didn't work. I tried again, thinking about how sad I'd be if Lorry died, and there was a bit of a prickle behind my eyes, but no real tears.

I hadn't seen Mally since the day he punched Tracy Powell. The memory of the bridge was still with me though, and when I hadn't been able to sleep I'd lain in bed and thought about those long fingers and touched myself.

The heatwave wore on, oppressive, endless, and Lorry and I had taken to lying on the concrete patch at the front of the cottage, dozing, listening for grasshoppers and watching for the rabbits that were even less cautious now, hopping down the stone steps and into the garden, desperate for water.

Lorry seemed happier, and had started talking more. The sores on his legs were clearing up and seemed to be healing. Janet had given my mother a poultice to put on them, something she made with the herbs and flowers in her garden, and each evening my mother would tend to Lorry's legs, washing them and applying the creamy ointment. He didn't need the bandages anymore, and he'd begun to get a tan on his legs too, matching that on his chest and shoulders. I was still mostly white, the pink patches where I'd got burnt and my freckles starting to join up across my nose the only visible signs that we were in the middle of a heatwave. I didn't know where I'd got my ginger hair and pale skin from. My dad was tawny and tanned easily. My mother, with her dark brown hair and deep eyes, like a raven. I was the odd one out. A cuckoo.

Lorry had picked up a stone and was scratching in the dust with it. I watched as he drew a triangle, and then a circle at the top, and when he scratched four lines jutting from the sides and bottom of the triangle, it suddenly took on the shape of a crudely depicted girl.

'Who's that?' I asked, thinking it was probably meant to be my mother.

'It's Petra,' he said, dragging the stone through the dust to carve two eyes and a straight line for a mouth. Lorry had never mentioned his twin sister before, and I hadn't spoken of her to him, thinking that it was kinder if he was allowed to forget about her.

'Mummy talks to her. At night.' He was adding hair now, long straight hair on either side of the circle.

'How do you know? Did you hear her?'

'In the night. If I get up. She's asleep but her eyes are open.'

'Asleep with her eyes open? Are you sure she's not awake?'

'No. She can't see me. She's talking to Petra. She says, "Love you, Petra" and then she smiles. Then I go back to bed.'

I took a deep breath. 'What do you remember about Petra?'

Lorry shook his head, but didn't look at me. 'Not much,' he said.

'Petra was our sister,' I said. 'Like I'm your sister as well. She was born at the same time as you, which means that she was your twin.' Lorry frowned, and I could tell he was working hard to process this information. He opened his mouth as if to ask another question, but his face froze as a loud jangling came from the house. He looked alarmed and put his hands over his ears and then he started rocking.

I felt a strange coldness on my shoulders, as though the sun had gone behind a cloud, but the sky was still clear and empty, the same opaque blue it had been for weeks. I felt silly for thinking it, but it was as though talking about Petra had summoned her up and I wondered fleetingly if she was somewhere, watching us, waiting to make her presence known. Was the telephone ringing a reminder of the circumstances of her death—a little joke? A sign from her that she was here with us, after all, exactly like my mother had said?

I could see that Lorry was becoming more and more disturbed, and was crying now as well as rocking and clamping his hands to his ears. I forced myself to stand up and walk to the house.

The white plastic telephone was still ringing, the trilling engulfing the hall, and I found myself expecting the handset to start vibrating, like in a cartoon. I made myself reach out to lift it, but another hand slammed down and grabbed it. My dad.

His frown was replaced with a smile after a couple of seconds, and he turned away from me, facing the stairs. He was holding the receiver close to his mouth, his lips almost touching the mouthpiece. Then he went red and smiled and put his hand round the handset so I couldn't hear much of what he was saying.

'Alright, in a minute,' I caught, and he put the receiver gently back on the cradle. There was paint on his hands and he rubbed them on his grubby jeans and muttered something about idle hands making work for the devil. Then he went outside and a couple of minutes later I heard the tell-tale squeak of the gate.

In my bedroom, I tugged on the only clean t-shirt I had and sniffed myself, thinking I should have had a wash when I'd taken Lorry to the stream that morning. I picked up the crow's skull from the altar on the mantelpiece and stroked the smooth arc of the cranium. The beak was glossy and black, reflecting the sunlight that poured in through the little window. I looked across at Mally's window, but the curtains there were closed. Down below I could see my dad and Janet, standing either side of her fence, our lawnmower lying discarded on the ground.

Janet was a good head shorter than my dad and she was looking up at him, her neck craned, one hand shielding her eyes from the sun. She was in her pink bikini again, a lipstick kiss against the parched yellow handkerchief of grass that was her front garden. She was like one of her flowers, the ones that thrived in the herb garden at the back of the house, a splash of vitality against a dull and barren background. Her other hand was on her hip. I could see the string from her bikini digging in to tanned flesh. She had no strap marks or anything on her shoulders, just bronzed, gleaming flesh. She must have been sunbathing topless.

I could make out the shape of her nipples through the fabric of her bikini top, and I watched, transfixed, as her hand went from shielding her eyes to playing with her hair, the fingers winding round and round the blonde tendrils, teasing them. She was smiling, then suddenly looked serious and began biting her lower lip.

My dad had his back to me, and he'd taken his shirt off and tied it round his waist, like the boys at school used to do with their jumpers. There was a peculiar intimacy to these two semi-naked people standing so close to each other, only a picket fence stopping them from touching, and for a moment I thought of my mother, asleep in her bedroom, pale and oblivious.

Janet stopped playing with her hair and her hand fluttered to the edge of her bikini top. Her fingers teased the fabric gently, stroking it, caressing it. I could tell from the way my dad was standing that he wasn't talking anymore. He was standing still, watching Janet. She was looking up into his eyes, but I didn't think he was looking at her face. Abruptly, as though waking suddenly from a dream, my dad shook his head and stepped backwards. When he turned around I could see that he was smiling to himself, and when he walked back towards the house, he kept on smiling and shaking his head.

Janet stood there for a few moments, watching him go, and then turned and went into her house. The lawnmower lay abandoned by the fence.

I was making a sandwich in the kitchen when my dad came back in. He looked surprised to see me, but busied himself by folding up the dustsheet that was under the window. He'd found some paintbrushes and paint in the shed and had made a start on painting the window frame. Fresh white gloss had taken the place of the wood he'd exposed and the window looked incongruous, the newness of the paint stark against the ancient glass. He cleared his throat.

'We'll need more water tomorrow, Nif. Can that be your job again?'

'S'pose so.' I thought of the climb up the hill, the heat on my back, the clinging sweat beneath my breasts. Then I thought of Mally. 'Yep. I can do that.'

'Can you make sure you go early, love? The Christians will be out in force, it being a Sunday and all, and it's probably best if you can go under the radar, so to speak.'

I nodded and crammed the sandwich into my mouth so I wouldn't have to say anything else.

I hadn't heard my mother coming into the room, but when I looked round she was standing in the doorway. She'd washed her hair and it lay in folds on her shoulders, glossy and smooth. She was wearing make-up, eyeshadow and a slick of lipstick that made her look younger and fresher. The dress she wore was one of her old ones that I hadn't see her wear for months, a long, silky white one with embroidery around the neckline. As she stood in front of the window, the light gathered around her, and it was like she'd regained her old radiance, that luminescence she used to have that made people flock to her. That contemplative, placid smile had found its way back to her lips and for a fleeting moment, I thought she looked like an angel.

My dad looked surprised to see her. 'I was just…making you a sandwich, love,' he managed, and held out a hand to gesture at the loaf of bread and the cheese I'd discarded on the sideboard. He picked up the knife.

My mother nodded, but didn't say anything.

'Cheese or ham?' My dad was really struggling now, but my mother just shook her head.

'I don't need food.' She spoke in a whisper, and her words hung smoke-like in the still air.

My dad put the knife down. He put his hands very gently onto my mother's shoulders, and steered her to a chair. He pushed her down and she complied, all the while with that strange smile on her lips.

'You've got to eat, love. Keep your strength up. You know what the doctor said: a healthy body equals a healthy mind.' As soon as he'd said it, my dad looked embarrassed, and he shuffled back to the sideboard and started making the sandwich. The butter had melted and he was scooping an ooze of yellow against the flabby bread.

'I don't need food. I already have all I need.' My mother had raised her voice slightly, but it still came out as barely a whisper. I saw my dad's shoulders tense, but he carried on scraping the liquid butter onto the bread. He didn't turn around, and when he spoke it was as though he was addressing the sideboard in front of him.

'Yes? And why's that then?' There was a deliberate lightness to his voice, but at the same time I could hear a new harshness, like the scrape of a knife against a plate.

'You know why, Clive. You know as well as I do that she's here.' My mother's voice was calm and smooth, but it also sounded smug, as though she was goading my dad. 'Janet says she can feel her as well. She says she has a way about her for things like that and she thinks Petra's here as well.'

My dad's shoulders twitched a little bit and I knew he was struggling to keep his temper. In the end, it was too much for him. He swung round, and little drops of liquid butter flew off the knife and spotted my mother's dress.

'Petra's…not…here.' He punctuated his speech with little jabs of the knife into the air in front of him, and he enunciated every word, speaking slowly to make sure she heard everything. 'You think our dead daughter is here, in this house? You think that she's come back to tell you that she forgives you? *That everything's OK?*' These last words were spat out, and when I looked at my mother I saw that the smile had slipped from her mouth and her lips were thin and straight. She'd made a spindly knot of her arms across her chest, and she looked as though she'd sunk into herself, made herself tiny.

When my dad spoke, there was a finality to his voice, a firmness, like that of an adult speaking to a truculent child.

'Just stop saying these things about Petra. You're making yourself ill and it's not fair on the children.'

My mother's face was white, and her smugness had turned to belligerence.

'Should I just keep quiet then? Not say anything? Is that what you want?'

My dad turned on her and there was real fury in his eyes.

'Yes. That's exactly what I want. For once I would like you to just shut the fuck up!'

My mother was stunned into silence. She placed her hands on the table in front of her, twining her fingers together, the knuckles forming bony white nuggets.

I waited for the drama to continue, but neither of them spoke. In the end my mother reached up one hand and pushed her hair behind her ear, the action a full stop punctuating the end of the conversation.

My dad stalked off in the direction of his studio, and I knew we'd see no more of him that afternoon.

Sixteen.

I woke up very early the next morning after a solid, dreamless sleep and got straight out of bed. I checked the relics. The sun wasn't quite up yet and in the pale light they looked unreal, the eggshells taking on a pearly glow, the crow's skull gleaming as if it bore a light of its own.

I was surprised to see that the curtains were already drawn in Mally's bedroom window and I half expected him to appear, but there was no-one.

I got dressed in a hurry. My t-shirt from the day before, my sole mini skirt that I'd worn that night to the pub, when Janet had flung her arms around my dad and had to be carried home. I thought there was probably something going on between them, but I didn't really care. Good luck to them, I thought, and where there should have been a pang of shame at my disloyalty to my mother, there was nothing. She was welcome to her fantasies about Petra. I was numb to her.

There was nobody in the kitchen when I went down, and the water bottles weren't there either. I thought they must be in my dad's studio. In the darkness of the back hall the temperature was comfortable but I was stunned by the wall of heat that met me when I pushed open the door. The clear plastic roof had been assaulted by the sun all the previous day, and the heat had built up like a furnace.

The bust of my mother stood on the wheel in the middle of the room. The hessian had been removed, and only the plastic remained, a transparent film made semi-opaque by smears of clay and a frosting of condensation. I went to open the window and my arm brushed against the plastic sheet. It floated to the ground, gliding elegantly. My mother's face looked back at me.

The forehead was high, the hairline arched. My dad had not yet carved out the detail of the eyes, and they remained blank, staring through me. The nose was long and aquiline and the sharp cheekbones gave way to the spaces below them, which were hollow and shadowed. And the mouth was gone. The lips had been removed, brushed away, no doubt by the strength of my dad's thumbs. Instead there was merely a space where the mouth should have been, a blank area between nose and chin, the clay there flat and smooth.

Outside, the lane sat quiet and empty. Day came slowly to this little corner of the world, and the sun peered over the horizon a little later than it did at home. As a result, it seemed that life was suspended, and that while darkness lay on the village, its heart temporarily stopped beating. The silence was absolute.

The gates at the front of the chapel were padlocked, an admonishment to intruders and outsiders. Like me. Like Mally. I crawled through the hole in the hedge, scrabbling my way up the bank, and into the field next to the chapel. Janet's field.

I chucked the bottles down next to the well. The plywood was still lying on top, the blue bucket next to it. I wanted to get to the top of the hill, to see the village before the sun came up. Already there was a shimmer of red on the horizon, and a sheen of orange that would soon become a flaming ball of sun. I wanted to see the village while it slept.

It didn't take me long to get to the top of the hill. I walked backwards part of the way, enjoying how the perspective changed as I got higher. The roofs of the houses became flatter, the windows grew squat and low, and even the fields became smaller, the squares of scorched grass making up what I knew would soon be a yellow and brown and ochre-coloured chessboard, but which in the early morning light looked blue and grey and opalescent.

Walking backwards up the hill meant that I stumbled a couple of times over divots in the baked earth. Finally, I reached the top and I sat, breathing heavily, waiting for the sun to come up. The sky was streaked with red by then, and a few meagre clouds sat above the horizon. I knew they would be gone in an hour, baked off by the sun's heat.

I didn't hear him until he was a few feet behind me, the crunch of the dried-out bracken making me turn around. He was wearing his usual tatty jeans, and the picture on the Bowie t-shirt he had on was partly obscured by the camera slung around his neck. I wasn't surprised to see him, and pleased that he'd come. He stopped walking when I turned around, but he didn't look at me. He stared at the other side of the valley, and when I turned back I saw that the first glimmer of the sun's sphere was sparkling over the horizon.

'It's magic, isn't it?' he said, still not looking at me, but with his eyes fixed straight ahead on the other side of the valley. 'The way the sun disappears at night and then comes up again the next morning. Every day. Every single day. You can depend on it.'

'It's not magic,' I said. 'It's physics. The earth turns as it goes round the sun, the sun disappears from view, the earth keeps turning and the sun reappears again. It's not like it's vanished, it's only moved. It's always daytime somewhere in the world.'

'And it's always night-time somewhere else.'

'Tell me a secret,' I said, and he laughed.

'Another secret? Now that's a big ask. I don't think I have any more secrets. Not ones I could tell you, anyway.'

'Why not? I told you about Petra.'

'Yeah, but I already knew about that 'cause your dad told my mum. You'd need to tell me something I don't know already for this to be worth my while.'

'Like what?' I said.

'Like…' he paused, as if trying to think of what to say, but I could tell he'd already decided on something. He sat down next to me and unhooked the Polaroid camera from around his neck and put it carefully on the ground. 'Like what do you think about when you're lying in bed at night, in that little attic room of yours, with no curtains and a nosy neighbour.'

I could feel the heat on my cheeks and looked at my feet. I tugged at my skirt.

'What do you think about when you wake up in the middle of the night, when the light has gone and the darkness is everywhere?'

The sun was halfway over the horizon now, and a great band of orange drenched the sky around it. I took a deep breath.

'I think about Petra,' I said. 'I think about my little sister and how she drowned that day in the bath when my mother went to answer the phone and left her on her own. And when she came back she started screaming and screaming and I ran in and there Petra was, her body completely still, but the water still moving, still washing over her.'

Before I could think better of it I started speaking again.

'And I think of how much I hate my mother and how it's her fault that Petra died. I think about who it was on the phone that was so important that she left Petra in the bath to go and answer it. And I think of how hard my dad's trying to make things right and that selfish bitch just lies there, off her face on Valium, staring at the wall or crying or screaming or just with that stupid smile on her face. And it's her fault. She let it happen.'

'What about the police? Didn't they get involved?'

'Yeah, they came round and asked us all a bunch of questions. They asked me if I'd seen anything and what I'd been doing and everything like that. But in the end, they decided it was an accident and they didn't press charges. They said it wasn't my mother's fault for leaving Petra alone in the bath, that she was four by then and could sit up by herself, so they didn't really know why it happened. They decided it was an accident. My mother still blames herself, though, and so do I.'

'And the dreams?' Mally's voice was low, calm, steady.

'I can never remember the dreams, but I know there's water and a phone ringing, so I know it's something to do with Petra. When I wake up I'm aware that I've had one of those dreams. It's like déjà vu or something. It's a feeling of…of…inevitability, I suppose. Of something that's happened that's important but I can only remember the feeling of it, the outline, and not the detail of it. It's a shimmer. A shiver.'

'Like someone walking on your grave?'

'Something like that.'

'And Lorry. What about Lorry?' Mally was sitting forward, his forearms resting on his knees, and he was looking at me intently. 'Why is Lorry...like he is?'

'He's always been that way,' I said. 'I suppose it has something to do with what happened when he was born—him and Petra, I mean.' I looked at Mally, but he was fiddling with his plimsoll.

'I don't remember much about when Lorry and Petra were born. My dad's told me a few things, and Mrs Akhar who lives next door to us, but I've kind of pieced it together over the last few years.

'I think my parents must have been trying for another baby for ages. I don't know how I knew that, it was just something that was always there, always around. Like, in the room there'd be me, my dad, my mother and this unborn child they wanted, and that was how it always was. I think I must have been about eleven or twelve when I first overheard them talking in the kitchen. They were excited and they were whispering about this baby they were going to have and what they'd call it and how they'd do up the spare room as a nursery. They didn't actually sit me down and tell me about it for another few months, when my mother got so big they couldn't hide it anymore.'

I'd never told anyone about this before, and now I'd started talking I couldn't stop.

'I remember my mother in the kitchen when she told me. She'd made a cup of tea and sat down opposite me, on the other side of the table. She told me that God had decided that we were going to have a new brother or sister in our lives. That we'd all been patient and had waited and prayed until God had decided that we were ready, and now it was happening. In a few weeks, the baby would be born and I would be a big sister.'

'Your mum doesn't look the religious sort,' Mally said, looking up from his plimsoll.

'What do you mean?'

'She doesn't look like the church-going type, that's all. I mean, you've seen all the people round here who go to the chapel. Your mum's different.' He shrugged.

'She doesn't go to church anymore,' I said. 'She gave all that up when Petra died. She said that if God existed he was a bastard and she took off her crucifix and threw it into the canal. She's never been back to church since.'

'What about you? Did you ever go to church?'

'I used to go sometimes, with my mother. Before the accident. I used to like the peace of the church, sitting there in the cool and the dark and the quiet. It was...soothing, I suppose.'

'So, were you ever, you know, confirmed?'

'No. My mother wanted me to be but my dad put his foot down. It's the only time I've ever seen him stand up to her. He said I should wait until I was old enough to make up my own mind and do it then if I still wanted to.'

'So, your dad's not religious then?'

'He never has been. He and my mother have this unspoken agreement that they just get on with things their own way. Some people believe in God, I suppose, and some people believe in nothing.' I shrugged. 'And some people believe in something else.'

'And what do you believe in?' Mally had pulled off a strip of the rubber from his shoe and was holding it in both hands and stretching it. I thought about telling him about the Creed, how it had found me exactly when I needed it, but I just smiled and shook my head.

'So *God* gave your parents a baby, then?' Mally said and the sarcasm in his voice was clear.

'I suppose so. Or at least that's what my mother said at the time. I was pleased, really I was. I was excited about being a big sister and helping my mother with a new baby, and I counted down the weeks and watched as her belly got bigger and bigger until one day her waters broke in the kitchen, this puddle of liquid that just appeared on the floor, and she just stood there, leaning on the worktop and clutching her belly.' I could picture my mother as she had been then: graceful, excited. Happy.

'My parents had arranged for me to go next door when this happened, and we stood there in the dark with my dad ringing and ringing the doorbell and there was no answer. It was raining, or sleeting or something like that, and really cold and we got soaked to the bone waiting for Mrs Akhar. In the end, we all had to go to the hospital, my dad, my mother and me.

'I remember how the car wouldn't start at first, and my dad had to get out and fiddle under the bonnet. Then it started and we drove to the hospital and I've never seen rain like it. The windscreen wipers could hardly keep up, and my dad had to sit forward in his seat so he could see out. It's funny, but I remember that better than any of the other things that happened.'

The sun was nearly all the way up now, and the sky had taken on the light of a new day.

'What did happen?' The piece of rubber Mally was stretching broke in two and snapped back against his fingers. He dropped it.

'When we got to the hospital I was made to sit on a chair outside the labour ward while my dad and my mother went in. I remember I was given a book—*Little Red Riding Hood*—by one of the nurses and I was cross because it was too young for me, but still I read it from cover to cover, over and over again, for hours and hours. Sometimes the same nurse would come and give me an orange or a biscuit or a glass of milk.

'The thing that I remember most about the hospital is the screaming. I'd never heard my mother scream before, and when it started it was the worst sound imaginable. Eventually my dad came out. He was crying—happy tears, I think—and he said that I had a little sister. He hugged me and then he went back in to the ward again. Then lots of stuff started happening all at once. Bells were ringing and more nurses came, walking quickly, not quite running but definitely in a hurry to get somewhere. I remember thinking *please make that not be for my mother or my sister, please make them be OK and for all this commotion to be happening for someone else*. But it was for them.'

'What happened?'

'There was a problem. All this time they'd thought there was only one baby, and so when Petra was born they thought that was it. It was only when my mother carried on bleeding that they examined her properly and they saw that there was another baby.'

'Lorry?'

I nodded. I couldn't remember the last time I'd spoken, uninterrupted, for that long, and I felt lighter as a result, but also afraid that by letting the words out into the world I'd never get them back again. Was this how it had felt for my mother, all those times I'd waited for her as she sat in the confessional box with Father Declan?

'So, what happened?' Mally was pulling again at the rubber from his plimsoll, stretching it out and letting it snap back into place.

'They got him out. He was small, a lot smaller than Petra, and the doctor told my dad that he'd probably been getting less of the nutrition, that Petra had been the stronger twin and in a way, had been starving Lorry of food and maybe oxygen. They thought he wouldn't survive, he was so small. But they kept him in hospital and he managed to pull through. My mother took Petra home and left the nurses to look after Lorry. She said that she thought it best if she gave her attention to one of the twins, and that when Lorry was better then he could come home and she'd look after him as well. I remember thinking that was a bit odd.'

'What happened after that?'

'My dad and I would go to visit Lorry in hospital—every day, this tiny bundle of skin and bones lying in the incubator. I remember my dad reaching in a finger and stroking Lorry and the nurse seeing him and telling him off and my dad getting angry with her and saying that was his child in that box and he'd touch him if he wanted to. I think that's the first time I ever saw my dad get really angry.

'After a few weeks, Lorry was strong enough to come home. My dad and I went to get him from the hospital, and I remember being really excited, and thinking that now we had a chance of being a proper family, that now I had not only a sister, but a brother too to help my mother look after.

'When we got back to the house with Lorry that day, my mother didn't even bother coming to meet us at the door. My dad let us in with his key, and called out to her. We went into the sitting room, and there she was, sitting on the sofa with Petra on her lap. She was feeding her, and singing to her. It was a song, a counting song that she used to sing to me when I was little. I thought she'd get up and come and pick up Lorry, her little boy, be pleased to have him home, but she didn't. She just said something about how he must be allowed to sleep, and that the car journey would have worn him out.'

I waited for Mally to say something, but he didn't, so I carried on.

'I should have known then that she was never really going to love Lorry, that Petra was all she needed. It took me a few months to realise this, and it came to me gradually. It was like when you get a cold and you can feel it building up over a few days and you know that there's nothing you can do to stop it and that very soon you're going to feel terrible. That's what it was like. And that was when I guessed that she'd never loved me either, and that was why she needed God to give her the perfect baby she thought she deserved.'

I couldn't believe I was telling Mally all this when I'd known him for little more than a week, but there was something about him, something that begged you to put your confidence in him.

The sun was fully over the horizon by then, a flaming ball threatening us with the knowledge of the oppressive heat it would bring later in the day.

'From then on, my dad looked after Lorry, or we dropped him off with Mrs Akhar from next door when my dad was teaching or had a commission he couldn't put off. When my dad started to get known a bit more for his sculptures, and things got busy for him, I did more for Lorry. I stopped going to school as much, which was fine as I couldn't stand it, and I fed Lorry from a bottle and waited for him to grow up.'

Sitting there in the early morning light I felt exhausted. I thought again about the church we used to go to, and sitting in the shadows while my mother asked God to give her a baby, watching as people slipped out of the confessional, having told the priest their sins. I wondered if they felt like I did now, unburdened yet shameful, having put into words the deeds they thought they should keep as mere thoughts.

'Two crows I see, good luck to me.' Mally's voice broke the silence.

'What?' I was impatient with him, and I said it sharply, the consonant sound clipped as my tongue clicked against my teeth. I wondered if he'd even been listening to me.

'It's a saying from round here. Goes way back, back to when

they were superstitious, even more superstitious than they are now.' He snorted out a laugh and then he pointed at a log a little way off. Two crows were perched there, their heads hunkered down into their necks. Mally lifted the camera and aimed it at the crows. It clicked.

'The locals think that if you see one crow it's bad luck. Kind of like a bad omen and it'll bring terrible things and doom and gloom to you and your family. But if you see two crows together, the second one balances out the bad luck from the first one.'

Despite myself, I was interested.

'You mean it reverses the bad luck? Stops the bad luck from taking hold if you see another one?'

'Something like that, yeah.' He was looking at the front of the camera, waiting for the photo to appear, and he'd lost interest in what I was saying. I persisted.

'So a bit like, say, if you broke something and it brought bad luck to you but then you broke something else to cancel out the bad luck? A bit like that?'

He was looking at me strangely now. His hand was shielding the sun from his eyes, but he was still frowning.

'I suppose so. What are you getting at?'

'So, like, I don't know, say if someone you really cared about, someone you loved and never wanted to hurt, say if they injured themselves and you knew that the only thing you could do to ward off the bad luck would be to make them hurt themselves again.' The words were all coming out in a rush now, and I had to pause for breath.

Mally was sitting up straight now. 'What's got into you?' he asked.

'Come on,' I said. 'It's my turn to show you something.'

Seventeen.

The morning we left for Wales I helped my dad pack the trailer. We hadn't needed to take much, as we were only planning on going for a month, but my dad had all his stuff for sculpting, which took up most of the space.

He went out after breakfast to pick up the trailer. He had arranged to borrow it from a friend of a friend, and had left me alone with my mother for the first time since the accident. He gave her a dose of Valium before he left, said she'd be asleep and that I was to leave her alone and just keep an eye on my brother.

After he'd gone I checked on Lorry, who was in the playpen in the living room, watching *Rentaghost* with the sound turned down. He had his thumb jammed in the corner of his mouth and didn't even look at me when I walked past.

My mother was lying in bed with her eyes open, staring at the ceiling. Her face was white, almost as white as the sheet drawn up around her chest, and there were deep shadows carved into her eye sockets and under her cheekbones. Her dark hair was fanned out on the pillow and the tendons on her neck were taut and stiff. If her eyes had been closed she would have looked like a corpse waiting to be buried, except that the sheet over her chest rose and fell a tiny amount with each breath she took.

I stood there for a while, watching her, thinking about Petra. I tried to match my breathing to hers, timing each inhalation to rise at the same time as hers did, and to exhale when she did, but her breathing was too slow for me, and I found myself struggling for air.

After a while I closed the door and went downstairs again.

It turned out that the man my dad had arranged to borrow the trailer from had forgotten all about it and gone out, so it took my dad ages to track him down and get the trailer back to our house. Finally, he got it onto the drive, and together with the car it took up most of the space. It was backed-up tight against the flower bed, which was devoid of any plants, all of them withered and dead from the drought. The plastic netting which my dad had tied against the wall to train clematis was now a graveyard for dead foliage, the neglected tendrils hanging in limp fingers.

I helped him fit other bits and pieces in the trailer around his potter's wheel and tubs of clay. We managed to fit in a few boxes of kitchen stuff and big gallon bottles of water. We worked in silence for an hour or so.

It was as we'd finished packing the trailer, and had started to secure the tarpaulin over the top, that my mother's voice emerged through the open bedroom window. It wasn't unusual for her to wake up and start shouting, and my dad hardly flinched, although I could see that he was trying hard not to meet my eye. He finished tying down the tarpaulin, then went in through the front door.

I had already noticed the wren that morning, and I watched it as it sat on a low branch of the rosebush. Now it was back again, all puffed up, its feathers fluffed out, stumpy wings with mottled stripes standing out from both sides of its body. There were tiny flashes of white over each eye, and it looked as though it was raising its eyebrows, asking me a question. It was chirruping out a song, its beak opening and closing as it turned left and right. A gobby, cocky little bird.

It hopped down and started scratching at the dust of the flower bed, occasionally flitting in and out of the holes in the plastic netting.

I moved towards it, but it didn't fly away as I'd expected. It stopped scratching and pecking and looked me straight in the eye. I wondered if it had a nest nearby. I edged closer, my hand out, palm upwards and flattened in a gesture of submission, as I'd seen my dad do with Mrs Akhar's cat. The wren just kept on looking at me. It didn't move, didn't even look away. I moved closer, inch by inch, and wondered if I might actually be able to grab it.

When I was about a foot away from the wren, it suddenly panicked. It hopped backwards a couple of times and then darted to the side, tucking its dumpy brown body through one of the holes in the plastic netting that had been meant to train the clematis.

The holes in the netting were too small for it to squeeze through easily, and it got stuck, one short wing sticking out at the side, trapped by the plastic. I moved closer to it and it tried to move away from me, but its trapped wing prevented it from flying away and it pulled and fluttered. I was so close by now that I could see its eye, the pupil dilating and contracting like the beam from a lighthouse.

As I reached out my hand to pick it up it flapped even more, and I could see that the plastic netting was twisted around its wing. When I knelt down and my fingers closed around the bird, I could feel how small its body was beneath the puffery of its feathers. Its breastbone was sharp and hard, and when I pressed a finger into the space beneath I could feel its heart battering in its chest. With one hand I held it, and with the other I tried to untangle it from the netting. It was no good. I was clumsy, working one-handed, and the netting had got wound tourniquet-tight around the top of the wren's wing, where it joined its body, and the bird's struggles had only made it tighter.

I was starting to get annoyed with it. Its beak was open now, its tiny tongue darting in and out as it panted in panic. If it would only stop struggling, I'd be able to get it free.

It was my mother who made me do what I did next. Her scream came bursting through the bedroom window, setting the air fizzing with nervous energy and my heart almost burst in my chest. My arm seemed to move of its own accord, pulling backwards, dragging the stupid wren clear of the netting in one swift movement, without me even thinking about it. I saw that I'd managed to free the tiny bird, that I was clutching it in my hand and that even though it was still panting and its eyes were still flashing, it was free.

Then I saw the feathers, still trapped in the netting, a collection of short, hard feathers about an inch long, joined at one end. But they weren't just feathers.

They were the bird's wing.

We left about an hour after that. My mother had calmed down enough to allow herself to be dressed by my dad, and had been put in the passenger seat where she sat nervously rubbing the fabric of her skirt. I'd cleaned the sores on Lorry's legs and changed his bandages for him, and he was sitting in the back seat, behind my mother, leaning against the window with his eyes half closed, his clown doll jammed between his knees. My dad was doing a final check of the house before we set off, closing windows and double-locking the front door.

He finished locking up and was about to get into the car when he seemed to hesitate. He went to the back, to the trailer, and rummaged around for a bit. Then he opened my door and handed me the hessian-wrapped package.

'Probably best if she sits on your lap, eh? Safer that way. Less likely to get damaged,' he said.

I put the treasure bag on the floor, careful to hold it safely in place between my feet, and took the bust of my mother. It was heavy and cold and I thought I could feel the dampness coming off it, even though I knew that under the hessian it would be wrapped in plastic.

My dad got in the driver's seat and started the engine. Lorry was scratching at his legs.

'Alright, Linda?' My mother didn't say anything, just gave an almost imperceptible nod and stared straight ahead.

The wren's wing had come away neatly enough, a smear of blood on the sinew and bone the only sign that it had been wrenched from the bird's body. It sat in the treasure bag with the other relics, wrapped in one of my mother's silk scarves. The rest of the bird I had thrown into the hedge, a gift for Mrs Akhar's cat. It occurred to me that it might still be alive, and the thought made me smile, the little bird flying helplessly in circles, one wing flapping, getting nowhere.

The treasure bag sat on the floor between my feet, and in my head I counted off the relics: *Robin's egg, magpie's egg, duckling bill and bone. Blackbird's egg, feathers of wren...* I knew that there was only one more to get. One missing relic that would make the incantation perfect.

'Right' my dad said. 'You ready, Jenny Wren?' His eyes met mine in the rear view mirror. My heart was jabbering in my chest.

'Oh yes,' I said, and I was smiling. 'I'm ready for anything,' and just like that we left.

Eighteen.

'Sometimes, you find out something about a person and it completely changes your perception of them.' There was the trace of a smile on Mally's lips. We were in my bedroom and he was holding the wren's wing in his hand, splaying the feathers out across his palm.

Nobody had been up when he and I had got back to the cottage. It was still early enough for the heat to be tolerable but I knew that later in the day, once the crucible of the valley had allowed the still air to stagnate, it would become insufferable.

In the hall it was still and silent, and as I closed the door behind us we stood close together and I could feel the heat from Mally's body. We'd managed to fill the water bottles and lug them back with us. We left them in the hall and I led the way up the stairs, quickly, running, conscious of Mally coming fast behind me. We turned the sharp corner of the staircase and started up the steep steps to my attic room, using the banister to haul ourselves up.

The relics were lined up on the mantelpiece, exactly as I'd left them. They weren't as awe-inspiring a sight as the skulls in Mally's bedroom, but they still made a fine display.

'This is my collection,' I said.

At first, he seemed unimpressed. He put his camera down on the bed and picked up the eggs one by one, first the robin, then the magpie, running his thumb over each one's surface and examining them in turn before returning them to their eggcups. When he came to the duckling a shadow of bemusement passed across his features, before he worked out what it was and a crescent of a smile touched his lips. He dealt with the blackbird's egg in a perfunctory manner, turning it over in his hand and nodding, but when he came to the wren he changed. At first, he held it between finger and thumb, spreading the feathers out across his palm. Then he brought it closer to his face and inspected the end where the feathers were joined. The bone.

'It's a wing', he said, and as I nodded, his sharp, bright white teeth appeared in a broad grin.

'From a wren,' I said, unable to keep the pride from my voice.

'Clever,' he said, and that was it. He approved.

'So, this is your collection, then? Like I have the skulls, this is what you collect?' He was facing the little arched window and the sun was streaming in, lighting up his eyes and causing his pupils to contract to pinpricks. In that light, I saw that his irises weren't brown as I'd thought, but a dark orange.

'They're the relics,' I said. 'That's what I call them.'

'Relics?'

'Yeah, I know. It sounds a bit religious, doesn't it? I don't know why I called them that, it just came to me one day.'

'Something to do with your Catholic upbringing, probably.'

He was still smiling, and his hand came up and I felt the tickle of the feathers against my cheek. He nodded, as if he wanted me to go on.

'It's all part of the Creed,' I said.

'And what's the Creed?'

I moved away from him and sat on the end of the bed.

'It's…it's kind of like a belief system, I suppose. Not a religion or anything like that, because I don't believe in God. It's kind of like a set of rules to live by to make life easier.'

He shifted the camera out of the way and sat down next to me, still holding the wing.

'Tell me about it.'

It felt strange talking about the Creed for the first time, and I was worried that I'd somehow make it less powerful by talking about it. But Mally had given me the crow's skull, the final relic that had allowed me to complete the incantation, and so he was a part of it too. I took a deep breath. I had rehearsed this speech in my head.

'The Creed is based on the relics. Each of these is a bird's egg or bone which is significant because of the circumstances in which it was obtained. The relics were found in a particular order. That's important. When I list them in the order they were found, their names form a rhythm, they have a…a cadence which is pleasing to the ear. This means that they were meant to be found in that order. It's a sign that the Creed is overseeing everything. I suppose you would call it a verse, but I call it the incantation.'

'The incantation?'

'Yeah.'

'Say it to me.'

'That's the thing. I mustn't tell anyone. If I do, it won't be as powerful.'

'But it's to do with the relics, right? Kind of listing them in order?'

'That's right.'

'OK. Got it. Carry on.'

'Well, I tell myself that if I say the incantation out loud before I go to sleep, then in the morning I'll be able to remember the dream.'

'Ah yes. The dream. The one about Petra?'

I nodded. 'I know it's about the night that Petra died. I know there's a phone ringing and there's water and that Petra drowned, but that's all I can remember. I can't remember who phoned, or why.'

'So you don't know for sure what happened the night that Petra died?'

'I know that my mother left her alone in the bath when she went to answer the phone and that when she came back Petra had drowned. That's all. My parents won't talk about it.'

'Can't you ask your dad?'

'I did ask him. Just the once, but he couldn't tell me.' The ashen face, the glassy eyes and the sagging jowls. I remembered my dad that evening when I'd finally summoned up the courage to ask him about Petra. He'd put his head in his hands and wept—great big real tears that ran in streams down his cheeks—and that was when I'd run upstairs and got into bed with Lorry and cuddled up to him and fallen asleep. I hadn't asked him about Petra again.

'OK. So what else is involved in the Creed?' Mally was turning the wing over in his hand, fanning out the feathers against his palm.

'Another part of the Creed is the balance. If a minor bad thing happens, I have to cancel out the negative energy by repeating it. It's about finding balance, equilibrium. So, for example, if Lorry falls over and grazes his knee, I have to make sure he grazes the other one, so that the bad luck is cancelled out.'

Mally looked thoughtful. 'Like the crows? *Two crows I see, good luck to me?* That's what you meant about repeating something?' He sat forward and pulled the photo out of his pocket. The crows stared back at us.

'Exactly. It's all about balancing out bad energy with other bad energy. People say that two wrongs don't make a right, but sometimes they do. It's all about finding the balance, achieving equilibrium. It's best if you can find an opposite action to the original one—for example, grazing the other knee, as that's better balance—but if that's not possible, it's OK to just repeat the action.'

'You seem to have it all worked out.'

'No, no I don't. That's the thing with the Creed: you have to work it out for yourself, and I'm still discovering things.'

'But it works for you?'

'I suppose so. After Petra died, I felt as though I didn't have any control over my life, but I realised that wasn't necessarily a bad thing. Now I don't feel as though I'm in control of my own destiny and that's a weight off my shoulders. As long as I can prove to the Creed that I am a loyal subject, it will look after me.'

'So does that mean you're no longer responsible for your own actions?'

I shrugged, but before I could answer him he picked up my hand and turned it over so it was palm upwards, and he placed the wren's wing onto it. It was barely there, weightless.

'You wanted me to tell you a secret,' he said. 'Another secret.'

'Do you have another secret?' I asked.

'Everyone has secrets. Look at you, and your collection. The relics and the Creed and the incantation. They were all secrets until just now.'

'So, what other secrets do you have to tell me?'

He was quiet for ages, and I thought he'd decided not to say anything. Then he took a deep breath.

'You remember me telling you about the plague cross? About how the plague was brought here by outsiders and about how half the village was wiped out?' I nodded, careful not to speak in case he changed his mind and didn't finish.

'Well, these people—two sisters, they were—came from a village in Derbyshire, a village that got the plague really badly. The rector there decided—decreed, in fact—that no-one should leave the village and risk spreading the plague germs. Just took it upon himself, just like that, to decide that no-one was going to be allowed to escape. He told them it was God's judgement and they would have to face it.' Mally gave a little snort of disgust.

'They were meant to stay there and die, you see, so these two sisters decided to escape, and they did and they ended up here. Only thing is, they didn't know they'd brought the plague with them.'

'How do you know all this?' I asked.

He took the wren's wing from me and very gently splayed the feathers out across his palm. Then he looked up at me.

'Because they were my ancestors.'

I sat still for a moment, until he carried on.

'It's all written down. My gran had some old papers which she passed on to my mum, and that's how she found out about our ancestors. She said she wanted to learn more about them—about her relatives from 300 years ago—wanted to get a feel for them and where they lived. This house was up for sale so she bought it, just like that—didn't even come to see it first—and because we own it, there's nothing they can do about us.'

He was looking down at the wren's wing again.

'So, you see, the reason the villagers hate us so much is because they blame us for what our ancestors did to their ancestors all those years ago.' When he looked up, there was the trace of a smile on his lips.

'Sometimes, you find out something about a person and it completely changes your perception of them.'

After Mally had gone, I spent the rest of the morning sitting on the patch of concrete at the front of the cottage, idly pulling up the withered dandelions that sprouted in the cracks. The relentless sunlight in my eyes got too much, so I turned onto my front and waited for the grasshoppers. I don't know why, but there seemed to be a huge number of them around, and it was easier than I thought to catch them.

All I had to do was sit very still and wait for them to land on the grass in front of me. I knew that once they started their creaking sound they were easier to catch, as if that distracted them somehow. Once I'd spotted one, I would slowly move both hands out, inching forward, little by little. At the last minute, when I was close and the grasshopper was still clicking away, I'd pounce on top of it with both hands. I would feel it hopping, little tickles against my palms and fingers as it tried to batter its way out. I'd let it do that for a few minutes to exhaust it, then, very carefully, I'd wriggle my fingers open and transfer the grasshopper to one hand, holding it tight, making sure there were no holes where it could escape.

Slowly, I'd ease my fingers open and before the grasshopper knew what was happening, I'd use two fingers to pinch it gently around its middle. Sometimes, this was when they escaped, and I learnt to put more pressure on the insect's thorax, the hard bit where the abdomen joined the head. Its antennae would wriggle wildly, and very delicately I would grip one of its legs between my finger and thumb and carefully pull. I would start with its powerful, jointed back legs, the ones it used to propel itself into the air, as they were the largest and would usually come away without difficulty. Then the two little hinged ones in the middle and the pathetic tiny front legs, the ones it used to prop itself up. These were more delicate and required a lighter touch, and could easily break if this part of the process was rushed. Finally, the wings and the antennae would come off and in my hand would be an inch-long twig.

I spent a couple of hours doing that and by the time I went in for lunch, I had a little pile of green and brown sticks on the concrete next to me, some of them still twitching, but most of them still.

When I went to bed that night, the relics were in their assigned positions on the altar. I picked them up in turn and rolled them over in my hand, examining them. By now I knew each one intimately. I knew how the robin's egg would feel chalky when I rubbed it, how the magpie's egg would snuggle neatly into my cupped hand, how the duckling's beak and bone would lie, grotesquely beautiful, on my palm. The mottled spots on the blackbird's egg would be clustered together in places, like my own freckles. And the feathers of the wren's wing would fan out in my fingers, still joined together by the tiny piece of bone and sinew. Finally, I picked up the crow's skull, the gift from Mally, and turned it over in my hand. I didn't know it as intimately as the other relics, and even though I'd examined it several times since I'd found it skewered on the railings, I'd never noticed before the weight of it, the density of the bone and the obsidian hardness of the beak.

I tried reciting the incantation, touching each of the relics as I named them, wondering if that was the missing ingredient that would make the Creed show me the details of how Petra had died. On the face of it, my memory of what happened that night was complete: it made an entire story—it had a beginning, a middle and an end. But still I had that niggle that there was something missing, the thing that appeared in my dreams that I could never recall. I played over in my mind what I could remember, trying to pin down exactly what it was.

I had already given Lorry his bath that night, and was in the bedroom with him, putting him into his pyjamas. My mother always did Petra's bath, and I was struggling to get Lorry to lie still so I could get his nappy on. I could hear my mother, her soft clear voice ringing out across the landing from the bathroom, singing as she played with Petra in the bath. 'Jack and Jill went up the hill, to fetch a pail of water. Jack fell down and broke his crown and Jill came flying after.'

It was the ringing of the telephone that cut her off. The white telephone that sat on a little teak table at the bottom of the stairs. I heard the singing stop, and then the splashing stopped as my mother hushed Petra. She rushed out of the bathroom and I heard the squeal of the creaky floorboard at the top of the stairs. I thought she said something, perhaps to me, as she started down the stairs, but I wasn't sure, and by that time Lorry was crawling to the doorway so I grabbed him

167

and put his pyjamas on. I remember wondering who could be on the phone, whose phone call could be so urgent that my mother would leave Petra in the bath on her own when she went to answer it. At least, perhaps I thought that; maybe it only occurred to me afterwards.

She was only gone for a few minutes.

There's a special time of day, when light is caught in limbo. Dusk: that time when the twilight dips to a level where light and dark start to merge, and everything takes on a silvery, ghost-like sheen, when it's difficult to tell where one thing ends and another begins, and the lines of things are all blurred together.

Standing at the altar, examining the relics, I could see that it was almost a full moon, hanging low, suspended in the pale grey light, a glowing orb. I realised I was still stroking the crow's skull, and put it back on the altar, back in its place at the end of the row. I said the incantation out loud again three times, then I lay in the dark with my eyes open.

Nineteen.

In the weeks after Petra died, I fantasised about drowning. I would lie in the bath and take great big lungfuls of air and let the warm water wash over my head and see how long I could hold my breath for. Just when my chest felt like it would burst, I would hold on for a few seconds longer and then let the air rush in, cold white oxygen filling my lungs. I wondered if it was actually possible to drown yourself, to keep yourself under the water until your lungs did burst, or until you passed out and started breathing in water—or whether human beings had some self-preservation gene that made them sit up out of the water and not drown.

I was thinking about this as I lay on Mally's bed. It was late morning and the sun was streaming in through the window. I'd left Lorry sitting with my dad in his studio. There had been an uneasy truce between my dad and my mother, and they circled each other like hyenas. I'd thought it best to get out of the house.

Mally was sitting on the chair, strumming softly on his guitar with those long fingers.

'Do you believe in ghosts, Nif?'

'What?' The question startled me.

'Ghosts. You know. Dead people. Spirits. Things that go bump in the night and all that.'

I thought again of water. Lying there on Mally's bed I could feel water closing in over my head. It was warm water, not cold, and it was comforting at first, pleasant. As soon as I thought this, the sensation disappeared.

'No,' I said. 'Why do you ask?'

'Your mum's been telling my mum that she talks to your sister. She says she comes to her in the night and stands next to the bed and talks to her.'

'Don't be ridiculous,' I said. 'Ghosts aren't real.' But even as I said it, I thought about Lorry telling me that he'd heard my mother talking to Petra. I thought about my mother, how she had hugged me and told me that Petra had appeared and said to her that it was alright, that it was fine to have left her in the bath on her own. That my mother had been forgiven for drowning her own daughter.

Mally shrugged, and stopped strumming.

'It's what they talk about, when they're sitting downstairs, drinking my mum's concoctions. I think my mum's been trying to help your mum.'

'What do you mean "concoctions"?' I sat up. 'She's trying to drown her sorrows with gooseberry wine?'

Mally started strumming away at the guitar again.

'Yeah, and the rest.' His eyes were focused on his fingers.

'What do you mean?' I asked again. 'The rest of what?'

'It's difficult to say,' he said and looked up at me. 'She makes…' He was searching for the right word. 'Well, she calls them "potions". They're just like the gooseberry wine, really, only they're made from the herbs and flowers and stuff that she grows in the back garden.'

I rolled this idea around in my mind. I could see Janet in her pink stringy bikini, her blonde hair piled up on her head, the blue eyeshadow creasing on her eyelids. She didn't look the hippy sort, the sort that would make medicines out of herbs and stuff.

Mally must have seen the doubt on my face.

'It's something she's always done. Her mother—my gran— did it as well, and she learnt it from her mother. She goes out and collects all these herbs and flowers and stuff and dries them out. You must have seen all that crap hanging up in our kitchen?'

I nodded, remembering the desiccated foliage brushing against the top of my head.

'When we moved here earlier in the year, she was planning to make all these potions and sell them at the market in town, but the chapel lot put the word out that they were wrong, somehow—tainted—and nobody would buy them.'

'So now she's making these "potions" for my mother and they're making her feel better?'

He shrugged again. 'That's only what I heard them saying. Your mother was thanking my mum for the potions and saying how much better she felt for them. Said they made her feel better than the Valium did.'

'Well, if it's stopping her from being a nutjob, I'm all for it,' I said. 'Maybe she can give me something to help me remember the dreams.' I was only half-joking when I said this, but Mally got up and put the guitar down. He came and sat on the bed next to me.

'Do you ever wonder if maybe you're trying too hard? If maybe you're over-thinking it?'

'What do you mean?'

'Well, you're thinking that the relics and the incantation are going to bring back the memory and let you remember the dream, but what if they're stopping you from remembering? What if you're concentrating too hard, and because of that you can't remember?'

It was my turn to shrug. 'Perhaps. So, what do you suggest?'

He got to his feet and stood squarely in front of me. 'I think you need to get rid of the relics. I think you should put them somewhere safe where you can't dwell on them. Then, when your conscious mind is freed up to think about other things, your unconscious mind will let you remember the dream.' He looked pleased with himself.

'OK, Freud.' I was smiling now. 'Where do you suggest we put the relics?'

He started moving towards the pine cupboard, then looked back at me over his shoulder. 'Give me a minute,' he said. 'Go and get them. I've got a plan.'

When he turned back to the cupboard and started unlocking it, I stood looking at him for a moment. The shaft of light fell directly onto the bare top of his arm, where the skin gleamed, pale and untainted by the sun.

The relics were in their places on the altar. I wrapped each of them carefully: the eggs in the cotton wool and then the egg box; the duckling bill and bone in its handkerchief; the feathers of wren in their silk scarf. I didn't have anything to wrap the crow's skull in, so I pulled one of my t-shirts out of the dirty washing pile and gave it a sniff. It was the usual, musky smell that I'd had since we'd arrived in the village. I wrapped it around the skull and put all the relics in the treasure bag.

I bounded down the stairs, curious to find out what Mally's plan was, but the sound of voices in the kitchen made me stop in the hall. Through the crack in the kitchen door I could see Janet and my mother, sitting at the pine table. As usual, they were leaning close together, whispering, hands clasped together on the tabletop. Lorry was with them, sitting on the floor, twisting the legs of his clown doll over and over each other.

As I listened, Janet's voice rose in intensity, and she was muttering something I couldn't fully make out in a language I didn't understand, like when the priest used to chant the Mass in Latin. It was familiar but foreign at the same time. Lorry was muttering too, making noises that could have been words or maybe weren't, and the two voices caught in the still air and mingled, together but separate, like oil on water.

I watched as Janet put her hand up to my mother's face, and my mother closed her eyes, a small smile forming on her lips. She looked beatific. She pressed her cheek against Janet's fingers, as though she was leaning into an embrace, and that's when Janet moved her hand down and, very gently, took hold of my mother's chin.

With her other hand, she picked up a delicate porcelain cup that I hadn't seen before, and lifted it to my mother's lips. My mother opened her mouth, greedily, her head thrown back, the tendons in her neck sticking out. Janet placed the cup on my mother's bottom lip and tipped it gently, and my mother made a gulping sound as some of the clear liquid escaped and cascaded down her chin. She opened her eyes and looked at Janet, and even from where I was standing out in the hall I could see that there was a light in her eyes that I hadn't seen for months. Her face was aflame with a joy that hadn't been there since we had last been to church and I'd watched her take Communion.

Mally was waiting for me by the chapel. The windows watched us, sombre in the sunlight.

'What kept you?'

'Nothing,' I said. 'I just needed to pack up the relics properly.' I lifted the treasure bag to show him. He, in turn, lifted a Tesco bag with a trowel poking through the side. There were some other things in there as well, nestled at the bottom, but I couldn't make out what they were.

'Come on then. We're going up into the field. Behind the chapel.'

'Why've you got a trowel?' I asked. 'You're not thinking of doing any digging in this heat, are you?'

He didn't answer me, and set off towards the hole in the hedge.

He dragged himself through and I followed, and we both brushed off the dust that clung to our arms and legs. Then we started walking up the slope.

It was almost midday by then, and the sun felt like it was burning a hole in my scalp. Sweat was prickling in my hair, and when I ran my hand through it I knew it would be left sticking up in spikes. Mally walked on ahead, just like that day when I'd first met him. That felt like a lifetime ago. It suddenly occurred to me that all the time we'd been in the village, I'd watched no TV, heard no radio. I hadn't even seen a newspaper.

Mally reached the top before I did and threw himself down onto the crunchy grass. I'd counted to 274 by the time I dragged myself up next to him, and we sat for a moment, getting our breath back, looking silently across at the sheer patchwork that formed the opposite side of the valley and down at the meagre stream that meandered along its base.

'It's a special place, this.' It was as though Mally could read my thoughts. 'It's this tiny village in the middle of nowhere. You could live here and not have anything to do with the rest of the world, if you wanted.'

'Apart from Tesco,' I said, and gave Mally's plastic bag a nudge with my foot. He picked it up and pulled out a packet of crisps which he tore open and held out to me. I took one. Salt and vinegar.

'Yeah, but you know what I mean.' He put some crisps into his mouth and didn't say anything for a bit while he crunched on them. 'It's like it's on the edge of the world. Did you know that a couple of hundred years ago the border between England and Wales was somewhere around here? It kept changing hands, depending on who won the most recent battle, the Welsh or the English. For centuries, this place didn't really know where it was, which country it was in.'

'A place on the edge,' I agreed. 'A threshold. It's like it's caught in the middle, like it's sitting between all the things we know about and all the things we don't.' And it was true. It was like the space between night and day, that time in the early morning or late at night when you don't really know which it is. A liminal place. I reached for the crisps and shovelled some into my mouth. The salt stung my lips where they were cracked from the sun, and instead of wiping it away, I let myself enjoy the tingling sensation.

Mally nodded, slowly. I swallowed and carried on.

'Or like that space between being asleep and being awake. When you're dreaming but you know you're also waking up and then when you wake up you can't remember the dream. This village is caught in the middle of real life and something else, a bit like that.'

'Ah. The dreams,' he said. 'That's why we're here, isn't it?' Without waiting for an answer, he sprang to his feet. He grabbed the crisp packet from me and upended the last of the crumbs into his mouth and then he jammed it into the back pocket of his jeans. He walked directly over to the log that lay about twenty feet from where we'd been sitting. It was where we'd seen the two crows the day before. He crouched down on his haunches and took the trowel from the Tesco bag. He put the bag down and it lay on the ground next to him, not even a breeze to make it twitch. Angling the trowel at the ground, he started making small stabbing motions, attempting to break up the hard surface.

'You'll be lucky,' I said, crouching down next to him 'The ground up here's going to be baked solid. It'll be like cutting into a brick.'

He didn't say anything, didn't even look up at me, just carried on jabbing away, and as I watched, little clods of earth sprang up. The dirt wasn't as dry as I'd been expecting, and looked darker, and moister. As he dug, the trowel turned up bigger and bigger lumps of soil, the earth getting richer and more loamy the deeper he dug. His hand movements started to get slower, gentler. Finally he put the trowel down and looked up at me, triumphant.

'And this, my dear, is one I prepared earlier.'

He reached into the hole he'd just dug and pulled out something that fitted neatly into his hand. It was brown and encased in soil. He cradled the object in his palm and, very gently, smoothed his thumb against the surface, smearing away the mud. Then he held it out to me. Here and there were tiny patches of creamy-beige against the brown, but mostly it was just earth.

Then I saw the beak.

As soon as I saw it I could also make out the smooth arc of the cranium, swelling back from the huge nostrils, and the eye sockets, clagged with mud.

'Of course, these conditions aren't perfect for the decomposition process,' he said, and I thought I could hear a swell of pride in his voice. He was back in teacher mode. 'Usually, flesh decomposes best under conditions of warmth and humidity.' He rolled the skull into my palm, where it sat, blank-eyed and impassive. 'The bacteria function better that way. But sometimes, one just doesn't have the choice.' He looked up at me briefly and smirked.

I thought about how I'd buried the duckling, not really planning to dig it up again, and then how I'd gone back to it and all the flesh had disappeared, leaving only the bill and bones. I snuck a look at the treasure bag on the ground next to me.

Mally reached into the Tesco bag and pulled out a toothbrush. He picked the skull out of my palm and set to work on it, using the fibres of the brush very gently to ease the soil away from the skull. Then he took out a little round-headed brush, the sort that my dad used to clean out his home-brew bottles, and inserted it into the skull, into the cavity where the brain would have been, and carefully eased it around the inside to remove all the soil. He produced pipe cleaners next, and angled them carefully into the rest of the skull's crevices—the eye sockets and the nostrils.

When he finished, he held the skull up to me. It shone dully in the sunlight, a muddied yellow colour.

'Is that the only one,' I asked. 'Or are there others?'

'What do you think?' When he looked at me, his pupils had shrunk to tiny dots, the irises flaming their peculiar orange-brown. He gestured with his hand, a lazy wave that took in the entirety of the field, from the top of the bank all the way down to the chapel and the well at the bottom of the hill. 'There are dozens. Perhaps a hundred or so. All dotted about.'

I looked around the field, thinking that perhaps the divots I could make out were in fact burial sites.

'We'll take this one and wash it in the water from the well,' he said, and I jumped to my feet and started walking, keen to examine the well again, already anticipating the cold water I'd throw on my face and my shoulders.

'But not just yet.' His voice was a reprimand, and I turned around and shielded my eyes with my hand. 'You can't just take something without giving something back,' he said, and gestured to the treasure bag I was swinging by my side.

'You want one of the relics?' I said, torn between my desire to please him and a protectiveness over my hoard. 'You want to bury one of the relics?' He was walking towards me down the slope.

'Not just one of them.' He stopped in front of me. 'All of them. That's the only way you're going to remember your dream: if we swap them for the skull—it's a raven, by the way—and bury them. You want to remember who phoned the night that Petra drowned, right? This way you'll stop obsessing about the relics and free your mind up to remember the dream.'

I thought about it. The relics were valuable, potentially powerful. They were the cornerstones of the Creed. But if Mally was right, and that by hiding them away and forgetting about them for a little while, I might stand a chance of remembering the dream, then it might be worth a try.

'Look,' he said. 'We'll bury them in the raven's hole. That way we'll remember where they are and we can come and dig them up at any time.' He looked thoughtful. 'It also means we won't have to dig another hole in this.' He stamped on the hard ground with his heel and smiled at me. 'Two birds, one stone, eh?'

After the burial, we hauled up water from the well using the blue bucket. We drank deeply from it, using our hands to cup the water to our faces—again, the distinctive taste of ancient landscapes and loam, like decaying leaf-matter. We washed the raven's skull until it was free of earth. It was still dirty though, little cracks running in a brown web across the dome of the cranium. From the Tesco bag, Mally pulled out a glass jar with a clear, viscous liquid inside. He carefully unscrewed the lid and dropped the skull in, before screwing the lid back on and swilling the contents around so the skull was fully immersed.

'Neat bleach,' he said. 'Gets rid of the last few bits of dirt. A couple of days and it'll be good as new.'

He dropped the jar into the plastic bag and handed it over to me.

'You have that,' he said. 'A swap for the relics.'

I took the jar and nestled it carefully into the bottom of the treasure bag, along with the empty egg box and the handkerchief and the silk scarf. Then I had a thought and took the jar out again, wrapped it in my old smelly t-shirt—the one I'd wrapped the crow's skull in—and put them both at the bottom of the treasure bag. Snug.

*

When I got back to the cottage Janet had gone. There was no-one in the kitchen. I went out to the back hall and saw that my dad's studio door was open.

Lorry was with him, sitting on a stool and watching him work, the clown doll sitting on his lap. My dad was silent, working intently on the bust in front of him. He didn't see me straight away, and I watched quietly as his hands moved over the form in front of him, smoothing, caressing, gently pinching.

He'd once explained to me, as I sat watching him working on my mother's sculpture one winter afternoon, that there were two main techniques involved in sculpting. The first was additive, where materials such as clay were added to the model and used to build up a resemblance of the subject, bit by bit, layer upon layer, adding to the detail. The second was called subtractive, where the clay was carved away to create the intricate details. My dad used both methods in a long process of building up and removing, adding and subtracting, that resulted in a striking facsimile of his subject.

Lorry saw me first. He clambered down from the stool and came over to me, his thumb jammed into his mouth. He looked tired. I picked him up and rested him on my hip. My dad was engrossed in what he was doing. He jumped when he saw me, and grabbed the hessian sheet that he used to wrap the sculpture. He draped it over the bust, making sure the edges were smoothed down around the wheel. Then he took off his glasses and looked at me.

'Hi Nif. How are you?'

'OK.'

His eyes flashed to the potter's wheel in front of him. 'I think it's nearly ready.'

'Good.'

'I think I'm going to carve the eyes soon.'

I was glad about that. I liked watching him carve out the eyes, watching the hooked wire work its way into the head and drag out a tiny nugget of clay. I liked how this one tiny act gave expression to the bust, made it seem real somehow. Brought it to life.

Lorry started whimpering, and I shifted him on my hip, but he held his arms out for my dad. I realised I'd been neglecting my brother over the last week or so. My dad yawned.

'I suppose those eyes will have to wait,' he said, and took my brother off me. My brother started crying, his fingers twisting into my dad's hair. 'OK. I know you're hungry. Let's get you fed, shall we?' My dad started towards the door, but then turned back. 'Have you seen your mother, Nif?'

'She was with Janet earlier, in the kitchen, but she'd gone when I got back just now.'

'Ah, yes, that reminds me.' He pushed his glasses up his nose and shuffled to readjust Lorry on his hip. He sounded hesitant, almost embarrassed. 'Janet's coming round tomorrow. She's going to dowse for water in the garden. Your mother's got a bee in her bonnet—reckons Janet has a knack for knowing where the springs are underground, and she thinks she might be able to find us one so we don't have to go to the well all the time. If it works it should make your job a bit easier, eh, love?'

I nodded, but I thought about all the time I'd spent at the well with Mally. The well and the field had taken on a special significance for the Creed, now that the relics were there.

'C'mon then, little feller,' my dad said. 'Let's go and find Mummy and have a snack. Come on, Nif.' He gave one last look at the bust.

I followed him out, but then I remembered that he hadn't sprayed the bust with water, to prevent it drying out. I doubled back into the studio. I picked up the water bottle and gave it a shake. It was full. There was a nozzle attached to it, so that it could spray a fine mist of water over the bust, and I tested it against my face. The water was lukewarm, but it still felt pleasant in the mugginess of the studio. I sat on my dad's stool, the one in front of the potter's wheel, and carefully lifted the hessian away from the sculpture.

It had changed since I last saw it. The hairline was lower and the forehead unlined and crease-free. The nose was shorter and tilted at the end. The cheeks had become plumper, and there was a hint of fullness under the chin. Now, it resembled Janet.

Twenty.

'Witches' knickers.'

'What?'

'Witches' knickers.' Mally pointed at a carrier bag that was hanging, snagged in the hedge. 'That's what some people call them. Witches' knickers.'

We were walking along the lane: me, Mally and Lorry. It was quite early in the morning, but already the sun was jabbing at us. I hadn't washed for a few days and the animal smell on me was ripe and raw, so I decided to take Lorry to the stream as soon as I got up. He'd still been eating his breakfast, a piece of bread smeared with jam, but I didn't want to hang around so I made him bring it with him.

Mally came out of his house just as we walked past and bounded into the lane next to us. He had a buzz about him, an energy that meant he was constantly twitching, or fiddling with his camera, and I suspected he'd been keeping a look out for us from his bedroom window. I hadn't said anything.

'So, did it work then? Did you remember the dream? Did you remember who was on the phone?' Mally was walking backwards, a couple of feet in front of me. He had his denim jacket on, but no shirt, and the Orion's Belt of moles across his belly winked at me as he moved.

'Nope. Nothing,' I said, and pulled Lorry away from the carrier bag.

I'd woken late that morning to the sound of someone tapping on my brain. At first, I couldn't work out if the sensation was sound, and I was hearing something loud and persistent, or if there really was someone standing next to me in my bedroom, their knuckles banging off my head. In the end, I'd dragged myself out of sleep and worked out that it was a noise—a loud, rhythmic, metallic noise.

The clanging continued as I pulled on my clothes and went downstairs. The front door was open and I could see my dad standing on the patch of concrete. He was holding a massive hammer, an enormous lump of metal on a wooden handle that must have been about four feet long. He'd stuck a crowbar into a crack in the concrete and was bringing the hammer down on top of it, each strike causing a loud and impertinent clang. There was sweat dripping off him, coursing down his bare back, but he didn't seem to be bothered by it. He just kept on swinging the hammer, hauling it up over his head and letting its own weight send it falling back down onto the crowbar. I remembered that he'd planned to dig up the concrete, that it was one of the jobs he'd decided to do to repay his colleague for letting us stay in the cottage.

'Maybe tonight then,' Mally said, and he spun round so he was walking next to Lorry and grabbed hold of his hand. I knew that the dream came in those few moments before I woke up, and the fact that I'd been woken before I was ready, artificially, meant that I hadn't had the dream. My dad's fault.

The plague cross had just loomed into sight when we saw the magpies sitting on the barbed-wire fence, heads hunkered down into their shoulders. There was a whole flock of them, seven in total, and they watched us, glass-eyed and judgmental. Mally slowed down as well when he saw them, and then we stopped—the three of us stood in a row across the width of the lane. The magpies were about twenty feet away.

Even before Mally's hand went to the inside pocket of his denim jacket, even before he pulled it out and showed me what it held, I knew what it would be.

'Lesson three, Nif?' He was smirking now. 'Think you're ready?'

I nodded. I knew I was ready. He handed me the wire.

It was wound up on itself, and as I loosened the end from where it was wrapped around the coil, I felt the spring of the energy within it, as though it had a life of its own and was trying to free itself. I flexed it in both hands, feeling the slight resistance of the metal as I pulled it through the loop at the end. It wasn't anything special, not a hangman's noose or anything like that, just a straightforward running knot with the tail stuck through. I uncoiled it, and saw that it was much longer than I'd been expecting, a good twelve feet or so.

'You've got to stand back from them, from the bait. If you're too close they won't come.' Mally had read my mind.

He lifted the camera strap over his head and hooked it around Lorry's neck. Lorry beamed. Then Mally took the wire from my hands and laid it out on the lane. It glinted, a metal snake on the dust. He grabbed the last bit of bread from Lorry's hand, and I thought Lorry might protest, but he was too intent on examining the camera.

Very slowly, crouching down, Mally walked towards the magpies, who lifted their heads up slightly, tilting them on their necks, but other than that they showed no signs of being bothered. When he was about ten feet away from them, he pushed the noose-end of the wire onto the lane in front of him, between him and the magpies. Then he bit off a piece of the bread and tossed it, without aiming, at the loop. It landed right in the centre. He turned to me and grinned.

Lorry started clapping, and I grabbed his hands and held them still and shushed him. The magpies still hadn't moved. Mally backed away from the birds and when he was down on his haunches next to the end of the wire he picked it up. Then he lay on his stomach in the dust and waited.

I had counted to 124 by the time anything happened. It was the middle magpie that moved first. Its head moved infinitesimally on its shoulders and it focused one eye down onto the ground, onto the bread. After a few seconds, it fluffed up its wings, a flutter of black and white, like it was getting ready for something. Then it stood up and hopped down onto the ground, landing a few feet away from the bread.

Although he hardly moved, I could tell that Mally was tensing, waiting for the magpie to put its head into the wire loop. It hopped forward, speculatively. Then it hopped back again, never taking its eyes off the piece of bread. It seemed to be considering its options. Then it hopped forward again and this time put out its beak to take the bait.

Very slowly, Mally tilted the wire ring so that it was at right angles to the ground. The magpie stopped and twisted its head again. It looked down at the trap with one eye, then reached its head forward through the loop, its beak already open to take the bread. Like lightning, Mally yanked the end of the wire.

The bird's wings flapped and flailed as the loop caught tight around its neck. A cloud of dust lifted around it, and it tried jumping backwards, away from the noose, but that only made the grip tighter. After a few seconds, it seemed to realise this, and it stopped moving and collapsed to the ground, its wings limp in the dust. The other magpies had already flown off in a clatter of black and white.

Mally pushed himself up onto his feet, brushing the dust off his jeans with one hand, but holding tight onto the end of the wire with the other. He held it out to me.

'Do you want to do the honours?' he asked. I couldn't tell if the light in his eyes was a reflection of the sun or something else.

I felt the now-familiar thrill in the pit of my stomach. It was the same feeling I'd had whenever I discovered a new relic, except each time it had got better, more intense—and now it felt like an electric current was passing through my body. The metal in my hand was warm, almost hot, when I took the wire from Mally, and I gripped it tightly.

The magpie was completely still by now, but its tongue was sticking out, pointed, pink and sharp. It was panting, little ragged breaths in and out. Mally had told me that the best way to kill a bird is to quickly yank on the end of the wire, cutting through the neck and severing the head. It would be over in an instant.

Instead, I pulled on the wire and dragged the magpie towards me, its body and tail feathers making a trail in the dust of the lane. When it was lying at my feet, I lifted it off the ground, and it hung there, swinging slightly in the stagnant air. Its head hung limply down, and its wings were slumped, and I thought for a moment it must have died. But then its eyes flickered and I knew it was still alive.

I found the words forming on my lips without me trying, and when I started singing my voice was soft, falling like silk over the dusty stillness of the lane.

'One for sorrow, two for joy. Three for a girl and four for a boy.'

I started swinging the magpie backwards and forwards, very gently at first, then quicker and quicker, like a pendulum. Even though I wasn't looking at him, I knew Mally was staring at me. I could feel the heat of his gaze, and I swung the magpie faster and faster.

'Five for silver, six for gold.' I found myself drawing my arm up and round, behind my head, like I'd seen my dad doing earlier that morning with the hammer. I thought of Little Red Riding Hood's father, the woodcutter, bringing the axe down onto the neck of the wolf.

'Seven for a secret…' There was a thumping sound in my ears and the sudden thought came to me that it was my heart pounding. I was about to swing the magpie down onto the ground, and I could already anticipate the pile of black and white feathers limp in the dust, when Lorry screamed.

I spun round and there he was behind me, his hands clamped over his eyes. He kept on screaming and then he started shaking his head, never once taking his hands away from his face.

I dropped the end of the wire and was barely aware of the magpie falling to the ground.

'Lorry! It's OK. Don't worry.' I put my arms round him and pulled him into me, breathing in his familiar biscuit smell.

'Nif hurt bird,' he panted, and took his hands away from his eyes. He looked at me in terror, but then his features shifted slightly and I saw suspicion and accusation.

I didn't know what to say. I picked him up and cuddled him, and that was when I saw Mally running back down the lane, back the way we'd come. I thought he'd lost his bottle and had decided to go home, but then I saw him stop and reach into the hedge. He pulled out the carrier bag and shook it. Then he ran back to us, and when he got close I could see that his eyes were still gleaming. He picked up the bird with one hand and let it fall into the carrier bag. He coiled up the wire that was still attached to the magpie's neck and placed it carefully into the bag as well. Then he grabbed the bag by the handles, for all the world like he was on his way back from the supermarket, and swung the bag towards me and Lorry.

'C'mon,' he said. 'Let's take it with us.'

The magpie lay on the grass in front of me, not moving. Only the odd tremor of the feathers on its ribcage gave away the fact that it was still breathing, and occasionally one of its eyes would spring open and then slowly close again.

Lorry had calmed down and was paddling in the shallow water next to the bank. He seemed to have forgotten all about the bird, and was splashing and laughing softly to himself. Mally lay next to me. He'd taken his denim jacket off and was lying on his back, soaking up the heat of the sun. His skin was so pale it was almost luminous, unscathed by the sun's vicious rays which had rendered my arms red and sore. He'd taken a couple of Polaroids of the magpie; they lay on top of the carrier bag in front of us. They were fuzzy and out of focus and didn't do justice to what we'd just achieved.

I could feel the prickle of the sun's needles on my back and wondered briefly if I should go into the stream with Lorry. The heat made it difficult to move so instead I concentrated on the feeling of the hard ground under me, the warmth pulsating from it through my t-shirt and into my belly. I felt Mally's hand reach out and grab mine across the scratchy grass. It was cool and dry.

We were waiting for the magpie to die. We'd decided not to upset Lorry any more by killing it ourselves, but instead to wait until it died and then bury it whole. It was an experiment. Mally wanted to see what would happen to the rest of the bones when they were buried. I just wanted to see how long it would take for death to come.

A raised voice made me look up. I could just about make out the lumpen forms of Tracy Powell and Fat Denise standing on the bridge. Their backs were to us, their fat arses propped against the stone wall. The bright colours of their t-shirts shimmered and looked as though they might disappear at any minute. I looked over at Mally. He still had his eyes closed.

Tracy and Denise hadn't seen us, and from their arm movements I guessed they were sharing a cigarette, passing it backwards and forwards between themselves. In front of me, the magpie twitched, one leg shooting out behind it, tipping it over onto its side. The wire was still around its neck. Mally had said that it was best to leave it there for now, until it died, and then take it off later. I didn't think we had much longer to wait.

'I'm going for a piss.' Mally was awake, and he hauled himself to his feet and slung his camera around his neck. I rolled onto my side and watched him saunter off towards the far end of the field and disappear behind the hedge.

Above my head, a dragonfly appeared and it dangled in the air, bobbing lazily. I wondered if I might be able to catch it and detach each of those glorious bottle-blue wings, one by one, and then its legs, but I decided it was too much effort and lay back down again. I put my head on my arms and after a couple of minutes, started to feel the tug of sleep.

'You're a fuckin' sicko, you are.' There was a foot on my back, planted between my shoulder blades, pushing me down and pinning me to the ground. Then I felt a hand on the back of my head, forcing my face into the sharp grass, and a pain in my temple where it was being pushed against the hard ground. Tracy Powell.

I could just about twist my head round far enough to see a shabby pair of sandals and red-chipped, ragged toenails. A pair of podgy hands appeared, the nails bitten down to the quick, and I guessed that was Fat Denise. I felt the pressure on the back of my head ease as Tracy let go of my hair, and the tendons in my neck strained as I tried to move my head. She stood up, but kept her foot on my back. I was trapped.

'What the fuck have you and that saddo been doin'?' Tracy's voice was shrill with incredulity, and I guessed she was talking about the magpie. 'That's fuckin' cruel, that is.'

I twisted my head round and could see that Fat Denise had picked the bird up and was cradling it. She tucked it under her armpit and used the other hand to ease the wire from the magpie's neck, surprisingly gently, and throw it onto the ground. The wire jerked slightly as it unwound, then it lay still, glittering in the grass.

The magpie wasn't moving, but after a moment it started panting again, harder and faster. It looked as though someone had breathed new life into it. There was light in its eyes again.

191

'What's wrong with you? Who'd do that sort of thing to a bird?' Tracy sounded properly upset. 'That's what hangin' round with Mally White does for you.' She grabbed my hair again and pushed my face back into the ground.

'Fuck off Tracy,' I managed to say, my mouth full of grass.

'He's a fuckin' nutter. Him and his mam should never have moved here. Nothin' but trouble since the day they arrived.' Fat Denise snorted her assent.

Tracy grabbed my hair again and yanked my head back. I tried to push myself up off the ground, but she put more weight onto the foot that she'd planted on my back and I was forced back down again. I used all the strength in my body to try to push myself up from the ground, but it still wasn't enough. I was trapped under the weight of Tracy Powell's bulk.

'Nif? What's happening?' Lorry's voice was small and plaintive and worried. I couldn't see him, but could tell he was standing next to me, about three feet away.

'Don't worry, Lorry,' I managed to get out, even though my face was being pushed into the ground. 'It's only a game. A game the big kids play.'

'I don't like it,' he said, and he started snivelling.

I managed to turn my head just enough to see that Fat Denise had got hold of him in one hand, her pudgy fingers making a bracelet around his wrist. He was twisting and turning, pulling away from her and trying to get free. She still had the magpie under her armpit, nudged up against her fat tits. Sick filled my mouth and I swallowed it back down.

Tracy leant down and pushed her face into mine. I could smell her breath, pungent with stale cigarettes.

'This your little brother?'

'Leave him alone,' I said. 'This is between you and me. Leave him out of it.'

She was quiet for a moment, as if gathering her thoughts, and when she spoke her voice wasn't shrill anymore, but quiet and considered.

'You know that night in the pub? When you all came in and tried to listen in on old Lyndon Vaughan's meeting?' She didn't wait for me to answer, but went on talking, her foul breath filling my nostrils. 'They carried on with their meeting after you left. They were saying stuff about you and your family, about how outsiders shouldn't just be allowed to arrive in the village like you did. They said that your mother's a nutter and your father's a lazy, good-for-nothing waster.' She leant even closer and the acrid stench was overpowering.

'But mostly they were saying that your brother's a mong and he should have been drowned at birth.'

I mustered all the strength I had into pushing myself up off the ground. I was going to punch her in that stupid, fat, doughy face until there was nothing left of it.

Abruptly, and before I could do anything, the pressure on the back of my head eased and Tracy was sprawled on the ground next to me. I looked up and Mally was there, panting. He had the look of the devil in his eyes. He drew back his foot, as if getting ready to take a penalty kick, and I realised he was going for Tracy. She'd guessed the same thing, and she curled herself up into a ball, foetal, her hands shielding her face. Lorry screamed.

The noise seemed to make Mally check himself. He took in a deep breath and relaxed his leg, planting his foot back on the ground. Denise let go of Lorry, who stood there, crying and rubbing at his wrist. Tracy struggled to push her bulk up off the ground, and at the same time pull down her skirt that had rucked up around her meaty thighs. Mally was by now bent over, panting. He was out of breath and clutching at his side, like he had a stitch.

Lorry ran towards me and I sat up and pulled him down onto my lap. He was snivelling, great gobbets of snot hanging from his nose. I grabbed a handful of grass and used it to wipe his face, the dried strands sticking to his nostrils. Then I chucked the grass away and pulled him into my chest and hugged him.

Tracy and Denise were about twenty feet away, heading back in the direction of the bridge. Denise was still holding the magpie, and it looked as though it was struggling to get free. It had survived. Then Tracy turned back and fired her parting shot.

'You know what? I think Lyndon Vaughan's lot are right. You're fuckin' evil you are. Evil. Doin' that to a poor bird. You and your mother and your girlfriend here. Fuckin' evil the lot of you.'

Mally stood up and watched Tracy and Denise clamber over the gate. He was still panting. Eventually, he managed to find enough breath to speak.

'I can't believe they took the magpie!' He was indignant. 'After all that.'

'Never mind the magpie. They hurt Lorry.' I held out my brother's wrist so that Mally could see the red marks, but he didn't even look. He bent down and picked up the wire from where it lay, only the glint of the metal making it visible in the scratchy grass. Still breathing heavily, he coiled it up, the wire resisting slightly, the tension in it causing it to fight back until he'd got it all wound up and the end tucked in.

'Here, you have this. I think you've earned it,' he said, and he passed it to me.

Twenty-one.

The altar was bare, except for the wire and the raven's skull in its glass jar. I held the jar up to the light. The bleach had a very faint yellowish tinge, but the skull itself had become paler, cleaner. Purer. The hairline cracks in the top had faded, and were barely visible now, and I knew in a couple of days I'd be able to take the skull out of the bleach and give it a final wash. I turned the jar round and round in my hand, watching the viscous liquid cling to the bone and slide over the tilt of the beak.

I still couldn't get rid of the smell of Tracy's breath. I hated how I'd felt so powerless, pinned to the ground, and how I hadn't been able to help Lorry. The red marks had gone from his wrists, but he looked worried all the time, and was nervous and twitchy, as though they might come back for him. I needed to get back at Tracy Powell for what she'd done. The blooming bruise from where she'd pushed my head into the ground was tender under my fingertips.

I put the jar back on the altar and looked out of the window, wondering if Mally's curtains would be open. They weren't.

When I went downstairs I was surprised to see that the front door was open, and the door to the kitchen had been propped wide. A wall of heat stopped me as I walked in. My mother was sitting at the pine table, with Lorry next to her. She'd washed her hair and it hung in a heavy, burnished curtain around her shoulders. She had on a dress, an orange-flowered one I hadn't seen her wear for months, and I thought she was even wearing lipstick. She was eating a boiled egg carefully, dipping the spoon into the shell and hooking out the white, and then a smear of the yolk, and putting it into her mouth with precision. Then she looked up at me and licked her lips and smiled, and I noticed again how her posture had changed: she seemed lighter, as if her grief had shifted slightly. She was sitting up straighter in her chair, as if the weight of Petra's death had literally been lifted from her shoulders.

'Hello, love,' she said. 'Fancy some breakfast? We've got boiled eggs and I even made some fresh bread.'

My dad caught my eye and I thought he made a tiny shrugging motion. He looked both confused and pleased. 'Your mother was up at the crack of dawn, kneading away. She even got me to light that bloody great big hunk of metal so she could bake it properly.' He nodded at the range cooker, which was still radiating waves of heat. The sweat was starting to prickle on my back.

I watched as my mother put down her own spoon and picked up Lorry's. He looked up at her and opened his mouth obediently, pushing his head back on his neck and sticking his tongue out. My mother scooped up some egg and put it in his mouth. He clamped his lips shut around it and started chewing. When he'd swallowed, he immediately opened his mouth again and held his face up for more. A baby bird waiting to be fed. My mother obliged, and all the time the same self-satisfied smile rested on her lips.

I grabbed an orange from the fruit bowl, peeled it, and chucked the peel in the bin. Then I sat down at the table opposite my mother and sunk my teeth into the orange and enjoyed feeling the juice drip down my chin. I watched in silence for a few minutes, chewing on the flesh of the fruit, as my mother carried on feeding herself and Lorry alternately. Then she turned to me and opened her mouth to say something, but abruptly she stopped, her mouth open. She was frowning.

'What happened there?' she asked, her hand moving up to her forehead. My hand mirrored hers and I touched my temple gently, feeling the faint spring of the budding bruise. I shrugged and chucked the orange peel into the bin. I reached for an apple.

'Must have been yesterday. I ran into a branch.' I looked at Lorry to see if he was going to contradict me, but he just sat there, waiting for his next spoonful of egg. My dad put down the plate he was wiping and peered at my forehead, frowning.

'It doesn't look too bad,' he said, and he held up two fingers in front of my face. 'How many fingers?' he asked.

'Just the two,' I said.

'I think she's OK, Linda. She'll survive.' He was smiling.

My mother didn't say anything for a moment, just carried on feeding Lorry. Then she cleared her throat.

'Janet's coming round in a bit,' she said, and her voice had a new softness to it.

I bit into the apple, and the flesh was mushy and too sweet in my mouth. It was bruised, a great brown arch of decay spreading through it. I spat it into my hand and chucked it in the bin.

'She's going to dowse for water.'

In the fruit bowl, there was only one apple left: it too was brown and decomposing. The rot had spread from one fruit to the other.

'What are you doing today, Nif?' My mother had lost her frown and was obviously trying to be pleasant. She had her eyebrows raised and there was a little tight smile on her lips. She looked stupid.

'Don't know,' I said. 'I'll probably just hang around here. There's not much to do, is there?' I remembered what Mally had said about teaching himself from books and the TV. 'We should have brought the telly with us.'

'There's no aerial,' my dad pointed out. 'So even if we'd brought it we wouldn't be able to get any signal. You can't even get any radio signal down here in the valley, and there's nowhere in this village to buy a newspaper. There could be anything going on in the big, wide world and we'd be none the wiser.' He turned back to the sink.

'You could stay here and watch Janet,' my mother said, ignoring my dad and talking directly to me. 'I think she has quite a skill for things like that.' She dug another gobbet of egg out for Lorry. 'She has a way about her.'

My dad's back straightened slightly, but he didn't say anything and he didn't turn around. He carried on washing up.

We were all quiet for a while, just the barely audible scrape of the teaspoon against the inside of the eggshell and the slosh of water in the sink to break the silence. My dad cleared his throat. Then he seemed to think that he'd better say something.

'So, Nif. School in a couple of weeks. Bet you can't wait, eh?'

My mother spooned some more egg into Lorry's mouth, but all the time her eyes were on me.

Just the thought of going back to school made me feel sick.

'I'm not going back.' I said it very quietly.

'Now, come on, love. Let's just talk about this.' My dad was drying his hands on a tea towel, and I forced myself to focus on the cloth in his hands, how the edges were ragged and the fabric had faded to the colour of porridge.

'I've decided I'm going to get a job,' I said, conscious of the waver in my voice. My mother snorted. My dad carried on rubbing the grey cloth over and over his hands.

'What sort of job?' he asked, and his voice was gentle enough, but there was a small hint of annoyance. 'You don't have any qualifications. You don't have any O-Levels—not through any fault of your own—but it's the truth. And there are already more than one-and-a-half million unemployed people in this country, despite Jim Callaghan's best efforts, so you really need to consider your options.'

'I don't know. I'll work in a shop or something. Or I'll go to night classes and get O-Levels, but I'm not going back to school.'

'I really think—'

My voice came out louder than I'd intended: 'I'm not going back to school. I'm sick of it and I'm not going back, no matter what you and Mr McPherson and all the rest of the fucking teachers have to say.'

Even Lorry looked shocked, and his mouth hung open, the pale yellow egg clagged around his teeth. My mother's pallid face was turning crimson from the blush that was edging its way up her cheeks. But it was my dad's reaction that was strangest. He just looked at me, his mouth turned down at the edges, for all the world like Lorry's clown doll. His eyes filled up with tears and he tried to blink them away. Then he turned away from me and pretended to wipe the sink.

If it hadn't been for the phone ringing, I think we could have stayed like that forever, frozen in a tableau. But as soon as the jangling rang out from the hall, my dad and my mother both jumped in their skins, and my mother got quickly to her feet.

'I'll get it,' she said and went towards the door. My dad hadn't turned around and he just stood there with his hands clutching onto the edge of the sink. The way my mother moved across the kitchen floor was timid, and she seemed to have become strangely compliant, as though my dad was a wild creature to be both feared and appeased. She went into the hall and closed the door softly behind her.

I strained to hear what she was saying, but all I could make out was a muffled buzz of one-sided conversation.

'That was Mally,' she said when she came back in, and my stomach flipped. My dad still didn't move.

'He was phoning to say that Janet can't come today, she's sick, but she'll try and come at the weekend instead.'

My dad turned around and passed his hand over his eyes. He and my mother looked at each other for an age before he finally spoke.

'Probably for the best,' he said, and went down to this studio.

*

After breakfast Lorry and I lay on our backs on the patchy lawn and counted swallows. Where the patch of concrete had been, there was now bare, loamy earth, but I knew that it wouldn't take long for it to be baked to dust. Lorry eventually dozed off and I closed my eyes and thought about getting revenge on Tracy Powell. Even though it was Fat Denise who'd hurt Lorry, Tracy was the one in charge; Fat Denise was just her sidekick. They'd done something bad to Lorry, and that had to be corrected, balanced out. It was what the Creed wanted. I wondered if somehow, by burying the relics, I'd managed to diminish the power of the Creed. I needed to give it something back. Something to let it know I was still its disciple.

I fingered the tender area on my forehead and then I had a thought. I sat up and scrabbled around in the grass until my fingers found a stone. It was about the size of a plum, with good, jagged edges.

The first time I hit my head with it, it didn't really hurt, so I guessed I hadn't done it hard enough. The second time I made sure to hit it really hard, and felt the lump rise almost instantly. I'd look ridiculous with two bruises on my forehead, one on either side, but I had to do it to balance out the bad luck. Two wrongs could make a right. I knew it wasn't enough to get back at Tracy and Fat Denise for what they'd done to Lorry, but it was a start; it showed willing. If I could appease the Creed, if I could demonstrate that I was still its disciple, I knew that I could make things alright for Lorry.

I looked over at my brother and was surprised to see that he had his eyes open, watching me.

'What's up, little feller?' I said, and reached my hand out to take his.

He was quiet for a moment, as if working himself up to being able to speak.

'They hurt me, Nif. Girls hurt me.' He lifted his wrist to show me the place where Fat Denise had grabbed him the day before.

'I'm sorry, Lorry,' I said, and shuffled over the grass to sit next to him. 'I should have been a better sister. I should have looked after you better.'

His eyes narrowed against the sun when he looked up at me.

'Mummy says Petra's looking after me. She says Petra's always watching over me and one day I can see her.'

'What?' Despite the still air, I felt the hairs on the back of my neck lift. 'You know Petra's dead, Lorry, right? You know that she's dead and she's never coming back?'

'Mummy says she is. She says she can feel her and that maybe she can see her if she keeps taking medicine.'

'What medicine, Lorry? The pills the doctor gave her? The little blue pills?'

He pulled away from me, and wrapped his arms around his legs. He shook his head.

'Medicine from lady,' was all he would say, and then he lay on his back and shut his eyes.

Twenty-two.

Sunday 15ᵗʰ August 1976

The long days wore on, with the same insolent weather, the same uninterrupted heat. Neither of my parents had mentioned our argument about school, and I was glad. There was a new tension between them, the air almost crackling when they were in the same room. I did my best to stay out of their way.

My dad gave up on the odd jobs he was doing around the cottage. He'd stripped and repainted the kitchen window, but with the other window frames he'd just painted on top of the old paint, and not too carefully either, so that some of it had encroached onto the glass. He removed some of the slipping tiles from the roof of the porch, but he hadn't bothered replacing them, and they sat in a stack next to the front door, giving the porch the look of a middle-aged man with a receding hairline. He hadn't bothered cleaning the gutters either, so the moss and weeds that grew there remained, although yellower and more withered than when we'd first arrived.

Mostly, my dad stayed in his studio, occasionally coming out to make a cup of tea or grab a scrap of bread. He didn't bother removing the clay from his hands anymore, but would appear in the kitchen with orange smears up to his elbows, layer upon layer building up, until eventually he'd have to wash.

The only time my parents seemed to have anything to do with each other was when they washed. My dad would heat up water on the camping stove. Pan after pan would be boiled and taken upstairs and poured into the bath, then cold water would be added until there were a few inches of tepid water in the bottom. My mother would go first, and I'd stand outside the bathroom door and listen to her washing herself, the strangely hypnotic sound of liquid being sloshed over skin. Then it would be my dad's turn, and he'd use the same water. It struck me that this sharing of bathwater, brought on by necessity, was the most intimate of exchanges I'd witnessed between them in a long time. This fusion of skin cells, of sweat and dust and clay, was the closest they'd been for months.

I'd forgotten it was a Sunday until I saw the people milling on the grass in front of the chapel. From my vantage point in the attic, I could see Lyndon Vaughan, his little dog running in circles, sniffing at ankles and scurrying from one person to the next. They all ignored it, talking among themselves, taking it in turns to be presented to Mr Beynon, who shook hands with all the men, just as I'd seen him do on that first Sunday.

There seemed to be a discussion going on between several of the men and Lyndon Vaughan, and it must have ended in an agreement, because one of them stepped forward towards Mally's house, with something in his hand. I couldn't quite see what he was doing, but he bent down in front of one of the wooden gateposts and reached out a hand, and he seemed to be marking it or drawing on it. He did this for a couple of minutes, then stepped back, as if surveying his work. The other men nodded their approval, and the first man moved back into the crowd again. I couldn't see what he'd done to the gatepost.

Lyndon Vaughan went to the boot of his car and brought out the same greengrocer's box I'd seen him with before. The bunches of leaves were handed out, and the ceremony with the water was performed again, each of the congregation taking it in turns to flick their bundles of herbs in the direction of Mally's house. It made me think of Janet, and the bunches of dried herbs in her kitchen, and the potions she made with them which Lorry had said she was giving to my mother. Perhaps they were more similar than they thought, the chapel-goers and Janet.

The chanting started, and hands were raised, the palms flat. As the voices got louder, and just like the last time, the words were incomprehensible, overlapping each other in a meaningless jumble, layer upon layer. Then, exactly as had happened before, the men and women paired up and trooped into the chapel.

I was sitting on the grass at the front of the cottage. It was late morning and the temperature was stealthily on the rise. There were no grasshoppers around, so I'd been pulling the peeling skin off my shoulders and rolling it into little balls. Even though the skin was white when I pulled it off, it would turn grey when I rubbed it between my fingers. I assumed that this was the dirt ingrained in my skin.

The gate squeaked and I looked over. Janet and Mally were coming down the stone steps. Janet had her hand raised in greeting. She had on a short denim skirt that stopped midway down her thighs and a skimpy red vest. A canvas bag was slung over one shoulder. Mally had both of his hands in his pockets and a big grin on his face, and his camera was hanging from his neck as usual. They walked across the flag-stoned path and around the patch of virgin earth where my dad had dug up the concrete. When I looked up at them I had to shield my eyes with one hand.

'Alright, Nif?' The sun made a halo of Janet's yellow curls.

'Hello,' I said, standing up. My mother came out of the house, and I thought she must have been standing at the kitchen window, waiting. She and Janet hugged—a long, lingering embrace. Janet was shorter than my mother, and her head fitted exactly into the space below my mother's chin, as if it had been carved especially for that purpose. I watched them hug and realised with a start that I couldn't remember the last time I'd seen my mother and my dad touch each other.

When Janet and my mother separated, their eyes remained locked together, and they were both smiling. Janet reached into the bag and pulled out a wine bottle with a cork in the end.

'Gooseberry wine,' she said. 'We'll need some refreshment in this heat.' My mother took the bottle from her and put it on the window sill behind her. When she turned back to Janet there was an air of expectancy about her, as if she was waiting for something else to appear from the bag. She seemed eager. Before either of them could say anything, my dad came out of the house, wiping his hands on his jeans. He took off his glasses and polished them on his shirt.

'Hello Janet,' he said. 'Feeling better?'

'Yes, thanks. Tummy bug. You know what it's like. You feel like death for a few days, and then it clears up and you feel right as rain again.'

'What's in the bag?'

'Tools of the trade,' she said and patted the canvas. 'Are you sure you want me to do this? I reckon there's a storm on the way. All this will probably be for nothing.'

My dad looked up at the sky, which was a lucid, cloudless blue.

'No chance. This heatwave's going to go on forever,' he said, and ran his clay-smeared hand through his hair.

Janet shook her head. 'No, there's definitely rain on the way. Trust me, I can feel it.' She tapped her nose and winked and my mother stuttered out a laugh.

'Well then,' Janet said. 'If you're sure, we'd better get on with it, before chapel kicks out. Unless you want a hostile audience?' She was smirking.

'I'll fetch some glasses,' my dad said, and ducked into the house.

Janet had spent at least twenty minutes walking backwards and forwards in straight lines over the scrappy lawn and the patch where the concrete had been cleared by my dad. He'd shifted all the broken pieces of concrete up to the parking area, and now there was a pile of jagged-edged grey slabs next to the Cortina.

We'd all watched in silence as Janet had taken a branch out of the canvas bag, a y-shaped thing about half an inch thick and the length of her forearm. She grabbed each of the handles of the branch—like the handlebars of a bike, with the long end pointing out in front of her—and had started pacing up and down, muttering to herself. A flush was rising up her neck, and for some reason I got the feeling that it wasn't caused by the heat, but by something deeper. Her concentration was palpable.

Every now and then the end of the branch would twitch, and Janet would stop and frown and lean down and point the stick at the ground, still muttering. Then she'd stand up again and carry on.

My dad was leaning against the porch, his arms crossed over his chest. His shirt was spattered with clay in little orange firework bursts. My mother stood a couple of feet away from him, Lorry clutching at her skirt with one hand, his clown doll with the other. She was biting her lip and looking intently at Janet. It was as though my parents had called a truce, and were both trying to act normally because Janet was there, but I could still feel the friction between them.

Both of my parents held a glass of wine, a cloudy green liquid that looked medicinal. My dad had given Janet a glass too, which she'd drained and put on the window sill. Mally stood next to me, by the patch of soil where my dad had been digging. No-one said anything.

Eventually Janet stopped and wiped her forearm over her face. Her hair was damp with sweat and stuck to her forehead, and her eyeshadow had settled into the creases of her eyelids. She puffed out a breath and walked over to where the wine bottle sat on the window sill. Having tucked the dowsing rod under her armpit, she poured herself a full glass and drank it down in one go, then put the bottle and the glass back down with a clink. She sat on the window sill.

'A little refresher,' she said, wiping her arm over her forehead again. 'It's thirsty work in this heat.'

'Oh, now there's a sight.'

I hadn't seen them at first. I'd been watching Janet, and so the voice which carried over the still air from the parking space made me jump. It was low and ripe, dripping with sarcasm. It came from Lyndon Vaughan who stood by the Cortina, behind the railings. His face was a mask of disgust, the bulbous bottom lip blubbery and wet and pink.

To his right stood Mr Beynon, staring unseeing in our direction, his eyes like pearls nestled in the white satin folds of his eyelids. I noticed again how his nose was long and hooked, his forehead high and arched, the black hair greased back, and I thought of the raven skull on the altar in my bedroom, the eye sockets just empty holes.

A foot or two behind the beetle man and the minister stood a dozen or so men from the chapel, dressed in their dark suits and looking for all the world like a flock of birds. The women were nowhere to be seen.

The beetle man's dog came running forward and planted itself at its master's feet. It drew its lips back over yellow teeth and quivered, its hackles raised in a ridge along its back.

'Still using the witching stick then, Janet?' I could hear the sneer in the beetle man's voice. 'Up to your funny business again, are you?'

Janet didn't even look at him. She placed the branch down very deliberately on the window sill, and then she picked up the wine bottle and emptied it into her glass. She lifted it to her mouth and took a deep swig. She wiped her mouth on the back of her hand, and only then did she turn to him.

'Mr Vaughan. Care for a drink?' She strode over towards him, and stood in front of the wall that separated the raised parking area from the lawn. He was a good couple of feet higher up than she was and she had to look up at him. She was a tiny splash of colour, standing there in her brazen clothing, her blonde hair springing out around her face, and she was fizzing with energy.

When the beetle man didn't answer, Janet turned to the minister.

'What about you, Reverend? Fancy a snifter?' She brandished her glass at him and the sudden movement caused her to stagger slightly. 'Or are you going to stand there all day gawping?' She smiled suddenly, a cruel grin that didn't quite reach her eyes. 'Oh no, you can't, can you? You can't see a bloody thing!'

It wasn't humour that fuelled Janet's laughter, but spite and alcohol, and again she raised her glass at the two men. I realised I hadn't once heard the minister speak; it was as if the beetle man was his mouth as well as his eyes.

'Heathen!' Mr Vaughan's voice was shrill, a knife cutting though the solid air. 'Leave these people alone and let us good folk carry on our lives in peace. There's no place here for people like you.'

'Oh, I'm no heathen, Mr Vaughan. I just have my own beliefs. Beliefs that are different from yours and that you can't abide.'

'Your beliefs are wicked, Miss White, and they have no place in this village.'

Janet sneered. 'I don't know what you're talking about, Mr Vaughan.' She turned away, as if dismissing him, and sauntered towards where my parents were standing, watching silently.

'Go on, off you go,' she said, and waved a hand in his direction. 'Take your crappy little dog and your…your "good folk" and get back to your bloody chapel and your lousy god and see where that gets you.' She stepped deliberately over the path and marched past my parents and in through the front door of the cottage.

Lyndon Vaughan's bottom lip was quivering dangerously as he watched Janet disappear. The minister stood next to him, unspeaking, eyebrows drawn together, his eyes empty. Slowly, the congregation started to disperse, moving backwards, returning to the cars that were parked on the verge.

Finally, the beetle man started to walk away, his hand supporting the minister's elbow. Abruptly, as if he'd had a second thought, he turned back and stepped forward, to the top of the steps, and leant over the gate. His voice was a whispered hiss, and I had to strain to hear his words as he spoke to my parents.

'Don't be taken in by her. I've warned you before, but you didn't listen. She's evil, that one. She'll draw you in, fill you with her beliefs, and you'll never be the same again.' Then he turned away and walked back towards where the minister stood, blind and helpless.

The little terrier started to follow, but then seemed to think better of it and stopped. It sniffed the gravel, and turned around a few times. It looked at my parents challengingly, and arched its back into a question mark, as if to say, 'What are you looking at?' Then it coiled out an enormous, mustard-coloured turd. Nonchalantly, it scratched the ground a few times with its back feet, then scampered after its master.

'What was all that about, then?' My dad plonked the empty glasses onto the sideboard. Janet and my mother were sitting next to each other at the kitchen table, both tugging roughly on cigarettes. Lorry had said he was too hot and had gone to sit in the relative cool of the living room.

Janet blew out smoke in a long stream before she replied.

'Oh, something and nothing. History. Bad feelings running high in a little village. Nothing to worry about. They're all

inbred anyway. Have you noticed how they all look the same?'
She snorted and then readjusted her face into a sneer; suddenly
she looked old and ragged. Her lipstick had worn off and the
wrinkles round her eyes looked deeper. She took another drag
on her fag and blew out smoke. 'They hate anyone who's not
like them, simple as that. When we moved here they instantly
took a dislike to us. It's because we're different. We're not like
them.' She shrugged.

I remembered what Mally had told me about the plague
coming to the village, brought by outsiders. Outsiders that had
been Mally and Janet's ancestors. Outsiders. The word had got
stuck in my head and the more I thought about it the less
meaning it had. I turned it round in my brain, the syllables
clicking, until it meant nothing. It was just a collection of
vowels and consonants.

My dad ducked out into the hall and I could hear him
rummaging in the cupboard under the stairs. No doubt Janet
thought she was being surreptitious when she dipped her
hand into the canvas bag that was hanging on the back of her
chair and handed a small, brown bottle to my mother, but her
actions were made clumsy by the wine she'd drunk, and her
hand slipped slightly as she slid it across the table. It made a
loud scraping noise. My mother didn't meet my eye, but at
least she looked embarrassed when she picked up the bottle
and put it in the cupboard of the sideboard behind her, just as
my dad came in with a bottle of wine.

'Well, we didn't find a spring, but at least we can water
ourselves,' he said, trying to be funny. No-one laughed, but
Janet managed a half-hearted smile.

My dad took a corkscrew from the drawer of the sideboard
and squeaked the cork out of the bottle. He poured the wine

into the glasses and handed them to my mother and Janet, who drank greedily. Mally looked at me, his eyebrows raised, and I gave him a tiny nod.

'But what does Lyndon Vaughan have against you? He's really got it into his head that you're trouble.' My dad was smiling to soften the significance of his words, but I could tell that the confrontation outside the cottage had shaken him. 'He actually said you were evil.'

Janet smiled back, a faded smirk that didn't quite reach her eyes.

'It's not Lyndon Vaughan who's the problem. It's the minister, old Beynon. Vaughan's nothing more than a mouthpiece for him. Beynon's the really nasty one.'

'Why, though,' asked my dad. 'I've never even heard him say anything. Even that night at the pub, you know, when you were…under the influence.' He smiled at this, and even my mother allowed a small smile to spread over her mouth.

It seemed to me that Janet's presence had brought about a thaw in my parents' relationship. They'd managed to be civil to each other and were more relaxed in the other's company. It was as though she had a soothing effect on them, as though she had charmed them. Maybe it was just the wine.

Janet grimaced. 'I know. Everyone round here thinks I drink too much.' She raised her glass in a mock salute. 'Well, the truth is, I probably do, but there's not a lot else to do around here is there?'

'So why do you live here, then?' my dad said. 'I mean, we're just here for a month or so to get our heads together. We don't live here like you do.' As he carried on speaking I saw my mother's shoulders slump a fraction of an inch. 'And I certainly wouldn't want to live in a backward place like this.'

Janet snorted and took a slug of her wine.

My dad persisted. 'So why do you stay? Why do you choose to live here when it's so awful? When they all hate you and things like…*that* happen?' He flung his hand out towards the window, gesturing at the parking space where the beetle man and the minister had stood just a few minutes before.

'Because I have history here,' was all Janet would say. She leant back in her chair, and took a swig of wine and a long pull on her cigarette. The smoke curled out of her nostrils and hung in the air in front of her when she spoke.

'What about you, Clive? What do you do?' She was looking my dad right in the eyes and a sly grin had attached itself to her mouth.

'He's a sculptor.' It was the first thing my mother had said since we came into the house, and her voice was so quiet I couldn't tell if she'd spoken those three words with pride or derision.

'A sculptor, eh?' Janet nodded slowly. 'What sort of things do you sculpt, then?'

'Busts, mostly,' my dad said. 'You know, head and shoulders, that sort of thing.' He took off his glasses and polished them on the hem of his shirt. He was blushing, and I thought he looked younger, almost like a boy. Janet was nodding slowly, and her head seemed to have grown heavy.

'Working on anything at the moment?' Despite the slur in her voice, it held a slippery slyness. She had her elbow on the table in front of her, her chin resting in her palm, and she was looking at him sideways. My dad opened his mouth to say something, but my mother was quicker and her answer darted out into the stillness of the kitchen.

'Me. He's working on a bust of me. He has been for months. And it's nearly finished now, Clive, isn't it?'

My dad carried on polishing his glasses, grinding away at them as if trying to remove some stubborn but invisible stain.

'Nearly. Nearly, love.' I thought of the bust in his studio, the bust that my mother had refused to look at since he'd started working on it. How he'd had to work on it from photographs and his memory because she refused to have anything to do with it. It was nearly finished the last time I'd seen it, with just the eyes left to be carved. And then it would be an exact replica of Janet.

'Can we see it?' Janet leant back in her chair, the end of her cigarette a trembling tower of ash. She seemed to be goading him, and I wondered if she knew about the bust.

'Not yet,' was all he would say. He looked defiant now, a man again and not a boy.

It was a sudden silence that filled the kitchen, and it was broken just as abruptly. My mother scraped her chair back and stood decisively.

'Well, look at that. Lunchtime already. You'll stay Janet? We've got ham and cheese and eggs. I could make you an omelette. Go on, say you'll stay?' My mother's voice was pleading, and she was gazing at Janet intently. Janet nodded and raised her wine glass in silent assent. My dad pushed his glasses higher up his nose.

Mally gave me another look and I nodded again. I slid backwards against the sideboard and in one smooth movement, grabbed the corkscrew and sidled towards the door, hoping my dad didn't notice. I stepped out into the hall and Mally followed me.

'Hey. No funny business, you two, OK?' My dad thought he was being funny and chuckled to himself. He still thought I was a child.

'No way, Mr Allen.' Mally's face was a study in innocence. 'Wouldn't dream of it.'

Twenty-three.

'So, what's the real story?' I was using the contraband corkscrew to attack the wine bottle we'd nicked from the cupboard under the stairs. The cork was stuck and had started to crumble.

Mally had given the skull in its jar of bleach a cursory inspection, and we agreed that it was ready for washing. I wanted to ask him about the relics, about digging them up again so that I could give the Creed the power it needed to get back at Tracy Powell, but he seemed preoccupied. I thought he might be upset about his mother's confrontation with the beetle man.

'What do you mean, "the real story"?' He didn't look at me, just flung himself onto my bed and stared up at the ceiling, arms behind his head.

'Well, all that stuff your mum told my dad, about them not liking you just because you're different? That's not quite everything, is it?' I managed to get the corkscrew in far enough to gain traction, and pulled at the cork. It came out with a pathetic plop and I took a mouthful. It tasted vinegary and vile. I wiped my mouth with the back of my hand.

'You told me about your ancestors being the ones who brought the plague to the village. I know about that. But that doesn't explain what Lyndon Vaughan just said to my dad. He said your mother was evil. Why would he say that?'

Mally sat up and grabbed the bottle from me. 'It's complicated,' he said.

'What do you mean?'

He took a massive swig from the bottle, then handed it back. He went and stood at the open window and took a packet of Benson and Hedges and a box of matches from the back pocket of his jeans. The flame was almost invisible in the stream of bright sunshine and the cigarette glowed a dull red when he took a drag. He leant out of the little window and blew out a steady stream of smoke. I stood next to him and together we looked down on the patch of grass at the front of the chapel, and the parking area where Lyndon Vaughan and Mr Beynon and the chapel-goers had congregated. The scent of the honeysuckle was clotting the the air again, languid and sickly.

'When we first moved here all sorts of heavy shit happened,' Mally said, and his voice was quiet and steady.

'What sort of shit?'

He took another drag on the cigarette and held the smoke in his lungs for a moment. He pushed his head out through the window before he exhaled. Then he handed me the fag.

'It was like they'd already made up their minds to hate us, before we even moved in. Like they knew who we were and didn't even give us a chance.'

'Like they knew about your ancestors?'

He nodded. I tapped the end of the cigarette on the outside window sill, and we watched as the little log of ash rolled away and disappeared over the edge.

'What happened to them?'

He didn't reply at first. He grabbed the wine bottle out of my hand and took a huge swallow. It was like he was steeling himself for something, and what he said next made me realise why.

'They said they were witches.'

'Witches?' He nodded.

'That's a bit extreme, isn't it?'

'Not really. This was 300 years ago, remember. People were nuts back then. Thought any woman who was a bit different or who acted strangely was a witch.'

I was quiet for a while, processing this information.

'But why would Lyndon Vaughan and the others hate you because of your ancestors? Surely they can't believe in all that?'

Mally took another swig of wine.

'It's…weird. After we moved here, back in January, strange things started to happen. People got sick and stuff. They started finding dead animals lying around, with no signs of how they'd been killed. You know, all that Hammer Horror bullshit.' I could tell he was trying to make a joke of it, but there was a tremor in his voice.

'Go on,' I said.

He took another drag on the cigarette then leant out of the window. When he spoke, his voice was so quiet that I had to strain to catch his words before they disappeared into the still air.

'Then they started saying that my mother was bewitching people.' He made little inverted commas in the air with his fingers. 'You know, making them fall in love with her. And it's true. There were lots of blokes in the village that did fancy her, including Beynon.'

I must have looked shocked, because he smiled briefly before he carried on.

'Some people in the village think my mother tried to seduce old Mr Beynon, that she tried to get him to screw her. They said that my mother wanted to shag that old man.' Disgust clouded his face. 'As if. He was the one hanging round her all the time, trying to get into her knickers.' Before I could say anything, he went on.

'Lyndon Vaughan backed him up of course, said he'd seen my mother collecting herbs at midnight under a full moon, or whatever other shit he'd seen on the telly. Honestly, it was like there was a witch hunt.' He stopped himself, realising what he'd said, and I was relieved when his scowl transformed into a grin. 'It was. It was just like a witch hunt. Whenever we left the house they'd be there, Beynon and Lyndon Vaughan, staring at us, not saying anything. And then they started doing this weird thing, shaking branches at our house and what-not, saying they were going to cleanse it.' He was rolling the cigarette in his finger and thumb, twisting it backwards and forwards.

'You've seen the circles they've scratched on our gatepost? The overlapping ones, all different sizes? They come along and make them with a compass, for fuck's sake. They call them witch marks. Say they're to ward off evil.' He'd grown angry again, and both his fists were clenched at his sides, the cigarette crushed between his fingers. The sinews stood out taut on his arms.

'They're like the circles in the pub,' I said. 'The ones over the fireplace. They're the same, scratched into the wood: sets of concentric circles that overlap. Did they put them there, as well?'

'They're old ones. Ancient. They're probably here from when our lot first moved here. The Derbyshire lot. This village has a long history.'

Mally had said that the chapel-goers thought that his ancestors were evil, that they practised witchcraft. Did they think that Janet was the same? Were they trying to defend themselves using their own type of magic? There was nothing overtly Christian about the ritual I was witnessing; it was more basic than that. The actions they were performing—the herbs and the water—were more like an ancient pagan ceremony, with none of the trappings of religion I'd grown used to when I went to church.

'I've seen them doing all that stuff. Making the circles and the stuff with the leaves and water.'

Mally nodded.

'What happened to make them start doing it all? Something must have happened to set them off?'

He took another swig of the wine before he went on. 'There was this…accident. Or…not really an accident. More of an incident. One day old Beynon woke up and he couldn't see anything. He'd got cataracts in both eyes and he just literally couldn't see. I mean, how does that happen to someone?'

Mally was holding the bottle in one hand, and I could see that it was nearly empty now, even though I'd only had one mouthful.

'He went to the hospital and they just told him to wait and see if he got his sight back. That was at Easter and the old guy's still blind as a bat.' He raised the cigarette to his mouth with his other hand and took a drag. There was a vertical furrow between his eyebrows, something I hadn't noticed before, and it made him look tired and cross, and older.

'Of course, they said it was our fault. That my mother was a witch, like her ancestors, and she'd put a spell on him to make him go blind. Can you believe that? In this day and age? For fuck's sake, Nif. It's 1976!'

I remembered what the beetle man had said to Janet outside the cottage, how he'd referred to her dowsing rod as a witch's stick, and how he'd warned my parents away from her.

'And what do you think?'

'Me? What do I think? I think that's ridiculous. She's my mum. She's not a witch for fuck's sake!' He stood at the window smoking angrily. After a couple of minutes, he stubbed the cigarette out on the window frame and strode over to the mantelpiece. He picked up the jar with the raven's skull in it. He held it up to the light and looked at it intently for a few moments.

'Tell me the incantation,' he said.

'What?'

'The incantation. Teach it to me. If you trusted me, you'd tell me.'

I turned this over in my mind. Part of me wanted to keep the Creed for myself. It was mine: it had chosen me. But the other part of me felt that Mally deserved to be in on it. He'd given me the crow's skull, the final relic which allowed me to complete the incantation, and now the raven's skull which was going to help me get revenge on Tracy Powell. Surely I could trust him?

I turned to face him. His hands were cool when I held them. I looked right into his eyes and started reciting. 'Robin's egg, magpie's egg, duckling bill and bone. Blackbird's egg, feathers of wren, the skull of a crow.'

He repeated it after me, and when he faltered a couple of times I corrected him. We said it together until he knew it perfectly, and then we chanted it over and over again, feeling the words surging around us. They melded together into something palpable, something greater than the sum of its parts. We bounced on the bed, chanting the incantation. We sang it and we shouted it and then we lay down, facing each other, laughing. There was something magical about it, about the two of us, there and then. There was an energy in the room, a feeling of anticipation, of something momentous about to happen.

When Mally put his hand under the waistband of my shorts, I was already expecting it. His long fingers inched lower, burrowing, searching, and then his hands moved round to my hips and deftly slid my shorts and my pants down, so that they bunched around my thighs. My fingers danced over his Orion's Belt of moles, and he grabbed at his belt and undid it in one movement, sliding it out of the belt loops and throwing it to the far corner of the room. It hit the chair with a loud clanking sound.

He rolled me onto my back and lay on top of me, his body surprisingly heavy for someone so lithe. I could feel him digging into my belly. I knew there was no turning back.

'Ready, Nif?' he asked. The sun was coming through the window and casting his face into shadows—and I thought then that was the reason the sun was so bright; it was to make the things in the shadows so much darker and hold their secrets away from the light—and then that little half-smile was back on his lips.

'Do you trust me, Nif?'

I nodded and his fingers were moving and there was the slow slide of denim against skin and then he was inside me.

Twenty-four.

Mally didn't stay long afterwards. He'd said he needed to get his mother home, that she'd be no good on her own after all the wine she'd drunk. When we heard the bottle smashing downstairs, we knew something was going on. I listened to his footsteps clatter down the attic stairs, and then I went to the open window and looked out onto the lane and the patch of grass in front of the chapel.

It was early afternoon, and even though the heat hadn't diminished at all, I began to wonder if Janet had been right about the weather turning. There was a new smell to the air. It was more robust, more substantial, and I thought I could taste it now, earthy and damp. It was just as heavy as before, but there was a definite shift. It was like the change that had come across my mother since we'd gone to stay in the cottage and she'd become friends with Janet: different, but not necessarily better.

The light had changed as well. The sky had lost the translucent glow I'd come to expect; now it looked weak and insipid. The blue no longer had the glossy sheen of satin, but instead was faded and worn like denim.

As I looked out of the window, Mally and Janet came into view and started climbing the steps to the little parking area. Janet was weaving all over the place and Mally was trying to prop her up and make her walk at the same time, and it would have been funny if it wasn't so pathetic. When they made it to the top of the steps I heard the familiar squeak as Mally opened the gate. Janet started to stumble forwards, propelled by her own weight, and her hands went out instinctively to break her fall, but she was too slow, and she landed awkwardly on the pile of broken concrete. She rolled over until she was lying on her back, slumped on the grey dusty mound, and she looked for all the world like a little girl, in her red vest and mini skirt, holding her arms up to Mally to be picked up. Mally stood there for a few moments, looking down at her, and I couldn't see his face. I was glad.

Eventually, he hauled her to her feet and they crossed the lane together. When they got to the gate, Mally reached out to push it open over the grass. It got stuck and he had to push at it awkwardly with his hip, all the time supporting his mother. Janet reached out a heavy arm towards the gatepost and her fingers dangled in the air in front of the circles that had been scratched there, not quite touching them. Then Mally managed to get the gate open and the pair of them made their way up the path and disappeared from view.

In our kitchen, my dad was clearing up after lunch. My mother was sitting at the kitchen table with her head resting on her arms. At her elbow, the ashtray was overflowing, the spilled butts trickling down onto the table in a wave, as though they were trying to escape from the filth. Next to the ashtray was the bust my dad had been working on, and I guessed that my mother had brought it up from the studio, intending to show it to Janet. It was still covered in its plastic and hessian wrapping. On the floor at my mother's feet were the shattered shards of brown glass that I recognised as being from the bottle Janet had given her: the potion.

I'd seen my dad drunk before, especially in the days after Petra died. He'd get my mother into bed and make sure she'd taken her Valium, and when he thought that Lorry and I were asleep, he'd sit in the brown Draylon armchair in the living room drinking glass after glass of whisky, the piss-coloured liquid slowly disappearing. From where I used to sit, huddled in the darkness at the top of the stairs, I would watch as his eyes started to get wet, usually after the third or fourth glass. Then he would start to let out short, sudden sobs, and as the level of the whisky in the bottle dropped his pain would grow, and he would let the tears flow, big fat drops that ran down his cheeks, past his chin and onto his neck. Once or twice I went down and stood in front of him, wondering if he could see me, but he looked through me as if I wasn't there.

The next morning, it would be as though nothing had happened, and the empty whisky bottle and the glass would be gone, and there would be no trace of my dad's grief from the night before except for the sagging around his eyes and the sour smell when he pulled me close to kiss me.

He was a different sort of drunk now. He was an angry drunk, and the tension was back in the room. It was as though Janet's calming influence had left with her, and my parents were back at war with each other.

My dad's movements as he tidied up the kitchen were jerky and sharp. His hands shook when he swept up the broken glass, and the ashtray tipped to the side when he went to lift it and it shed even more of the fugitive cigarette ends. There were broken eggshells on the sideboard, and the plates in the sink held the congealing traces of omelette. He was muttering to himself, his lips moving rapidly, his face set in a scowl. He didn't notice me when I walked in.

I grabbed an orange from the fruit bowl and was making for the door again when my mother lifted her head up off her arms. She seemed to struggle to focus on me, and then it was as though she decided she couldn't be bothered. She looked at my dad instead.

'Clive?' Her voice was a croak. He didn't turn around from the sink where he was scrubbing plates. 'Clive?' I could tell there was going to be a scene, so I crouched down in the back hall, at the top of the steps down to my dad's studio, and began to peel the orange.

My mother pulled herself to her feet, unsteady at first, and then, with great care, she crossed the floor to stand behind him. He was rigid, his spine straight and tight, and he didn't move when she placed a hand on each of his shoulders.

'Don't be like this. It's not Janet's fault. I asked her to help me.' My dad shook her off and dried his hands on the tea towel that hung next to the sink. He took his time, very slowly and deliberately drying each finger in turn, all the time keeping his back turned towards my mother.

'I asked her to make me the potions, and they help, they really do.' My mother's voice was wheedling, a whining drawl that made me want to punch her in the face, and when my dad spun round and lifted his hands I wondered if that was what he was going to do. Instead, he grabbed her shoulders.

'Please, Clive,' she wheedled. 'You didn't have to smash it. It's not Janet's—'

'Janet! That bloody woman. She's always here, hanging around, touching you and…and giving you those bloody *potions*!'

My mother's face was impassive. He gave her shoulders a tiny shake.

'You know what they'd be saying at home about the two of you, don't you? They'd say you were a pair of dykes, the way you're always together and hugging and what-have-you. You should be ashamed.'

'Ashamed?' My mother sounded incredulous but calm. 'Ashamed? Of what we have? I don't think so. What we have is beautiful. It's nothing to be ashamed of.'

'It's not right. It's…weird.'

My mother's mouth twisted into a sly smile.

'You think she's put a spell on me, is that it?'

'Don't be ridiculous.'

'Or are you jealous?'

'What do you mean?' My dad was suspicious.

'I've seen you looking. I've seen you watching her sunbathing. Don't tell me you're not interested.'

My dad drew his hand over his eyes and let out a long breath. He'd gone from angry to weary in a few moments.

'It's true, isn't it? You fancy her.' My mother sounded like a teenager, teasing her friend about a boy.

My dad snorted. 'OK, if you want to know, there is something about her.' He shrugged. 'Something that drew me to her. She's very charming, fascinating, I suppose. But the truth of the matter is that *she* tried it on with *me*. She threw herself at me. She was all over me.'

My mother's smile fell slightly as if she was made uncertain by this revelation and my dad seemed to gain strength from her weakness.

'You know what? She even tried to get me to screw her on her kitchen table.'

The smile froze on my mother's face and then disappeared. I'd managed to remove the orange peel in one go, and I let it fall to the floor.

'I don't believe you,' my mother said, shaking her head. 'She's my friend and she wouldn't do that.'

My dad carried on talking as if he hadn't heard her.

'But I didn't do anything. I stopped myself. Even when she was throwing herself at me, I stopped myself.'

'No. It's not true. I don't believe you.' She was still shaking her head, tiny brittle movements to and fro.

'And it's a shame you couldn't have done the same.'

My parents looked at each other, my dad's eyes wide and his mouth downturned. When he spoke, his voice had a finality to it.

'We'll go home. We'll go home tomorrow. We'll just pack the trailer and leave and go back to our lives and try to start again. This was a mistake.'

'We can't go.' My mother's voice was quiet. 'We can't go because Petra's here and I can't leave her.'

This was the final straw for my father.

'She's not here, you stupid woman. She isn't here and she never has been here. She's dead.' My dad was speaking slowly and carefully, and enunciating every word, as if he was talking to a child or an imbecile. 'She hasn't come back to tell you that she's forgiven you. You've made that up to make yourself feel better. She's not here because you drowned her, don't you remember? You left her in the bath on her own when you went to answer the phone and our little girl—my little girl—drowned.' As he spoke his voice was getting louder and louder, until he was leaning into her face and shouting.

'It was him, wasn't it? On the phone? I *know*. And I know that *you* know. Did you really think I didn't realise? All those times, those parents' evenings, when you'd smile and giggle and act like a bloody teenager. It was embarrassing. I felt ashamed for you. And all those times when I got back from work and you weren't there, and then Mrs Akhar would come out with Petra, and you'd left her there, with the bloody neighbour, so that you could go off and carry on with him. With him. With Peter-Fucking-McPherson. Jesus Christ, woman. With Nif's teacher! What were you thinking? Did you really think I didn't know?'

My dad had run out of words. He stared at my mother, waiting for her to reply. Her face had turned to marble. She looked about a hundred years old. She stood, looking up at my dad, her mouth open, little jagged breaths coming quick and fast. She looked like the magpie we'd trapped, unable to escape, panic coming off her in waves.

She turned away from him, as though she couldn't bear to look at him, or couldn't bear for him to see her face. My dad carried on speaking quietly, his voice measured and calm and accusing.

'It *was* him, wasn't it? Him who phoned that night. The night she drowned. Just tell me, Linda.'

At first I couldn't imagine my mother screwing Mr McPherson, but then I remembered her how she was before Petra died, when she was shiny and glossy and all the things she'd stopped being since. Even though I couldn't have defined it as such back then, there had been a feral side to her, a wantonness that should have made an affair with my teacher unsurprising, a sexuality that had been detected by the boys at the school gates all those months ago. All this time, when I'd tried to remember my dream, maybe I had known that my mother was having it off with Mr McPherson, but I'd blocked it out. I peeled off a segment of the orange and popped it in my mouth.

I couldn't see my mother's face from where I was sitting, but I knew what it would look like. Her eyes would be closed, the eyeballs bouncing against the papery skin of her eyelids. Her thin lips would have made a deep scratch across her face and her cheeks would be hollow and shadowed. In my mouth the orange was sharp, almost bitter, the flesh slightly dry and woolly, as though the juice had been leached from it.

'I'm sorry.' At first I wasn't sure that she'd said anything, her voice was so low. I don't think my dad heard her, because he didn't respond. 'I'm sorry,' she said again, and this time her voice was loud enough to carry through the heavy air. My mother took a step towards him, and reached a hand up, as though she was going to touch his cheek. My dad flinched and pulled away, and there was sadness as well as anger on his face.

I peeled off another orange segment and sucked on it.

My mother took hold of my dad's hand and clutched it. She went down onto her knees in front of him. She had her eyes closed, but her face was turned up towards him. She started muttering.

'Forgive me father, for I have sinned. Forgive me father, for I have sinned. Forgive me father, for I have sinned—'

My dad pulled his hand from hers with a violence that caused her to fall backwards.

'You stupid woman. You stupid bloody woman!' There was a new energy in him, something I'd not seen before. He

230

leant down and put his hands on her shoulders, and there was real violence in his eyes. He moved his hands up to her neck and the skin there grew even paler where his fingers applied pressure. She didn't fight him off, just looked up at him, all the time her eyes closed and her lips moving silently.

My dad roared, a feral noise, and threw his hands into the air. He stalked over to the bust which sat on the table and ripped off the hessian and plastic wrapping. From where I was sitting I couldn't see the face, but I was looking forward to seeing my mother's reaction when she saw that it was now a bust of Janet.

I put the final piece of orange into my mouth.

My dad walked back towards my mother, the bust held in front of him, and when he was standing a couple of feet from her I could see it properly. I could see the changes that had been made to it. I could see that it wasn't Janet anymore, but it wasn't my mother either.

It had my mother's high forehead and swooping eyebrows, but Janet's shorter, tilted nose and full mouth. The plump cheeks were Janet's as well, but the chin was my mother's, sharp and pointed, and the tendons, taut in the neck, also suggested my mother. My dad still hadn't carved the eyes, and the blank stare made it impossible to tell whose they were. It was a strange amalgamation of the two women.

My mother now had her hand at the place on her neck where her crucifix used to hang, her fingers plucking away at the hollow in the middle of her collarbone. She was still mumbling to herself, 'Forgive me father for I have sinned,' over and over again, and she still had her eyes closed. She didn't see my father when he rested the bust on his thighs, both hands taking the weight of the top of the head.

But I could see, in the whiteness of his knuckles, the effort that it took for him to use his thumbs to gouge out the eyes.

I sniffed my fingers. They smelt of oranges.

Lorry was asleep on the sofa in the living room when I crept in. He was lying with his arms thrown back over his head, like he used to sleep when he was a baby, and his bottom lip was sticking out. His legs were almost completely healed, the skin on them fresh and shiny and taut, with just a hint of redness here and there to suggest that there was ever anything wrong with them. I lay down next to him and nuzzled into his little body, enjoying his warm biscuit smell and the softness of his skin.

I don't know how long I lay there, drifting in and out of sleep, listening to Lorry's soft snores and gentle grunting. When I got up and went to my bedroom the sky outside was getting dark, but it wasn't just the impending night that brought the darkness. It was a different sort of darkness, a gloom that came from the clouds that were massing on the horizon, drawing a curtain over the valley.

Twenty-five.

Monday 16ᵗʰ August 1976

I felt the change as soon as I woke up the next morning. I opened my eyes and everything felt different. I couldn't work it out at first. There was a soreness between my legs that made me think of Mally, but that wasn't just it. There was something else.

I got out of bed and the air was heavier. Looking out of the window, I could see that the sky was stained grey. Everything was eerily quiet; not just an impenetrable silence, but a complete absence of sound, a vacuum. No birds singing, no cows or sheep or lawnmowers. Not even a grasshopper. The weather was on the turn and the thought excited me. There was a storm on its way.

Downstairs, I filled the kettle from one of the bottles and lit the camping stove.

I could only remember one summer storm, from when I was very little, before Lorry and Petra were born. I must have been about six or seven. My mother and my dad had taken me out for a picnic and we were sitting at the top of a hill, the red and blue checked picnic blanket laid out on the grass. There were sausages on sticks and orange juice and egg sandwiches that smelt like farts. The air was getting heavier, and my mother was complaining that it was giving her a headache.

The dog had followed us from the car park, and it came over and started sniffing at the food. It was a spaniel, I think, although I didn't know that then. My dad shooed it away but it always came back again, curling around us, its tail tucked between its legs. It was a scruffy thing, and it didn't seem to have an owner. It was all on its own.

It had already stolen a sandwich off the plate, and then it came back for a sausage. I had the cocktail stick half-way to my mouth when, quick as lightning, it leant in, and with its horrible damp mouth, pulled the sausage off the stick in one swift movement.

I don't know why I did it, but I grabbed it by the scruff of its neck and held it steady and I jabbed the cocktail stick into its eye. The dog started yelping, and put its chin down on the floor and started pawing at its face. It was funny, seeing it like that, and I remember thinking that it served it right for stealing food. I had a well-developed moral code, even at that age. Then the first drops of rain came and we grabbed everything and bundled it into the picnic basket and ran for shelter.

I don't remember what happened after that. I don't know if I was told off or punished in any way, and I don't know what happened to the dog, but my dad said later that it was because of the incident at the picnic that we never had pets of our own.

The kettle boiled and I made a cup of tea.

Mally had said that we were going to get revenge on Tracy Powell. I didn't have the relics anymore to give me strength, so instead I'd put the jar with the raven's skull in the treasure bag. I'd put the wire, coiled up into a circle, in the back pocket of my shorts. I was aware of the strength of it, the tension wound up in that one length of metal, pressing against me through the fabric.

I drank my tea and let myself out of the front door. I anticipated the squeaking of the gate before I opened it, so I climbed over and onto the patch of gravel next to the Cortina and the pile of broken concrete. I stood in the lane for a moment, in the space between the two cottages, and breathed in the musky air. Still hot and dry but with a definite suggestion of change. The clouds that gathered over the top of the valley had grown heavier, even greyer and more ominous than the night before, and their reflections were suspended in the blank eyes of the chapel windows.

The gate outside Mally's house still hung on its hinges and I scraped it open over the grass. I made sure not to touch the circles scratched into the gatepost—the witching circles—and pulled the gate closed behind me. The gravel path sounded brittle under my feet as I made my way to the back of the house, where the vibrant colours of the flowers in Janet's garden shrieked even louder in the accumulating gloom.

The top part of the stable door was open and I peered in. Janet was sitting at the kitchen table, her face resting on the heel of one hand, elbow on the Formica. She was sucking on a cigarette, the lines around her mouth scored deep into the beige skin as she took drag after drag. It was as if she was trying to get as much of the smoke into her lungs as she possibly could, and she would suck in three or four times before letting out a long stream of smoke and then start sucking again. The hand holding the cigarette was trembling and the fag-end was glowing red, on-off-on-off like a beacon.

She looked up as I pulled the door open.

'Alright, love?' She was wearing a grubby white dressing gown and when she spoke she moved her hand away from her face and the movement caused the fabric to shift slightly. I caught a glimpse of the pale brown swell of a breast. Her voice was croaky and sore. 'You looking for my boy?' She leaned back in her chair, the dressing gown coming together again with the pull of the fabric. She didn't wait for me to answer. 'You'd better watch him. He's one for the ladies he is. I've lost track of the number of girls I've had to help out. Keep your legs shut near that one, I'm telling you!' She chuckled, a deep, throaty sound that set her off coughing.

I wanted to turn around and leave, but instead I found myself pulling out a chair and sitting down at the table, the treasure bag on my lap. I was facing Janet over the scratched tabletop. My dad was right: there was something about her, something mesmerising. Sitting there in her dirty dressing gown with her hair sticking up in tufts and her smeared make-up, she was both repulsive and compelling. There was an aura about her, a fascinating sexuality that was almost tangible. I remembered what my dad had said about her, and I had the absurd thought that maybe he was right: maybe she had bewitched him and my mother after all.

Behind Janet stood some shelves, each one crammed with little brown bottles, like the one I'd seen her give my mother that had ended up smashed on the kitchen floor. Above our heads, the bunches of drying herbs hung like bats in a cave. She saw me looking.

'My herbs,' she said. 'I collect them and dry them out and use them to make my medicines.' She ground out the cigarette into a tin ashtray.

'Like the ones you give my mother,' I said. 'And the poultice for Lorry's legs.' Even I could hear the hostility in my voice. She must have heard it too. She shrugged.

'It's working though, isn't it?'

'Mally told me about you,' I said. 'About you being outsiders and all of the people in the village hating you because of your ancestors. Is it true?'

'Mally's a sensitive boy,' she said. 'The people round here think he's just a good-for-nothing waster, screwing the girls and then dumping them.' She cackled out a laugh, a brief stuttering sound that stopped abruptly. She picked up a packet of Benson and Hedges from the table and tapped one out with a yellow-stained finger, the nail varnish old and chipped. 'And he is a bit lazy, to be fair, but for some reason the girls can't leave him alone. He's even had that Fat Denise, and the ugly one, Tracy.'

My cheeks caught fire, and she laughed again.

'Oh, don't look like that. There's not much going on round here that I don't know about. Small place this. Not a lot to do. Kids will make their own amusements.' She sniffed. 'Adults too, I reckon.'

She was looking at me intently now, scrutinising me. She put the fag between her lips and picked up a small silver lighter. My mother's lighter. The flame licked at the tip of the cigarette. She inhaled, causing the lines between her eyebrows to sink deeper. She kept her eyes on me the whole time.

'Took it, did he?'

'What?' I looked straight back at her.

'Your virginity. Pop your cherry, did he? That's his thing, see. He likes to be the first one. He's a bit of a maverick, my boy. A pioneer. I'll give him that.' I could feel the heat edging its way up the back of my neck, making me bolder.

'I know you tried it on with my dad.'

She blew out the smoke and at the same time waved her hand, clearing the air but dismissing me at the same time.

'Oh, that was nothing love,' she said. 'That's nothing to worry about. Just pretend, that was. Just a bit of fun.'

She rested the cigarette in the ashtray and walked around the table. She stood next to me and when she put a hand on my shoulder it felt cool, even through my t-shirt.

'Just a bit of fun, Nif, my love.' I looked to the side and saw that her dressing gown had fallen loose again. Her breast was exposed, the nipple standing hard and proud against the soft flesh. I looked away, but I knew she'd seen me looking.

She took her hand away, but slowly; there was no urgency to her movements. She reached behind her and I heard her pick up the kettle from the worktop, then the glug of water as she filled the kettle from a bottle and the scrape and pop of it being plugged in. A click.

She walked back around the table and sat down again. She picked up the cigarette and flicked the ash off the end into the ashtray. She rested her elbows on the table, holding the cigarette an inch away from her mouth. The smoke curled up between us.

'Look. I like you Nif. I like your family. I think you've been through a lot and I'd like to help you. There's nothing going on between me and your dad. Not for want of trying on my part, I can tell you, but he's just not interested. Told me as much himself.' She smiled, a tired smirk that made the eyeshadow in the corners of her eyes crinkle. 'Truth is, a woman can get pretty lonely round here.'

'Why do you stay here then? Mally told me no-one here likes you. You're like us. You're outsiders. Nobody wants you here. The chapel lot made that clear. Even Tracy Powell thinks you should leave.'

She took another drag on her cigarette and held it in for a few seconds before blowing it out in one long puff of smoke.

'What else did he tell you?' She looked at me through the smoke, and for a long moment her features were clouded and hazy.

'He said that the people here, Mr Vaughan and Mr Beynon and all the rest, don't like people like us—outsiders—because of what your ancestors did. He told me that they came here and brought the plague with them and wiped out half the village and that's why they don't like outsiders.'

The cigarette had quickly burnt down to a stump, and she placed it tip-down in the ashtray and ground it out, her knuckles whitening against the brown skin. She looked up at me through narrowed eyes. Her eyeshadow was smeared and mascara had found its way onto her cheeks. Still, she was enchanting to look at.

'Did he tell you that they accused them of being witches?'

I nodded, unable to say anything.

'Did he tell you that the villagers thought they'd put a hex on the village and that's why so many people caught the plague and died? Did he tell you that they said my ancestors—Sarah and Elspeth, they were called—didn't get the plague because they used *the devil's magic* to protect themselves?' As she spoke, she made little curlicues in the air with her fingers, but her voice was bitter.

'Tell me about them. Your ancestors. What else do you know about them?'

Janet sighed. 'Do you really want to know?'

'Yes,' I said. It was important to me to find out as much about Mally as I could. Janet tapped her fingers on the tabletop for a few seconds, drumming out a rhythm. Then she stopped.

'They were only young—both in their early twenties—and Sarah had a child, a daughter called Alice. Only four years old, she was. They came from Derbyshire, from a village that had quarantined itself. Cut itself off from the world, on the instructions of the rector.'

'Mally told me that. He said that Sarah and Elspeth escaped.'

'They did. They fled in the middle of the night, them and Alice, and they walked for days until they came here. Nobody knows why they chose this village. There's nothing about that in the papers my mother left me. It was all written down, you see? After the event. It was all put down on paper. Evidence.

'Anyway, at first, they were welcomed here, by the men at least. Two young women, single and unattached—and they were lookers as well, by all accounts—turning up out of the blue. Why wouldn't they be welcomed?'

'But they brought the plague with them.'

Janet shifted in her seat. 'That's what they all said. Who knows, it could have come from somewhere else; there were merchants and drovers and all sorts going backwards and forwards in those days. But not long after Sarah and Elspeth and Alice arrived, the rumours started.

'Rumours that they were witches?'

Janet nodded. She plucked another cigarette from the packet and held it between her fingers, unlit.

'Apparently, it started out with just a few of the women, speculating about why so many folk suddenly caught the plague, and why it had started just after Sarah and Elspeth arrived. It's my guess that they didn't like the fact that their men were having their heads turned by these newcomers, and put the word out as a way of getting their own back. But you know what these places are like; once a rumour starts it soon spreads.'

'So, what happened?'

'They came for them in the middle of the night, that's what happened. Not just the women; the menfolk as well. Said they were witches, and that they would pay a heavy price. They formed a mob and they took them from their beds and they dragged the three of them—Sarah, Elspeth and Alice—down to the stream.'

Behind me, I could hear the kettle making the first noises of boiling, the sound of tiny fizzing bubbles rising to the surface.

'The stream?'

Janet nodded. 'There's a part where it gets deep, down past the bridge, next to the oak tree.'

I pictured myself bathing, enjoying the touch of the water against my skin.

'Why did they take them to the stream?'

When she said it, Janet's voice was matter-of-fact.

'To drown them.'

The bubbling sound from the kettle was getting louder.

'To drown them? The villagers drowned them for being witches?'

'That's what they wanted to do. They tried to make them confess first, of course. They held Sarah under the water until she was almost dead, and then they brought her out again. But she wouldn't confess, wouldn't say she was a witch.'

'What else did the villagers do?'

Janet stood up, the chair scraping on the tiles. She took her time to push it in under the table and then she stood behind it with her hands resting on the chair back, the unlit cigarette dangling between two fingers. She leant forwards and I could see the curve of a breast again where her dressing gown gaped.

'They drowned Alice.'

'Alice? The little girl?'

The kettle had started to make a low whining sound. Janet nodded slowly.

'They drowned Alice to get Sarah to confess. Four years old she was. Four. Can you imagine that? Drowning a four-year-old?'

Without warning, her face changed. The skin around her eyes and her jowls sagged. She seemed to grasp the meaning of what she'd said as suddenly as I did. She looked away from me, down at the tabletop. She bunched the fabric of her dressing gown around her, covering herself up, and when she spoke, she did so without looking at me, keeping her eyes firmly on the Formica.

'They drowned Alice and then they drowned Sarah.'

The kettle screamed and Janet moved quickly behind me to turn it off. I felt the steam against the back of my neck.

'What about Elspeth?'

Janet only paused for a moment before she took in a deep breath and replied in a brisk voice.

'Elspeth got away. She managed to escape from them and she ran away and hid. Again, she walked for days to another village, a village where no-one knew her or what had been said about her and she settled there and had a family.'

'How do you know all this?' I asked.

'She wrote it down. Elspeth wrote it all down and passed it on to her daughter, who passed it on to hers, and so on. When my mother thought I was old enough to know about it, she passed it on to me.'

There was a thump and Mally appeared at the bottom of the stairs. He looked like he'd just woken up: his hair was flattened against one side of his head and he wasn't wearing a shirt. He had sunglasses on, despite the gloom of the kitchen, and I couldn't see his eyes at all.

'Cosy,' he said, nodding at the pair of us. He had something in his hand, something that looked like a pack of playing cards, which he slid into the back pocket of his jeans.

He walked behind me and I heard a cupboard click open. Then the squelch of the fridge door and the clank of mugs. I didn't turn around.

Mally put a teapot on the table in front of me. A bottle of milk appeared, sugar in a pot and then three teaspoons landed with a clatter. He put a couple of teabags in the teapot and then appeared again with the kettle. He leant over me, the kettle inches from my face, the heat from the metal radiating onto my cheek. He poured boiling water over the teabags.

'What have you two been talking about then, eh?' The smell from his skin was sour and musky and animal. I breathed in greedily before he moved away.

'I was just telling Nif what happened to Sarah and Elspeth and Alice.'

Mally nodded slowly and went and stood behind his mother. Janet picked up my mother's lighter and there was a tiny spark and then a flame flickered. The lines appeared around her mouth again, etched in deeper as she inhaled. Mally put one hand on her shoulder and I watched as he pressed, his fingers making the skin on her collarbone grow white against the tanned flesh. Janet breathed out the smoke, and started toying with her cigarette, rolling it and tapping it over the ashtray.

'And?' he said, his eyes still blank behind the sunglasses.

'And what?' I countered.

'What do you think? About us? About our ancestors? Everyone round here…disapproves of us. What about you?'

My eyes followed his hand as it moved down, the long fingers still pressing, but now on the soft flesh at the top of Janet's breast. His fingers disappeared beneath the fabric of her dressing gown. Janet had turned her face and was looking up at him, her face soft and adoring.

In one swift movement, Mally took his hand away and plucked the cigarette from his mother's fingers. He held the butt in his finger and thumb and rolled it around before putting it in his mouth. He sucked hungrily, and when he blew out the smoke, it filled the space between me and them, and for a moment they were faded, caught behind a veil.

'Come on, Nif. We're waiting.' He was challenging me.

'OK then. I think you're weird, if you really want to know. I think you're really weird for wanting to live in a shit place like this, where nothing ever happens and everyone hates you. Why do they despise you so much for something that happened hundreds of years ago?'

Neither of them said anything at first. Then Janet coughed and cleared her throat. She took the cigarette from Mally gently, as if silently requesting permission, and when she spoke her voice was quiet, not much louder than a whisper.

'It's about revenge, simple as that.' She shrugged. 'It's about the children being made to pay for the sins of their forefathers.'

I looked at her face for clues. Who were the children and who were the forefathers? Were the villagers trying to avenge their predecessors who had died from the plague? Or were Janet and Mally trying to get back at the descendants of the people who had drowned their ancestors—who had drowned a four-year-old girl?

I couldn't help it. My eyes were drawn to the herbs hanging from the ceiling and the shelf with the brown glass bottles. Even before I said it, I knew how ridiculous it was going to sound.

'And were they witches? Your ancestors, Sarah and Elspeth. Were they witches?'

Janet snorted. 'Witches? Who believes in witches these days?'

'The people who go to the chapel certainly do. Mr Beynon and Mr Vaughan and all the others. They think your ancestors were…' I couldn't bring myself to say the word evil. 'They think your ancestors were up to no good and because of that, they think you're doing the same. I've seen them, with their cleansing rituals and their witch marks on your gatepost.'

Janet sniffed. 'It's not as easy as that. It's not a question of good and bad or anything as cut and dried as that. It's…it's a question of what you believe in. Where your faith lies.' She looked up at Mally and then back at me.

'There are hundreds, maybe thousands, of religions in the world. All of them have their own beliefs and philosophies, their own structures and rituals. The chapel-goers here have a belief in their god that they think allows them to take the moral high ground. They think theirs is the only religion that should be allowed to exist and that all the others are…illegitimate.'

She paused for a second to take a drag on the cigarette.

'Now, take your mother. She lost her faith in her god after your sister died, but that doesn't mean she can't believe in something else. She can be more…flexible about what she believes in. It's a case of picking and choosing, of finding the path that's right for you. Isn't that right, Mally?' She looked up at him again and he nodded.

He reached round and took the pack of cards from his pocket, and that's when I saw that it wasn't a pack of cards, but a stack of photos, Polaroids, like the ones I'd seen on his bedroom wall. Like the ones he'd taken of me by the plague cross and at the stream. He started shuffling them, as if they really were just a pack of playing cards.

'And who are you to judge?' he said, and I still couldn't see his eyes behind the sunglasses. 'What about you and the Creed, eh? How is that any different from the things other people believe in?'

I looked quickly at Janet and there was no sign of surprise or interest on her face. He'd already told her. I felt another rush of heat up my neck. All the time he kept on shuffling.

'You're just a little girl who's angry because her sister's died and you want to blame everyone else. You've made up this stupid thing, with relics and incantations and shit like that. It's bollocks, the lot of it. If you really want to get revenge, you need to know how to do it properly.'

'What do you mean?'

Mally fanned the Polaroids out face down in his hand and offered them to me.

'Go on,' he said. 'Take one.'

'What?'

'Pick a card, any card. But don't look at it.' I hesitated.

'Go on,' he said. 'Humour me. Mally the Marvellous, remember?'

I felt stupid, but I reached out and took a card from the middle of the pack.

'The thing is, Nif, you're just a little girl playing with things you don't know anything about. You're just a kid. It won't be long before you go back to school and it'll be like these last couple of weeks never happened.' The thought of going back to school stung.

'But you said we were the same,' I said. 'You said that we needed to stick together, that we were both outsiders and needed to form an allegiance.' I could hear the wheedling in my voice and felt the tears prickle the backs of my eyes and I hated myself for it.

'That's shit, Nif. You just seemed like someone who needed to get laid and so I obliged.' Mally took his sunglasses off and his eyes looked more deep-set and dark-smudged, and the line between his eyebrows was now etched deeper. 'And it wasn't easy,' he said. His mouth was twisted into a cruel, sharp-toothed smile. 'Take some advice from me. Try having a wash now and again, and brushing your teeth, and basic things like that. A change of clothes wouldn't go amiss either.'

My hand was sweaty where it clutched the Polaroid and I curled my fingers into my palm.

'You can look now,' he said, nodding at the photo in my hand.

'What?'

'Go on, turn it over. Look at it.'

The paper of the Polaroid was creased where I'd been clutching it, and the edges were furled. I was still holding it like a playing card, face down on the palm of one hand, gripped between my thumb and my fingers. I knew what I was going to see when I turned it over. It was something that had always been at the back of my mind, ever since I'd seen the photos arranged on Mally's bedroom wall. But even then, that inkling of knowledge, that foreshadowing of an idea, didn't quite prepare me for the violence of the image.

It was a picture of Mr Beynon, and it was similar to all the other photos I'd seen stuck to Mally's bedroom wall. It had the same orange-brown glow to it, and it showed just the minister's head and shoulders. He was facing the camera full on, and had his mouth open, as if castigating the person taking the photo. But there was one difference between this picture and the other Polaroids I'd seen. In this one, the minister's eyes had been scratched out. Something sharp had been rubbed over them again and again, removing the shiny surface of the photograph and revealing the white paper beneath.

The last thing I saw before I left was Janet, the smirk firmly in place on her lips, even as she dragged on her cigarette.

Twenty-six.

I found myself standing in the lane outside Mally's house. I was holding the treasure bag with the raven's skull and I was trembling. Almost without thinking, I'd put my hand to the back pocket of my shorts, to check that the wire was still there, and I'd been relieved to feel its powerful presence through the fabric.

Then I saw my dad. He was standing next to the Cortina and he'd hitched the trailer back onto the car. Some of his sculpting stuff was scattered around on the parking area and I knew straight away that he was packing to go home. I knew immediately what this was. This was the end.

When he saw me he tried to smile, but it didn't work and he gave up.

'You're up early, Nif,' he said, and his face had a grey tinge to it that matched the sky behind him. 'Storm's on its way, I think.'

'Yeah. Looks like she was right.' I couldn't bring myself to speak Janet's name, yet still I was testing my dad. It worked. He refused to meet my eye and shuffled his feet in the gravel, flipping the stones over with the toe of one sandal. I thought he was going to say something. He even opened his mouth but then he closed it again and wiped his hand over his eyes and down his face, drawing his eyelids closed. He stood like that for a moment, his head thrown back, shoulders slumped, looking defeated and wan. Then he made a real effort to draw his shoulders up again, to open his eyes and look at me.

'We need to go home, Nif. This place isn't right for us.' It was the simplicity of his words that did it, I think, the pure statement of fact. He didn't even try to persuade or cajole me, and I think that was what made me just nod back at him. He was right. We weren't welcome here.

'If we crack on, we can get the trailer filled before the rain comes.' He nodded towards the horizon which was already darker, drabber than it had been when I came out that morning, as grey as the shadows under his eyes.

Again, I nodded, silent. I was numb. Then I had a sudden feeling of being inexplicably drawn to the plague cross. An invisible thread drew me towards it, and I knew I would acquiesce. I mumbled something to my dad and set off down the lane, still conscious of the wire in my pocket. I thought of the sisters, Sarah and Elspeth, but mostly of Alice, little four-year-old Alice who had drowned at the hands of the villagers.

That was when I heard the first rumble of thunder.

The cows were still in the field when I rounded the corner, and they were lying down, their skeletal ribs bulging. The air was cooler now. It was still warm, still eerily quiet, but now it was muggy as well; there was a humidity that promised change.

Ahead of me stood the plague cross, taller than I remembered and more imposing. I had become used to seeing the cross at the top silhouetted against a cobalt sky, a stark shape out of the blue, but now it seemed to merge into the sky, dissolving as the grey met grey and mingled.

I stood for a moment at the base of the plague cross and passed my fingers over one of the indentations at the base. That was when the first drop of rain hit me squarely on the nape of my neck, and then another and another, dozens of them falling suddenly across my shoulders and over my arms and bouncing off the stone. I stood at the bottom of the steps and held out my arms and surrendered myself to the rain. I threw my head back and let it fall on my face, washing my tears away and cleansing me. I stood like that for ages and when I was soaked through and my arms were aching, I sat down on the steps and hugged the treasure bag to my chest.

I don't know how long I sat like that. It could have been minutes or hours. Time vanished. It was just me, alone, and that was how it was meant to be.

The last person I wanted to see was Tracy Powell. Her sallow, pimply face filled my field of vision, distorted by my tears. She was bending down, right into my face and her breath had the sour tang of vinegar and cigarettes. I put out a hand to push her away, but she moved aside before I could make contact. When I looked up, I could see that she had Fat Denise with her, and that they were both soaked to the skin. Their hair hung in sodden tendrils and the rain had glued their t-shirts to their fleshy torsos.

'You alright?' she said. 'You look like shit.'

There was something approaching empathy in Tracy's voice, so when she held out the vodka bottle to me, I took it without hesitating. I took a deep swig on it, and then another and another, and the alcohol mingled with the rainwater and the tears that were cascading down my chin and I felt better, cleansed.

'Hey, steady on, girl.' Tracy made to grab the bottle back off me, but I held on tight and turned away from her, tipping it up into my mouth again. Already I could feel the welcome warmth of the alcohol mixing with my blood. All the while, the rain continued to batter down.

Tracy started after me, and I ducked away from her, the treasure bag clutched under one arm, the half-empty vodka bottle held in my other hand. I ran back the way I'd come, my feet splashing along the lane. The dust had turned to mud already, and I could feel the splashes against my calves as I ran. I was a lot faster than Tracy and Fat Denise, so I slowed down when I got to the bridge and propped myself against the low wall that ran along the side of the bridge. The stream was still a meagre thing, but it was flowing swiftly now, the water having taken on a new urgency since the storm began. I cast a glance downstream, towards the oak tree that jutted out into the water.

I took another couple of swigs of vodka and thought again about Alice. Would she have fought back? Would she have tried to get away? How many of them were there, the villagers who took her to the stream and drowned her? She would have been terrified, confused. She would have pleaded with her mother, Sarah, to help her. She would have looked to her aunt, Elspeth, with desperation in her eyes. How long had they held her there, under the water that I had washed in only days ago, until the air left her lungs and her body floated, lifeless?

It was Tracy who drew up first—she stopped a couple of feet in front of me and leant forward and put her hands on her knees. Fat Denise arrived a couple of seconds later, red-cheeked and wheezing. I grinned at them and took another chug from the bottle. It was now only a quarter-full and the world was spinning.

'Give it back.' Tracy's face was thunder and she was standing up, stepping towards me. I held the bottle out to the side and behind me and laughed into her face, and when she reached forward to grab it I pushed her in the chest. The flesh there was wobbly and wet and warm.

I didn't expect her to push me back quite so hard.

The stream was cool, but it was still shallow, and when I landed on my back it took me a moment to realise what had happened. I was still holding the vodka bottle, and the treasure bag was still under my arm, but it was soaked through now. An absurd thought flashed into my mind: it was time to wash the raven's skull.

I'd turned myself over onto my front so that I could push myself up, and was crouched on all fours when Tracy landed with a massive splash next to me. She'd jumped down from the bridge, and had managed to land on her feet. She grabbed me by the shoulders, pushed me forward and straddled me— and my face was under the water. I was blinking and trying to push back, but she was stronger than me and I could feel the weight of her forearm against the back of my neck. I counted to twenty-three and the oxygen was thin in my lungs and I was getting light-headed when it came to me. I would be Alice. I would be the little girl who drowned—but in my version, I would come back to life. I let my body go limp. I let my arms fall underneath me and my legs give way and then I was face down, prone in the water. I let go of the vodka bottle and in my mind's eye I saw it bob away from me, floating downstream. Tracy's confusion was almost tangible. The pressure on the back of my neck eased, and I could feel her sitting up, even though she was still straddling me. I pictured her turning to Fat Denise, a frown puckering her forehead, concern clouding her stupid scrunched up face—and that was when I pushed myself up and all the air rushed back into my lungs. She staggered backwards and I threw myself at her and grabbed her round the waist, and the next thing we were grappling like wrestlers and splashing ineffectually.

I knew the effects of the alcohol were making my movements clumsy and slow, but Tracy was too heavy and cumbersome to put up a proper fight. She squared up to me, but before she could land a punch I grabbed her by the hair and yanked her backwards. I could feel the grease on my palm even through the water. She fell over onto her back and I was on top of her, my hands on her neck, and I could feel her starting to weaken, tiring under my strength.

Then I remembered the treasure bag and looked around, panic rising like bile into my mouth. I fumbled one-handed in the water around me, still holding onto Tracy's throat with the other hand. My chest flooded with relief when my hand touched the sodden fabric, and then the hard glass of the raven jar.

When the thought came into my mind, it was as though it had been put there by someone else. It just appeared, as if by magic. I saw myself holding the jar with the raven's skull in it, smashing the rim of the jar against the rocks at the bottom of the stream, so that the lid came away and left a jagged edge. I saw Tracy, her mouth gaping, wider than it should be, and very red as I forced the broken glass into her mouth, making her smile grow and grow, even though she was screaming at the same time. I saw the bleach, thick and viscous like egg white, but now streaming with red, falling over her ruined mouth and down her chin.

But I knew that was not how it would end.

I felt very calm. I let go of the treasure bag and adjusted my hands around Tracy's throat. I pushed her face slowly and gently under the water. I was focusing on the row of pimples around her hairline, little white pustules against angry red bumps. I looked down and she was blinking and trying to say something, but I couldn't hear her. Everything had gone silent. It was as though someone had switched off the world, and there was just me and Tracy Powell, and the cool water washing over us. A baptism.

Then there's a bird. It's a bird that sounds like a phone, a trilling that won't stop, and my mother goes to answer it. It's not a phone, it's a bird, no it's a phone and it stops ringing and she's gone for ages and I'm in the bathroom. Petra is little. Pink skin under water. Dark hair spreading like a bruise. She's smiling and I'm smiling and she's precious like a flower and she's my mother's favourite and I must look after Lorry because he's more special and my mother doesn't want us and she loves Petra and my hands are gentle on her shoulders. I'm pushing her under the water and she's stopped smiling and she's splashing, legs and arms, and there's water over her face and her eyes are open and I'm stronger than she is and she's weak and I've counted to 197 and she's limp under my hands and she's got her eyes open. Bubbles. A stream of bubbles from her nose is all.

And I dry my hands and go to make sure that Lorry's OK.

When I woke, there was the taste of vomit in my mouth. It was like the morning after Petra's funeral, when I woke up covered in puke and bile, but now there was blood there too. I was lying on the bank of the stream, soaked to my core, and I was shivering, even though the rain had stopped and the sun had reappeared. There was no sign of Tracy or Fat Denise.

I sat up and felt my chin. One of my teeth was loose and I worked my tongue around it, feeling it start to come free. Then a jab of pain shot through my jaw, and instantly the numbness was gone. The numbness I felt around Petra's death was gone and all of a sudden my instincts were twitching, my synapses were firing and all my senses were interwoven. I could hear the shriek in the hairs on the back of my neck and the look of the rain as it hit the stream tasted salty. The treasure bag was lying next to me and it sounded blue and heavenly and when I picked it up the fabric tasted of sunlight.

I pulled out the jar with the raven's skull and unscrewed the musty lid. The bleach smelt shiny as I poured it away into the stream and I tipped the feathery-whiskered skull onto my palm and washed it in the sweet water.

The incantation came to me, unbidden, and I let it skip through my brain.

Robin's egg, magpie's egg, duckling bill and bone. Blackbird's egg, feathers of wren, the skull of a crow.

And then I was flying. I was a bird. I was outside of myself and I was lifted up, hovering in the sky above. I was flying above the lane and I could see the bridge and the plague cross and the stream, and I flew even higher and I could see the pub and the chapel and the cottage, and even Lyndon Vaughan's little dog, skittering around on the verge.

And Mally's house.

And all of a sudden I was back down again, walking along the lane, the dust turned to mud by the rain. I was drenched to the skin, my orange hair made auburn by the water, my pale skin shining, translucent and radiant.

My hand was at the back pocket of my shorts and the wire was still there. I nipped it out with two fingers and felt the strength of it as it sprang open in my hand. It was burning with power. The raven's skull was in my other hand, its empty eyes now full of meaning and urging me onwards.

First of all, I decided, I was going to go and dig up the relics and put them back in their rightful place on the altar.

Then I was going to find Lorry and kiss him and hug him harder that I'd ever hugged him before.

And then I was going to go back to Mally's house.

My sister was dead, and I had killed her.

That was OK. I could fix that. The Creed had taught me that.

Because sometimes two wrongs can make a right, right?

Acknowledgements

My thanks go to Nathan Connolly for recognising the merit in my peculiar little book and for wanting to publish it. I am also grateful to Gary Budden for excellent editing skills and insightful comments.

This book was written while I was studying for an MA in Creative Writing at Manchester Metropolitan University. During that time I was very fortunate to attend the writing centre at Moniack Mhor on two occasions, as part of a group of students and tutors. The first time, I was close to giving up on this book. The second time was after it had been accepted for publication and I was struggling with the edits. On each occasion, the camaraderie and support of the other attendees kept me going. There were many people involved; I am grateful to them all and it would be wrong to name individuals (oh, go on then: Nick Royle, Livi Michael, Matthew Adamson and Charis Wightman).

Sincere thanks are also due to Georgia Davies, Jacqui Grima and Rianne Harney whose friendship and feedback on my writing have been invaluable. Ladies, I salute you. My thanks also go to my dear friend and staunchest advocate, Sara Cox.

I am also grateful to my parents Chris and Toni, and my sister Emma, for the gifts of a happy, loving childhood and a curiosity about words.

Finally, and most of all, thank you to Dom, and to Ted, Ben and Florence, for providing love and inspiration on a daily basis.

About the Author

Lucie McKnight Hardy grew up in rural West Wales, the daughter of London immigrants. She speaks Welsh and her education was through the medium of Welsh. She studied English at the University of Liverpool and after falling in love with the city, stayed on to work for an advertising agency there.

From Liverpool she moved to Cardiff to study journalism, and then worked for a not-for-profit organisation as public relations and corporate policy officer. She then moved to Zurich where she worked, for four years, in marketing.

After moving back to the UK, she worked as a freelancer before taking a break from work to have a family. During this time she studied creative writing with the Open University and then completed the MA in Creative Writing at Manchester Metropolitan University. She has now settled in Herefordshire with her family.

similar titles from

dead ink

Hollow Shores
Gary Budden

'Budden's writing is sparse, terse even, but perfectly suited to the landscapes of dislocation and alienation that are his natural milieu'.

– Nina Allan, *The Race*

'These stories, these words, represent an honest, scalpel-sharp, and unafraid dissection of the collective British psyche. Here is a country and a world teetering on the lip of apocalyptic void. And here are, too, insanities, desperate longings, great loves and rages and beauties. Completely absorbing.'

– Niall Griffiths, *Runt*

Budden's debut collection blends the traditions of weird fiction and landscape writing in an interlinked set of stories from the emotional geographies of London, Kent, Finland and a place known as the Hollow Shore.

The Hollow Shore is both fictional and real. It is a place where flowers undermine railway tracks, relationships decay and monsters lurk. It is the shoreline of a receeding, retreating England. This is where things fall apart, waste away and fade from memory.

Finding horror and ecstasy in the mundane, *Hollow Shores* follows characters on the cusp of change in broken-down environments and the landscapes of the mind.

Sealed
Naomi Booth

"Sealed is the perfect modern horror novel."
– Helen Marshall, *World Fantasy Award-Winning Author*

*'An accomplished, slow-burning meditation on motherhood,
pregnancy and love. […] A marvellous first novel.'*
– *The Guardian*

*'A brilliant dystopian distillation of just about all the ecological
fears a young parent can suffer.'*
– Books of the Year 2017, *the White Review*

Timely and suspenseful, *Sealed* is a gripping modern fable on
motherhood, a terrifying portrait of ordinary people under
threat from their own bodies and from the world around them.
With elements of speculative fiction and the macabre, this is
also an unforgettable story about a mother's fight to survive.

Heavily pregnant Alice and her partner Pete are done with
the city. Above all, Alice is haunted by the rumours of the
skin sealing epidemic starting to infect the urban population.
Surely their new remote mountain house will offer safety, a
place to forget the nightmares and start their little family. But
the mountains and their people hold a different kind of danger.
With their relationship under intolerable pressure, violence
erupts and Alice is faced with the unthinkable as she fights to
protect her unborn child.

dead ink

Dead Ink is an independent press based in Liverpool and supported by Arts Council England. We publish bold and groundbreaking books from emerging authors.

We see it as our job to find the new talent and bring it out from the underground. We're a small team, but an award winning one. From literary novels to non-fiction anthologies, we work hard to make sure that everything we produce is beautiful and brilliant.

Northern Publisher of the Year 2018
Northern Soul Awards

Regional Finalist, Small Press of the Year 2019
The British Book Awards

deadinkbooks.com
@deadinkbooks